Murder for Love

It's the Ultimate Act of Passion . . .

16 new original stories, including

JOYCE CAROL OATES

"AT THE PARADISE MOTEL, SPARKS, NEVADA"

He's a man away on business. She an exotic dancer who's just away. In a fast gray Infiniti, on a warm Nevada night, they're headed for the Paradise Motel, where sparks are going to fly. . . .

JONATHAN KELLERMAN

"THE THINGS WE DO FOR LOVE"

They were the perfect couple with the perfect child and the perfect career . . . as long as they didn't get caught. . . .

ED McBAIN

"RUNNING FROM LEGS"

On a train rollicking to Chattanooga, a beautiful Frenchwoman in silk underwear and a young war veteran find out that danger is the strongest aphrodisiac of all. . . .

FAYE KELLERMAN

"THE STALKER"

"It had been pure magic. That night she felt as if she had died and gone to heaven. Looking back on everything that had transpired since, she wished she had."

and 12 More Superb Short Mysteries

EDITED BY OTTO PENZLER

Delta
Trade Paperbacks

A Delta Book
Published by
Dell Publishing
a division of
Bantam Doubleday Dell Publishing Group, Inc.
1540 Broadway
New York, New York 10036

ISBN: 0-385-31840-5

Reprinted by arrangement with Delacorte Press

Manufactured in the United States of America
Published simultaneously in Canada

February 1997

10 9 8 7 6 5 4 3 2 1

BVG

To Carolyn

The love of my life

Contents

Murder for Love

Introduction

Contrary to popular usage, the opposite of love is not hate. It is indifference. Love and hate are too closely connected to be separated by time or circumstance. As long as one exists, the potential for the other also lives. Only when love, or hate, fades into indifference do those two passionate emotions no longer share a chamber of the heart.

The stories that follow are a celebration of love. All right, let's concede that in most of these tales at least one person dies a violent death. It's just love gone wrong. There's nothing wrong with the love—it's just the people who experience it, sometimes, or those who don't.

In order for a crime of passion to occur, there must be, naturally (or, from time to time, unnaturally), a passion. Can you imagine how much one person has to love another person to want to *kill*? That is not a manifestation of liking someone a lot.

Feeling the urge—no, the *need*—to kill someone is proof of truly deep emotion. Unless one is a nut case, of course, and the whole thing makes sense only to the murderer.

While some would make the argument that anyone who murders another human being is insane, one could easily take the position that there are times when killing someone is the most appropriate behavior, under the proper circumstances. Unfaithfulness is the best reason for killing a loved one. One really can't be blamed for falling out of love; tragically, it happens. But to be truly loved and to turn away from that passion, to take it for granted and risk losing it for momentary pleasure, is to be a prime target for a passionate retaliation.

Does such extremity seem pathological, or implausibly cold, or so outré that it does not touch ordinary lives or ordinary people? Reconsider. Such stories appear with regularity in movies, novels, television shows, newspapers and, most important, on the following pages.

Every one of the stories in this collection has been written especially for it, having appeared nowhere else prior to this volume. The subject moved some of the most outstanding writers in America to tell a story of lovers who took a wrong turn on the road, and the consequences of their folly, whether motivated by greed, or lust, or fear.

There are stories in this anthology for everyone, but especially for lovers. The diversity of authors to be found here assures pleasure for the reader of crime fiction, of romance fiction, and of distinguished fiction in general. Included are works by such prolific short story writers as Joyce Carol Oates, Ed McBain, and Mary Higgins Clark, as well as those who write them rarely (Elmore Leonard's first short story in thirty years, James Crumley's first in twenty-three) and even some who had never before written a short crime story (William J. Caunitz, Carol Higgins Clark, and Shel Silverstein).

In these stories people get hurt and people die. Some of the stories are a little more romantic than others, some are grittier than others, some are less traditional than others, but all have great pleasures to give. It is hoped that you will find this richly flavored cornucopia of crime rewarding enough to reread on special occasions, like St. Valentine's Day or your wedding anniversary. Or the anniversary of the time you thought about being unfaithful and resisted. Or, if you didn't resist, when you were lucky enough to not get caught and didn't have to pay the consequences.

—Otto Penzler

WILLIAM J. CAUNITZ

No matter how much research an author does, no matter how meticulously facts are checked, no one can bring a sense of verisimilitude to a police story the way a cop can. Joseph Wambaugh was the first important author to illustrate this, but no one during the past decade has had greater success writing police stories than William J. Caunitz.

A New York City policeman for thirty years (well, actually twenty-nine years and a few months, since he retired from the force after the enormous success of his first novel, One Police Plaza*), he worked his way up from patrolman to sergeant, during which time he saw as much as there was to see of the low side of human life. Apart from the bureaucracy that seems to pervade all government departments, he loved the life. His enthusiasm was conveyed to those around him, evidently, as one of his daughters has also become a police officer.*

This is the first short story William J. Caunitz has ever written. Life—and, often, death—is too complex to try to describe in just a few pages, he says. But the passionate elements of life have been superbly conveyed in the pages that follow.

—O.P.

Dying Time

BY WILLIAM J. CAUNITZ

Detective John Parker walked into the Seventeenth Squad's second-floor squad room, went directly over to the command log, and signed himself present for duty at 0800 hours. The heading on the top of the page read: Sunday, April 23, 1995.

Joe Carney, a burly guy with a shiny bald head, was finishing up a night duty, typing furiously. He was clearly a man in a hurry.

"Anything doin'?" Parker asked.

"Naw. The usual Saturday-night bullshit." Carney pulled the report out of the typewriter and said, "I'm out of here for three days."

"Have a good swing," Parker said, and walked around the room emptying overflowing wastebaskets into a large cardboard barrel. Going back to his desk, he raised the window up as far as it would go. A spring breeze blew across the squad room. Outside, police cars were double parked on East Fifty-first Street and along Third Avenue. He watched churchgoers, dressed in their spring fineries, strolling west on Fifty-first to catch the nine o'clock Mass at St. Patrick's Cathedral, four blocks away. He sighed at the thought of having to work on such a beautiful day and, savoring the scent of spring, went back to his desk.

Sunday day duties were usually quiet in the Seventeenth, a good time for a detective to play catch-up on his paperwork. Parker rolled a case follow-up report into the typewriter.

John Calvin Parker had broad shoulders and deep blue eyes. At forty-seven his hair was still black and wavy, without a trace of gray. The faded razor scar that edged along his right eyelid gave his weather-beaten face a dashing air. He had just finished closing out an old robbery case with "No results" when the telephone rang. He snapped it up. "Seventeenth Squad, Detective Parker."

"Hey, Parker, we just caught a double homicide at Forty-two Sutton Place South," the crusty desk sergeant reported.

Parker cursed and slammed down the phone.

The crime scene was in the north penthouse apartment of a luxury co-op that stood at the edge of the East River. Two liveried doormen worked the entrance while the concierge, who stood behind a waist-high mahogany desk in the center of the elegant lobby, tended to the needs of the tenants and their guests.

As Parker stepped off the elevator into the vaulted marble foyer of the north penthouse, he was greeted by Sergeant Luther Johnston, the Seventeenth's patrol supervisor. "It's a bad one, Parker."

"They usually are." Parker looked at the three cops trying to console the well-dressed woman slumped on one of the foyer's gold brocaded armchairs. Her face was buried in her palms; she was crying. "Who's the lady?"

"Mrs. Elizabeth Gardner. This is her daughter's apartment."

Parker looked at the yellow ribbon of crime-scene tape stretched across the archway leading into the living room.

"What's the story, Sarge?" Parker asked.

The patrol supervisor read from his notes. "Mary Ann Gardner, age twenty-nine, lived alone, her mother arrives around nine-thirty this morning to have brunch later with her, lets herself in with her own key, discovers her daughter and another woman dead in the living room, she starts screaming, a neighbor hears her and phones down to the concierge."

"And the other woman?"

"Mrs. Adele Harrison, age forty-six, lives in apartment sixteen-AS in the south wing of this building. Married to J. Franklin Harrison."

"As in Harrison Pharmaceuticals and Harrison Aviation?"

" 'At's the one."

"Has the husband been notified?"

"Not yet. According to the concierge, he left Saturday on a business trip and hasn't returned yet."

Parker went over and stood next to the yellow tape, his practiced eyes roaming the crime scene. The large room had a glass wall that overlooked the river and a wide terrace with lots of plants. The thick pile of the carpet was beige, and the sofas and easy chairs were covered in white moiré silk. On the walls hung five Muehl paintings from his Greek Island period. Two women lay dead on the floor, their bodies about twenty feet apart. The body nearest the terrace was wearing a white silk bathrobe over a white nightgown. Her bare feet were facing the other body. Adele Harrison lay on her back about three feet in front of the steps that led down from the foyer. The corpse was dressed in an orange-and-white Chanel suit. A .32 S&W revolver lay beside the right foot, next to an open lizard pocketbook.

Parker became aware of Elizabeth Gardner's moans and the soothing words of the cops trying to comfort her.

Sergeant Johnston whispered to Parker, "Looks like the Harrison dame comes in, shoots Gardner, then does herself."

Parker looked into the sergeant's young face, smiled, and, bending under the tape, walked into the living room.

Death's rancid stench already polluted the air. It's amazing how some of us get used to that stink, he thought, crossing the room to Mary Ann Gardner's body. She lay on her back with her arms spread out at her sides; the left eye was open, the right one closed. A jagged bullet hole gaped from the center of her forehead; blood pooled around the head, caking her long blond hair in crimson mud. The body was stiff from rigor mortis. All the blood had settled to the bottom of the body, causing lividity's blue discoloration to show through her bathrobe.

Adele Harrison's skirt was hitched up above her knees, and her left leg was bent awkwardly under the right one. Both eyes were closed and her mouth was open. Heavy powder tattooing surrounded the bullet hole in her right temple. Parker got down on all fours and, lowering his face close to the revolver, peered into the cylinder. Two rounds had been spent. He got to his feet just as Sergeant Johnston called to him, "Crime Scene just arrived."

Parker looked around and saw two detectives lugging black valises coming into the foyer. "Gimme a few more minutes alone," he called to the familiar faces.

"No problem, John," the older one said.

Parker looked at Mary Ann Gardner's mother. She was dabbing her eyes with a handkerchief. She caught his curious stare and made an attempt to tidy her hair. He walked away into the master bedroom. The king-size bed was messed up with disheveled sheets hanging over the sides. The top left side of the fitted sheet had come undone from the mattress. Two of the four pillows were on the floor. The center of the fitted sheet was stained, and a single strand of black curled-up hair lay in the stain. He moved his nose close to it and smelled the unmistakable musk of sex. He looked around the tastefully furnished room for Mary Ann Gardner's pocketbook. He didn't see it. He hadn't noticed it in the foyer or the living room either. He stepped into the bathroom; it wasn't there. Coming back into the bedroom he focused his eyes on the messed-up bed. He went over and knelt, running his hand under the sheets. Not feeling anything, he lifted them up and looked under the bed, spotting the pocketbook standing up against the wall on the bed's right side. He pulled it out and, sitting on the floor with his back up against the bed, opened it. He took out her cosmetics pouch. The thick wallet was stuffed with credit cards, three hundred ten dollars, driver's license, and her car registration. There were several photographs of Mary Ann with girlfriends. A photograph of her and her parents. He slid the photographs into his pocket and took out her appointment/telephone book. He flipped the pages to yesterday, Saturday, April 22. The one P.M. entry read: "Jean for lunch at JD's." The next entry caught his attention: "3 P.M. lover boy." He flipped pages, scanning entries. There were a lot of lover-boy entries.

Parker told the crime-scene detectives that he wanted exact measurements and a crime-scene sketch in addition to photographs and fingerprints. "There's some love juice and a black pubic hair on the bed. I'd like you to run DNA on both of them." He suddenly walked away from the crime-scene detectives and lifted Mary Ann Gardner's nightgown. Her pubic hair was blond. Walking back to them, he said, "I'd also like you to vacuum the pillow and the bed."

The detectives opened their valises and went to work.

"Hello, Jack." Dr. John Goldman had been with the Manhattan ME's office for over ten years. He was a short guy with thin lips and a cheerful smile.

"What brings you out, Doc? You usually tell us to tag 'em and bag 'em."

"We have standing orders to respond to all high-profile homicides. And Sutton Place South is about as high profile as they go in this town."

Parker agreed and watched him kneel to examine Adele Harrison's body. After he finished there he walked over and examined the other corpse. After five minutes he came back over to Parker and said, "I can't be sure until I get them on the table, but my guess is sometime between ten and midnight." A strange expression came over the ME as he looked down at the body with the bullet hole in the temple and said dryly, "Looks like someone hit you a ground ball."

"Grounders aren't always grounders, Doc. You know that."

"Why is every detective I know a philosopher?"

"Because we deal with the shits of the world."

The guest bedroom had a brass trundle bed against one wall and a bookcase on the other. A desk stood by the window that overlooked the river. On it were a computer, a laser printer, and a fax machine. Parker's attention was drawn to the blinking e-mail cursor on the computer's screen. A template sat on top of the keyboard above the function keys, denoting the various functions each key performed. F-10 was the e-mail key; he pressed it. "You have one personal message" came onto the screen. He touched the key again. The message came up. "I love you and can't wait to be with you again. I'll be home Sunday evening around six. I'll come right up to you. Frank."

Walking out into the foyer, Parker motioned the uniformed cops away from the victim's mother. He dragged a chair over, sat down in front of her, and said, softly, "I'm John Parker, Mrs. Gardner. I've been assigned to investigate this tragedy."

She looked at him, disbelief clouding her face. "Why

would anyone want to hurt my Mary Ann? She never harmed anyone in her life. Why? Why?"

"Did your daughter live alone?"

"Yes. She wasn't married."

"How well did she know Mrs. Harrison?"

She shook her head and said, "Mary Ann never once mentioned her name to me. I don't think she knew her."

"What about her boyfriends?"

"My daughter never talked to me about that part of her life."

"Was your Mary Ann expecting you today?"

"Yes. We spoke yesterday and arranged to have brunch together today. I have my own key, and she left word with the concierge not to announce me. She was afraid that she might be in the shower when I arrived and didn't want me to have to wait in the lobby."

"Tell me what happened when you arrived here this morning."

Her face set as she tried to recall everything. "I got off the elevator and walked down the corridor to the door. I took out my key and let myself inside. As soon as I stepped into the foyer I knew something was wrong. That awful smell and the silence. Mary Ann's apartment was always noisy: music, the television, her on the phone. I called her name and there was no answer. I went to walk into the living room and saw them, dead on the floor. I lost control and started to scream. The next thing I knew the apartment was full of policemen."

"Do you remember touching anything in the living room, or rushing in to hold your daughter?"

"I don't remember. I don't think I left the foyer."

Parker heard the photographer snapping pictures of the crime scene. "Mrs. Gardner, can you think of any reason why anyone would want to hurt your daughter?"

"No."

"Have you told your husband what happened?"

"David passed on four years ago."

"Did your daughter work?"

"Not really. She had several trust funds from her grandparents and her father. She dreamed of becoming a screenwriter. She must have written a dozen screenplays, but none of them was ever produced. She was very excited about her latest one. It was about 'relationships.' "

"When you spoke to Mary Ann yesterday, how did she sound?"

"Very upbeat. She'd found a producer who was interested in her screenplay."

"Did she tell you the producer's name?"

"No, she never mentioned it."

"Weren't you curious?"

"Of course I was. But if Mary Ann had wanted me to know, she would have told me."

"Who is Jean?"

"Jean Bailey was Mary Ann's closest friend." Elizabeth Gardner's tears had caused her makeup to run; mascara smudged her eyes. She was a beautiful woman with long legs, high cheekbones, and full lips. She had deep brown eyes that looked almost black. Parker continued the interview for another fifteen minutes and then asked one of the uniformed cops to drive the bereaved woman home.

The doormen had locked the front entrance in order to keep out the haughty media crowd that had descended on the Sutton Place co-op.

The doormen turned their backs on the horde, ignoring them.

Walking over to the concierge, Parker looked out at the black-tipped microphones pressed up against the glass doors and asked the man behind the desk, "How long has the wolf pack been outside?"

"They arrived shortly after you did."

Parker extended his hand. "I'm John Parker."

"Frank Baffin," said the concierge, shaking hands.

"How long you been working the desk?" Parker asked.

"Twenty-one years come December." He was a short, wiry man with wisps of gray hair sprouting around his otherwise bald head. Small, round green eyes peered out from under his overhanging brow.

"Guess you could tell some stories, huh?"

"Hey, when I retire I'm thinkin' of writing a book about the shenanigans of the people who live on Sutton Place."

Looking down at the visitors' log, Parker asked, "Are all visitors entered in that book?"

"Yes, 'cept when a tenant accompanies them into the building."

"Are all unaccompanied visitors announced?"

"Yes, 'cept when a tenant leaves word not to. But they only do that for close family members."

"Was Mrs. Harrison listed as a visitor to Mary Ann Gardner's apartment yesterday?"

"No. I looked. I phoned the guys who were on duty last night and evening, and they both said that they never even saw Mrs. Harrison yesterday."

"Was there any way for her to get there without passing through the lobby?"

Baffin explained that the lobby separated the north and south wings of the building, but that in the basement a corridor connected both elevator banks.

Parker said: "So anybody who is in the basement can walk to the north or south elevator bank and ride up to any apartment they choose without being seen or announced."

"Yeah. But only tenants have free access to the basement."

"What about deliveries?"

"They all come in through the service entrance and are accompanied by porters up to the apartment."

"When is the service entrance open?"

"From eight in the morning until six o'clock in the evening, and up to five on Saturday. Closed on Sunday."

"What about the garage?"

"It's on the Fifty-fourth Street side of the building, and it's only for the tenants. There's a slot that they stick a plastic key into that opens the door, or they can use an automatic door opener. They park the car and walk through a door in the back that leads into the basement."

Parker pointed to the visitors' log. "How long are these kept?"

"Two years, then they're thrown out."

"Mind if I look through it?"

"Go ahead."

The first entry was on December 10 of last year. The day and date headed each page. The left-hand column listed the time, followed by the visitor's name and the tenant and apartment number. The last column listed the time the guest left the building. As he scanned the pages he saw that Mary Ann Gardner had many male guests, all at night. None of them stayed overnight. "Do you know any of these men?"

"Naw. They'd come over to me, give me their names, and I'd call up to her and she'd say 'Send 'em on up.' "

Parker picked up the log and walked over to the grouping of blue sofas. After taking out Mary Ann's appointment book, Parker turned to the first "lover boy" entry on Sunday, January 15, 1995, at 7:00 P.M. He opened the visitors' log to that time and date and saw no corresponding entry, nor was there one for any of the other fifteen "lover boy" entries in her appointment book. The page that held yesterday's entries had a slip of paper stapled to the top. He took it off. It contained a list of names. "What's this?" he asked, holding it up.

"The Goldmans in apartment twelve-CS had a party last night. That's the list of their guests. They left it here at the desk. That way we check them off as they arrive and don't have to bother the Goldmans with announcing each of their guests."

Parker folded up the slip of paper and slid it into his pocket. He returned the visitors' log and asked Baffin, "Did Miss Gardner bring a lot of men home with her?"

"I don't know what you'd call a lot, but she certainly never got lonely. She was always bringing guys home with her. Most of them I'd never see again."

Jean Bailey, an attractive brunette in her early thirties, was nervous. Sitting on the terrace of her East Seventy-ninth Street apartment, toying with a spoon, she looked across the glass table and said to Parker, "I couldn't believe it when I heard it on the radio."

"I understand you were one of her closest friends."

"Yes, we were very close."

"Tell me about her. What was she like?"

"She had a great sense of humor, loved to be with people, and wanted more than anything else to be a screenwriter."

"How long had she known Adele Harrison?"

"I don't think Mary Ann knew her. She never mentioned her name to me."

"What about her boyfriends?"

Jean's eyes fell to the empty coffee cup; she began gnawing at the edge of her lower lip. "I don't know about any of that." Her words lacked conviction.

"It's important that I find out all there is to know about Mary Ann's life. Please."

She grabbed a package of cigarettes up off the table and lit one. Blowing out the smoke, she relented. "Mary Ann didn't have one boyfriend, she had lots of them. She never wanted any of them to take her out for dinner or anything like that. All she wanted was for them to come to her apartment and take her to bed." She took another pull of her cigarette.

"Did you know any of her lovers?"

"No."

"Where did she meet these guys?"

"In the neighborhood. At the New School where she took courses. She liked to go to Johnny Diamond's; she'd meet them there." She flicked the cigarette ash and asked softly, "Why did she kill Mary Ann?"

"We're not sure yet. Was Mary Ann into married men?"

"I don't know. She was very secretive about her love life."

"How long had she known Adele Harrison?"

"I already told you, as far as I know, Mary Ann didn't know her."

"You had lunch together yesterday, right?"

"No. Mary Ann canceled. She said she was expecting company. Which meant one of her lovers was coming over. We dished on the phone for a while and made plans to do lunch on Monday."

"Did she tell you who she was seeing?"

"No, she didn't. As I already told you, Mary Ann wasn't big on giving out the names of the men she was sleeping with."

"I always thought that women confided that stuff to their close girlfriends."

Jean smiled as she crushed the cigarette in the ashtray. "Women are not all the same, Detective."

"What did you two talk about?"

"She was excited about her latest screenplay. She told me that a producer was interested in making it into a movie."

"Did she tell you his name?"

"No."

"Mary Ann must have been happy over that."

"She was thrilled. I've never seen her so excited."

"I'm surprised she didn't tell you the name of the producer. I would think that she'd do that."

"I know, that was strange. Not like her. I had the feeling . . ."

"What?"

"From the way she was gushing on and on about this producer, I had the feeling that he was the one she was seeing yesterday."

The man opened the door and stole into Mary Ann Gardner's apartment. When he saw Parker sitting in the foyer with his shield case dangling from his right hand, he froze. "Who the hell are you?" he demanded.

"Detective John Parker, Seventeenth Squad." He studied the handsome, well-dressed man for a few seconds before he said, "Mr. Harrison, your wife and Mary Ann are both dead." Harrison's legs sagged. He looked with stunned silence at Parker, digesting the words he had just heard.

"What did you say?"

Parker told him again. "How?" Harrison said.

"It appears that your wife shot Miss Gardner and then took her own life. The revolver she used was registered to you."

Harrison staggered against the wall. Parker rushed over to him and helped him onto a chair.

"I don't believe this," Harrison said.

"I'm afraid it's true."

"I kept that damn gun in a shoe box on top of the closet in our bedroom. I hadn't touched it in years. I decided on Friday to sell it to one of the gun dealers around police headquarters, and took it down. I left it on my dresser. I was going to get rid of it on Monday."

"When did your wife find out about the affair?"

Shaking his head with disbelief, he said, "I didn't think she knew."

"How long had you been having a thing with Miss Gardner?"

"We met in January at Johnny Diamond's. The affair began immediately, the first night."

"How did you manage crossing over to her side of the building without being seen by the doormen or the concierge?"

"I'd take the elevator to the basement and cross over to the north-side elevators."

"No one ever saw you riding up and down?"

"No. Half the tenants in this building have other homes."

"When did you last see Mary Ann?"

"Saturday. I left my apartment at one. I had an appointment in Philadelphia last night. I left Mary Ann's apartment at three."

"How did you get to Philadelphia?"

"Amtrak."

"What hotel did you stay at?"

"The Winston."

"Didn't any of the doormen or the concierge tell you what had happened when you came home?"

"They didn't see me. I entered through the garage and came right here."

"Were you going to produce Mary Ann's screenplay?"

"I'm not in the movie business. I showed her story to a producer friend of mine and he was interested." His eyes narrowed. "How did you know I was seeing Mary Ann?"

"I read her e-mail."

"I told her to use a password but she didn't think she needed it because she lived alone."

"Can I assume that you have a password for your e-mail?"

"Of course I do."

"Did your wife know it?"

"No. Adele and I respected each other's privacy." His eyes focused on the bloodstains on the living room rug. "Who found them?"

"Mary Ann's mother."

"Her stepmother," he blurted. "They couldn't stand each other."

"I got the impression that they were close to each other."

"Just the opposite. Mary Ann's father left her his entire estate. He'd been married to Elizabeth for only three years, and she signed a prenuptial that left her three hundred thousand in the event of his death. That's not a lot of money for a woman with her lifestyle."

"Mr. Harrison, I need to go with you to your apartment."

"Why?"

"Do you have an answering machine on your phone?"

"Yes."

"I need to listen to it."

"My wife hated guns. I don't think she ever held one in her hand. Detective, Adele was a religious woman. She would never kill another human being, and she certainly would never kill herself."

"I know."

"May I come in?" Parker asked forty minutes later, his hard eyes fixed on Elizabeth Gardner's face. She stepped aside. He walked into her fourteenth-floor Park Avenue apartment, his eyes sweeping the large living room. He turned to face her. A nervous twitch invaded her right eyelid. He said: "Women never commit suicide by blowing out their brains, they just don't."

Her mouth fell open.

"Adele Harrison recorded your conversation on her answering machine. It's all there, you telling her about the affair, suggesting that you come to her apartment to discuss it. You weren't sure what you were going to do, were you? All you knew for sure was that Mary Ann was happy over her screenplay and you hated her all the more for it and wanted to cause her pain. You told the concierge you were going to the Goldmans' party. You went to the Harrison apartment instead. At some point Adele Harrison excused herself. That was when you saw her husband's gun on his dresser. It all came together then, didn't it? You quickly snuck into the bedroom, took the gun, and stuck it into your pocketbook. Then the two of you went to Mary Ann's apartment. During their confrontation you stood beside Adele. At some point you took out the revolver, shot her in the temple and then killed Mary Ann. You then wiped the gun clean of your fingerprints, pressed it into Adele's hand in order to get her prints on the gun, dropped it on the floor next to her body, and then went to the Goldmans' party."

"You can't prove any of that."

"I'm getting a warrant to take your clothes to the lab. Our forensics people are going to find particles of gunpowder that match the powder tattooing on Adele Harrison's temple. That and the tape will convict you."

The color drained from her face.

"Why, Elizabeth?"

"Money. I stood to inherit if Mary Ann died."

"How did you find out about the affair?"

"I dropped by Mary Ann's unexpectedly. The concierge was busy and didn't see me, so I just went on up. I walked in and found them in bed." She started to shake. "What's going to happen to me?"

"You'll probably spend the rest of your life in prison."

She got up slowly and darted out onto the terrace. He ran after her. She threw herself over the railing. He leapt to grab her, but she was gone. Watching her silent plunge to the street, he thought of the two murdered women and realized that everyone has their own dying time.

CAROL HIGGINS CLARK

It would be naive, even downright foolish, to suppose that Carol Higgins Clark didn't have an advantage when she completed her first mystery novel, Decked. *Her mother, Mary, was firmly established as the bestselling female mystery writer in the world, and it was expected that some of that fame and affection would spill over to her daughter.*

In fact, the first book had numerous hardcover reprints and then made the paperback bestseller lists. All went as hoped and predicted. But affection for a writer's book, while it may make a reader curious enough to buy one book by a relative, cannot extend to a second purchase. If readers bought Decked *because they liked Mary Higgins Clark, they bought* Snagged *because they liked Carol Higgins Clark. And* Snagged, *about murder at a panty-hose convention being held in the same hotel as a funeral directors' convention, did even better than her first book. It made the national bestseller lists both as a hardcover and as a paperback. Her third book,* Iced, *has been the biggest success of all.*

The beautiful actress-turned-writer has enjoyed success in two careers, her bestselling status as an author having been preceded by starring roles in made-for-television movies, among other vehicles.

With "For Whom the Beep Tolls," she sets off in yet another direction. The creator of the humorous Regan Reilly mysteries has produced her first short story ever, a few elements of which are based—believe it or not—on real-life incidents.

—O.P.

For Whom the Beep Tolls

BY CAROL HIGGINS CLARK

If only the answering machine hadn't stopped working. . . .

Ellie Butternut pushed open the door of her apartment with a sigh of relief and then slammed it shut behind her. The sight of her small but cozy apartment on the ground floor of an old two-story building in West Hollywood always eased the tension that had been building up all day. She plopped on her couch, pulled off her shoes, and stretched her aching feet out onto the ancient coffee table as her cat, Twister, jumped up to join her.

Ellie had been running around the whole hot afternoon, from audition to audition, praying against the odds that she'd finally land some sort of stint. The thought that she hadn't gotten a single acting job for three months was dispiriting. She'd auditioned for everything from a mother superior who always turns out the lights in a South Coast Power industrial film to a two-layered shortbread cookie doing jumping jacks for a national commercial. All for naught. "Thank you for coming in," they'd say in a flat voice. Or even worse, a resounding "Next!"

The last job she had had was playing in a safety video that the owner of the local car wash decided to produce. He figured it would be a good item to sell by the cash register, where an array of whatchamacallits for use inside a car was already on display. While customers waited for wheels to get shined, they often couldn't resist another plastic drink holder or dangling air freshener. Why not a reasonably priced video on how to protect yourself while getting to and from your car in dark parking lots and garages?

That's show biz, Ellie thought as she glanced out her window, which was flanked by overgrown bushes. It's a tropical look, she decided. Raising her eyes, she gazed up at the Hollywood Hills in the distance beyond Sunset Boulevard and her local 7-Eleven. Everyone out here is chasing some sort of dream. Or has a screenplay. Including me, she thought, as she stared at a mansion way up yonder that from her vantage point was no bigger than a speck. Someday I'd like to have that speck, she thought. Or at least live in its neighborhood.

Wiggling the toes of her swollen feet, she picked up the remote control and flicked on the television.

"Oh, God," she murmured as she watched the face of her biggest rival, Lucy Farnsworth, playing the part of a harried housewife complaining about her husband's dirty socks on a commercial for Force, the latest sensational laundry detergent. "If it weren't for you, that would be my face peering into that washing machine," Ellie said aloud.

Ellie had been on first refusal, which meant that she couldn't accept another job doing a laundry-detergent commercial without first alerting the folks from Force, but she had ultimately been released from her obligation. She had already been planning how she would spend the residual checks that would have arrived in her mailbox with a pleasing regularity, but the part had gone to Lucy. Now her cash was once again running low and there were so many things she needed.

"Oh, well," Ellie said to herself with her usual optimism, "maybe it means a better commercial will come along."

She hoisted her sturdy 5′4″ frame off the couch and stood up, glancing into the gold-leaf mirror that her aunt Evelyn had given to Ellie just last year. "I know how you like to collect old stuff for your apartment," she'd said. "I'd like for you to enjoy this mirror before I die."

Ellie pushed back her frizzy auburn hair. Her pale skin was dotted with freckles and beads of sweat from the California heat. Stretching out her arms like a singer in agony, she smiled a crooked smile at her reflection and her green eyes glinted. "So I'm a character actor, what can I say?" She knew that she would always play the best friend. Thirty-four years old and slightly overweight, she also knew that if she could only land that one great comedic role, her life would change. She didn't have to play opposite a gorgeous leading man, but a leading man in her life wouldn't be so bad. It was just so hard to find Mr. Right. She couldn't even scrape up a Mr. Right Now.

She walked into the hallway, which was the size of a telephone booth, and glanced at her answering machine on the shelf. If there were messages, there would have been an audible beep. But now the red light was blinking too quickly and *ERR*, meaning screw-up, was flashing on its tiny screen.

"For Pete's sake," she muttered. "I was afraid this thing that ties me to the outside world was on its last legs. My lifeline is dead." She sighed. Everything has to come through this machine, she thought. Vital information about auditions, jobs, the occasional date, or news about how easy it was to switch long distance companies was all filtered through this most wondrous, at times most provoking, electronic device.

Tomorrow morning I'm going to have to go buy a new one, she thought. With my weary charge card. At least it'll be Saturday and I won't miss any calls from my agent when I'm out. With a sigh, Ellie headed into the bathroom to the turn-of-the-century tub, turned on the faucets full force, and prepared to take a much-needed cool soak.

Ellie spent a blessedly restful night. The usual sounds of car alarms going off, booming stereos from passing hot rods, and deranged recyclers passing outside her bedroom window with their squeaky shopping carts full of rattling bottles and cans did not awaken her. Not even the usual sounds of her lead-footed neighbor upstairs, Toni-Anne Loskow, coming in from her late-night job as a phone psychic, disturbed Ellie's slumber. Her baby greens were slammed shut. It was nearly 9:00 A.M. when she heard the sound of Frances's voice haggling with someone over the price of a set of old pots and pans. Frances was the building manager, who lived next door to Ellie and had a fondness for garage sales.

As Ellie struggled into consciousness, she sat up and peered past the flimsy shade she had bought at a hardware-store closeout and surveyed the situation. Sure enough, Frances had covered the lawn with everything from old appliances to sleeveless blouses with darts in the bust that Frances had probably worn as an extra in a film shot in the sixties. Like everyone else in the building, Frances was a card-carrying member of the Screen Actors Guild. And, also like everyone else in the building, Frances had gotten her share of little parts over the years but was still waiting for the big break that would free her from her years of scrimping to get by. In her late fifties, Frances had done some stand-up comedy. Recently someone had asked her if she didn't wish she'd moved home to Oregon a long time ago and settled into a "normal" life. "What—and give up show biz?" Frances had answered. "No way, José."

Ellie climbed out of bed and stumbled into the kitchen. Quickly she put on a pot of coffee and then dressed in a pair of sweats. She washed her face, brushed her teeth, grabbed a mug of coffee, and walked outside onto the lawn where the early birds were picking through the loot. Not only did Frances sell her own possessions but she also sold anything her friends wanted to get rid of. For a slight fee, of course.

"Morning, Ellie," Frances called from her lawn chair perched in the shade of the one big tree. She had her coffee mug in hand as well. It depicted Snoopy in a gleeful pose. Frances's dark curly hair was pulled back with a headband and her reed-thin body was dressed in an old pair of jeans and a T-shirt.

"Morning." Ellie sat down on the ground next to Frances's chair. Her eyes landed on an answering machine complete with a telephone that was resting on a towel nearby.

Ellie put down her cup on the scruffy lawn and reached out for it. "Where did you get this? It still looks pretty good."

"Toni-Anne gave it to me to sell yesterday. She was the eighty-seventh customer at the bank and since they opened in 1987 and it was their anniversary they decided to give away a few prizes. The teller handed her a brand-new answering machine, so she decided to get rid of her old one." Frances sighed. "To think I was going to stop at the bank yesterday. . . ."

Ellie smiled as she looked over the machine. "Maybe she had a premonition something was going to happen to her. She predicted the bank would be a good place to go yesterday."

Frances waved a hand at her. "She doesn't believe in that psychic stuff. She said she makes it up as she goes along."

Ellie frowned. "She's been doing it for over forty years, hasn't she?"

"In one form or another. She started at a carnival in her

hometown at the Jersey shore when she was about twenty. She couldn't believe the money she could make telling people what they wanted to hear. When she came out here to act, she kept it up, which led to the psychic hot line."

"Well, maybe her machine will bring some sort of psychic good vibes to me. Mine gave up the ghost yesterday. How much is it?"

"Thirty dollars."

Ellie, ever the bargainer—which made her quite a match for Frances—held it up and smirked. "Is that the best you can do?"

Frances laughed. She gave her voice a gravelly edge and said, "With that you even get a fresh pack of tapes she just bought recently. They don't fit her new machine. And you get the owner's manual too."

"Such a deal. I'll take it." Ellie looked around and whispered, "Where is our favorite neighbor, anyway? I never heard old lead-foot come in last night. Maybe she wasn't wearing those green combat boots of hers."

Draining the remains of her Snoopy cup, Frances shrugged. "I haven't seen her this morning. Maybe she's still sleeping."

Across town, Harold Pinsworth, a forty-four-year-old accountant, woke up in a cold sweat. He had had wild dreams in the little time he managed to get some sleep. He looked over at his twenty-five-year-old sleeping wife, the beautiful Corinne, who was as far away on the mattress as she could possibly get without falling off.

She'd fallen out of love and he was doing anything and everything he could to get her back. When they met through the personal ads, he had believed that true recognition of his worth would soon be realized at the investment firm where he had been employed for twenty-two uneventful years. Corinne had just come to Hollywood from smalltown U.S.A. because she liked to get tan. Answering the ad written by the sophisticated forty-three-year-old bachelor who yearned to meet a young, attractive woman with sound family values, Corrine had been impressed on their first date. Twelve other women had refused to answer his calls after the first meeting. But Corinne had welcomed the second and the third. When she looked at him adoringly with those big brown eyes, he knew that no promise was too big to make.

But now, eleven months into the marriage, Corinne's patience was growing thin. She'd begun to realize that the plans he'd shown her for the house he would build her as a wedding present were just that. Plans. "Where's the land for this house?" she kept asking. "Where's the new car? The designer clothes you promised me? I don't mean to be greedy but . . ."

Harold had gotten desperate. He couldn't lose her. So his love for his gorgeous young wife had clouded his judgment and he became tempted to "borrow" some money from his firm. He had known so many who had used in-house money to make a killing and then had put it back. He had regretted he had never done it. But this time, this week, he knew he had to try. He'd always been chicken before, thinking supposed he lost it. There'd be no place to run or hide. He'd be sent to prison, disgraced.

But now Corinne had married him, looking for love and security. For four months they had been blissfully happy. But then she started getting restless.

The other night they'd been watching television in bed and she had fallen asleep. He'd been thinking all night about a get-rich-quick scheme that required a million dollars of the firm's money. Then the commercial for the psychic hot line had come across the screen. A crystal ball and the soothing sounds of a woman's voice saying, "Call us. We'll help you with your problems. We'll help you make your important decisions."

In a trance, Harold had snuck out of bed, slipped into the kitchen, and dialed their number. He'd been hooked up with Esmerelda. Harold remembered how he could barely talk to the woman on the other end with the deep, rich voice.

"I'm considering a business investment," he sputtered.

"Invest. Invest. Invest," she'd said. "I see a wonderful aura around you. Brilliant colors. You will be lucky. It will change your life, you'll see."

The next day Harold bought a million dollars' worth of stock in a company that was supposed to release a secret patent in electronics. At three the stock plummeted. He almost went crazy. Instead he called the psychic hot line that night and told Esmerelda how well he had done with her advice. "I want to take you out to dinner," he'd said.

"We're not supposed to do that," Esmerelda had whispered.

"Oh, come on. What's the harm? Whisper your real name and home number to me. I'll call you there."

Esmerelda relented. "My name is Toni-Anne," she'd breathed.

The next day, Friday, he was practically apoplectic. He called her a number of times during the day but hung up when he got the machine. Finally he decided to leave a message, thinking she might be the type to screen her calls. But she hadn't picked up. He said he'd call back later, he wanted to see her that night. He felt desperate, knowing that the firm would discover the loss the next week. He had to release his anger somehow. The next time he called, Toni-Anne answered the phone and he arranged to meet her in the big parking lot at Ralph's grocery store and walk to a little Italian place nearby.

Instead, he persuaded her to get into his car and let him drive her to a nicer restaurant a few miles down the road. When she got in she seemed pleased. But the pleasure ended abruptly when he pulled over in a park and strangled her, dumping her body in a wooded area.

It was all like a blur to him, a dream.

Now, as he lay in bed, he trembled at the thought of the message he had left on her machine. He had to get that tape. She might not have erased it, because he left it only yesterday, and he couldn't take a chance that his voice would ever be identified. As it was, he was nervous about the call to the psychic hot line, which would show up on his telephone bill.

Luckily he had her pocketbook with her keys in his trunk. He'd even driven by her building on the way home.

Harold gazed at the back of his sleeping wife. I did this all for you and now I'm going to end up in prison for embezzling. Maybe then you'll understand how much I love you. How I risked everything for you. Maybe then you'll love me and understand me and stand by my side. But before that can happen, he thought, I'm going to do whatever it takes to get that tape back tonight so I'm not convicted of murder. Whatever it takes.

Ellie had had a pleasant, relaxing day, puttering around her apartment and getting ready for the group of friends who were coming over for pasta and wine. She did some cleaning, talked on the phone, played with her cat, and even did laundry. It was nice to not go rushing around in the car.

She had been in an acting class for several years and from time to time a number of her classmates, anywhere from three to ten, would get together for some laughs and to gossip about the business. Tonight they would be six.

Ellie cut up some cheese, took out some crackers, and put them on the top of the refrigerator to keep them away from Twister. That all set, she went into the bedroom to get changed, passing her new answering machine that was still sitting on the shelf unplugged.

I'll have to figure out how it works later, she thought. Or I could always get Toni-Anne to explain it to me. Come to think of it, she hadn't seen Toni-Anne all day. Oh, well, she thought, I'll probably hear her later.

Harold glanced at his watch. It was 10:00 P.M. Do you know where your tape is? he thought.

"I'm going out for a pack of cigarettes," he said to Corinne as the closing credits of the movie on cable came across the screen.

"Suit yourself," she replied, not even bothering to look in his direction.

He got in the car and drove to Toni-Anne's neighborhood, looking for a parking space that was close to her building but not too close. He didn't have to worry. There were no spaces available in the immediate area. He pulled down the block, turned the corner, and finally found one. Turning off the engine, he exhaled deeply. Here goes everything, he thought.

One minute later he was climbing the creaky outside steps to her apartment. Quickly he let himself in with her keys and sighed with relief. His heart was pounding. The apartment was totally still.

Suddenly something rubbed against his leg and he jumped into the air.

"Meowww." A cat was reaching out its paws in an attempt to snuggle with his leg.

"Jesus!" he murmured as he shook the cat off. He'd always hated them.

A faint glow from the streetlight shone through the window and onto the floor. The dejected cat slithered past an envelope that was marked "Toni-Anne."

Regaining his composure, Harold bent over and picked it up. With the aid of his flashlight he read the contents.

Dear Toni-Anne,

Guess what? Ellie from downstairs bought your answering machine. Isn't that great? She was so happy to get the new package of tapes too. The old one was still in there so if you want it just let her know. Enclosed is $25. See you around.

Frances

Harold stood there trembling. Oh, God. Oh, God, he thought. Stuffing the money into his pocket, he shined the flashlight around the apartment, then crept into the bedroom. The empty cardboard box for a new answering machine was on the bed. On the nightstand a machine sat, its red light blinking.

He pressed the rewind button, praying that his message was on this machine. Holding his breath he listened to the first message.

"Toni-Anne, this is Ruthie. I found a good scene we can do for the acting workshop. Give me a call. Bye." An electronic voice recorded the time. "Friday. 8:32 P.M."

It's not on there, Harold thought frantically. I called Friday afternoon. Did she set up this new machine after I called? Or did she erase my message? I have to find out!

Stealing out of the apartment, he went down the steps on his toes. Voices could be heard floating from the window of the apartment below.

"Ellie, that was great pasta!"

Harold stopped in his tracks and crouched down in the heavy bushes outside her window. This must be the apartment!

"Hey, Ellie, can I use your phone? I want to check my messages," a guy's voice was saying.

"At 10:30 on a Saturday night?" Ellie laughed.

"Maybe my agent called with a great opportunity. An actor could have dropped out of a film that starts tomorrow. . . ."

"Sure. Go ahead. One of us has to get a big job soon."

"Your machine here isn't plugged in."

"I just bought it from the woman upstairs today. I've got to figure out how to use it."

"I'll plug it in," he offered.

The next thing he knew, Harold could hear the messages being played.

"Toni-Anne, are you there? Are you there?"

Ellie's guest remarked, "I guess she left the tape with her old messages in the machine."

Then Toni-Anne's voice came on. A rambunctious "Hello. Don't hang up. I'm here." It was followed by that electronic voice. "Friday, 4:30 P.M."

"Hey, guys, we shouldn't listen to her messages," Ellie started to say as the next voice came on.

"Toni-Anne, I've got to see you tonight. I want to reward you for what you've done. Your advice was wonderful. I'll call you back later."

Harold's blood froze as he listened carefully to what another one of Ellie's guests was saying about him.

"He wouldn't make a good actor. That voice doesn't sound too happy to me."

"Next!" another voice cried, and the whole group laughed heartily.

Luckily for Harold, the guests didn't stay much longer. I've got to get through this window before she shuts it for the night, he thought. He had heard her take the tape out of the machine after his message. It has to be right there.

Slowly starting to stand, he glanced into the apartment.

She had gone into the kitchen and was doing the dishes. Luckily she had turned on the radio. Now, he thought. I've got to get in there and hide.

Boosting himself up, he climbed in the window. Another damn cat was standing in his path!

He took three quick steps across the room and slipped into the closet just as Ellie came back and asked her cat, "Twister, what's the matter? Don't scratch the door, honey."

A few minutes later, Ellie got into bed with a sense of contentment. It always made her feel good to spend time with her friends. She sank into the pillow and turned to the news station on her radio.

"An unidentified woman was found in a wooded area a few hours ago by a group of hikers," a report began. "Apparently she had been left for dead. Someone had attempted to strangle her but she is still alive. She's in a coma and the doctors are not sure of her chances. They believe her to be about sixty. She has platinum-blond hair, was wearing a long skirt and a peasant-type blouse and a pair of unusual green boots."

Ellie bolted upright in bed. That sounds like Toni-Anne! she thought. Those crazy boots. Ellie hadn't seen her all day. That weird message on the tape. I've got to listen to it right now, she thought wildly.

Jumping out of bed, she darted into the hallway and put the tape in the machine and listened.

"I've got to play this for Frances!" she said aloud, pulling the cassette out of the machine and running to her front door. Suddenly she felt a hand go around her mouth.

"You don't have to play that for anyone."

It was the voice she had just heard on the tape!

* * *

Frances was relaxing in her bedroom, watching the eleven o'clock news, when Toni-Anne's cat jumped on the ledge outside her window and scratched at the screen.

"What's the matter, baby?" Frances asked. "Where's your mama?" She opened the screen and let the cat jump in on her bed.

With that, the report came on about the unidentified woman with the green boots.

"Toni-Anne!" Frances gasped. She picked up the cat and her master key ring and hurried out of her apartment.

This can't be happening, Ellie thought as she tried to slide away from him. The audition for the shortbread cookie flashed into her mind. Jumping jacks. If only she could free her body. But in the safety video they'd said to go for the bridge of an attacker's nose. With all her might she jabbed her hand behind her but missed. They struggled to the floor and the television fell off the stand. She could hear Frances's voice outside.

"What's going on in there?"

Her attacker was distracted for a moment and Ellie gave him a good whack across the nostrils. Blood started spurting as she managed to scream and Frances unlocked the door. Twister had jumped on Harold's legs and was scratching him when Frances hurried in. Toni-Anne's cat leapt from her arms and jumped on his face as he yelped in pain.

"Call the police!" Ellie yelled to Frances, standing up and grabbing the can of Mace she'd been given when she did the video. It was right in the drawer of the table next to the couch.

"Watch out, kitties," she ordered, dramatically spraying his face. "Mister, you're not going anywhere!"

* * *

Three weeks later, Frances and Ellie brought a paler Toni-Anne home from the hospital. Ellie made a pot of tea and they sat around her living room, rehashing everything.

"I tell you," Toni-Anne was saying as she petted her cat, whose purring motor was in overdrive as he cuddled in her lap. "I would have had a premonition if I were going to die. But I still shouldn't have gotten into that car with him. Hey, I never said I was the world's greatest psychic."

"Well, thank God you're okay," Ellie said as she poured her another cup of tea and broke off a piece of cookie for Twister.

Frances was drinking out of her ever-present Snoopy cup. "I always knew garage sales were exciting. I just never knew how exciting they could be."

The phone in the hallway began to ring. They all looked at each other and laughed.

"Uh-oh," Ellie said. "I think I'll just let the famous machine pick it up."

It was the owner of the car wash. "Ellie, those safety videos have been selling like hotcakes since you got all that publicity. I'd like to get a photo of you with Toni-Anne and Frances for a new cover. And guess what? A producer who bought the video thinks I have real talent. He's optioning my screenplay. I told him I'd sell it to him as long as there are parts for the three of you. . . ."

That night, when Ellie got into bed and turned out the light, all was quiet. Then she heard Toni-Anne clomp into her bedroom directly above. Ahhhhh. That's the sweetest sound I've heard in a long time, Ellie thought as she drifted off to sleep.

Mary Higgins Clark

Happily married with five young children, Mary Higgins Clark's husband came home from work one day and, having just announced his arrival, had a heart attack and died. His mother, who lived with the family, heard the commotion and ran out of her upstairs bedroom, asking what had happened. Mary said, "It's Warren; he's dead." Shocked by the news, his mother immediately had a heart attack and died too. It is the sort of incredibly melodramatic tragedy that could never appear in fiction.

The young widow then had to get on with life. Each morning, she rose at 5:00 A.M., carried her portable typewriter to the kitchen table, and wrote for two hours before getting her children up, dressed, fed, and off to school, after which she went to her full-time job. After work, she made sure the kids were fed, bathed, got their homework done, and off to bed before she collapsed herself. The next morning, more of the same. I confess to being unimpressed when aspiring writers speak of their passion for writing being unfulfilled because they are simply too busy to get words on paper.

As perhaps the bestselling mystery writer in the world, Mary Higgins Clark is most closely associated with suspense fiction in which a woman or child is in peril. In "Definitely, a Crime of Passion," she has written a somewhat different story, a breezy throwback to the married couple as sleuths. Here, a handsome and much-loved former president who flies his own plane, and his gorgeous and energetic young wife (think James Bond meets Mr. and Mrs. North) appear in the first of what will surely be a series of adventures.

—O.P.

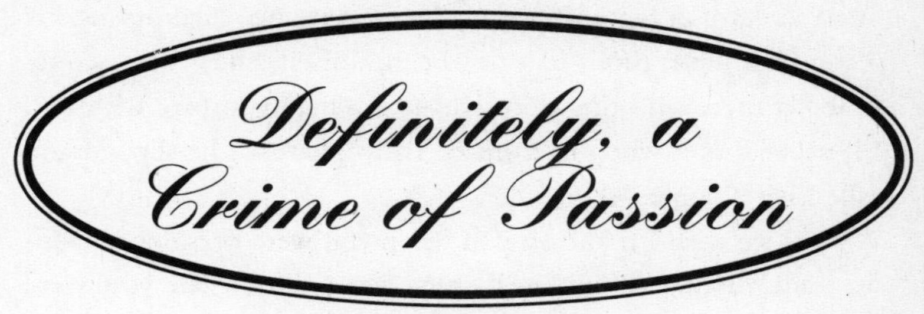

Definitely, a Crime of Passion

BY MARY HIGGINS CLARK

"Beware of the fury of a patient man," Henry Parker Britland IV observed sadly as he studied the picture of his former Secretary of State who had just been indicted for the murder of his lover, Arabella Young.

"Then you think poor Tommy did it?" Sandra O'Brien Britland sighed as she delicately patted homemade jam onto a delightfully hot scone.

The couple was comfortably ensconced in their king-size bed at Drumdoe, their country estate in Peapack, New Jersey. Matching breakfast trays complete with a single rose in a narrow silver vase were in front of them. *The Washington Post, The Wall Street Journal, The New York Times,* the London *Times,* and *L'Observateur* were scattered on the delicately flowered gossamer-soft quilt.

"I find it impossible to believe," Henry said slowly. "Tom

always had such iron self-control. That's what made him such a fine Secretary of State. But ever since Constance died during my second administration, he's not been himself, and when he met Arabella there's no question that he fell madly in love with her. I'll never forget when in front of Lady Thatcher he slipped and called her Poopie."

"I do wish I'd known you when you were president," Sandra said ruefully. "Oh, well, nine years ago when you were sworn in for the first time you'd have found me boring, I'm sure. How interesting could a law student be to the President of the United States? At least when you met me as a member of Congress, you thought of me with respect."

Henry turned and looked benevolently at his bride of eight months. Her hair, the color of winter wheat, was tousled. The expression in her intensely blue eyes somehow managed to simultaneously convey intelligence, warmth, wit, and humor. And sometimes childlike wonder. At their first meeting Henry had asked her if she still believed in Santa Claus.

That was the evening before the inauguration of his successor. He'd thrown a cocktail party at the White House for the about to be sworn in members of Congress.

"I believe in what Santa Claus represents, sir," she'd replied. "Don't you?"

At seven o'clock when the guests were leaving, he'd invited her to stay for a quiet dinner.

"I'm so sorry. I'm meeting my parents. I can't disappoint them."

Henry had thought of all the women who at his invitation changed their plans in a fraction of a second and realized that at last he'd found the girl of his dreams. They were married six weeks later.

The marriage of the country's most eligible bachelor, the forty-four-year-old ex-president, to the beautiful young congresswoman twelve years his junior had set off a media hype that threatened to be unending.

The fact that Sandra's father was a motorman on the New Jersey Central Railroad, that she had worked her way through St. Peter's College and Fordham Law School, spent two years as a public defender, and then in a stunning upset won the congressional seat of the Jersey City longtime incumbent, earned her the cheers of womankind.

Henry's status as one of the most popular United States presidents of the twentieth century as well as possessor of a great private fortune and his regular appearance at the top of the list of the sexiest men in America made other men wonder why the gods had so favored him.

On their wedding day one tabloid had run the headline: LORD HENRY BRINTHROP MARRIES OUR GAL SUNDAY, a takeoff on the popular radio soap opera of the 1930s that five days a week had asked the question "Can a girl from a mining town in the West find happiness as the wife of England's richest, most handsome lord, Lord Henry Brinthrop?"

Sandra had immediately become known to one and all, including her doting husband, as Sunday. She hated the nickname but had become resigned when Henry pointed out that he thought of her as a Sunday kind of love, which was his favorite song, and how people who voted for her embraced it. "Like Tip O'Neill," he said. "That suited him. Sunday suits you."

Now seeing the genuine concern in Henry's eyes, she covered his hand with hers. "You're worried about Tommy. What can we do to help him?"

"Not very much, I'm afraid. I'll certainly check to see if the defense lawyer he hired is good, but no matter whom he gets it's a particularly vicious crime. Think about it. The woman was shot three times with Tommy's gun in his library right after he told people that she had broken up with him."

Sunday examined the front page picture of a beaming

Thomas Shipman, his arm around the dazzling thirty-year-old who had helped to dry his tears after his wife's death. "How old is Tommy?" Sunday asked.

"Sixty-five, give or take a year."

Together they soberly studied the photograph. Tommy was a trim, lean man with thinning gray hair, and a scholarly face. Arabella Young's wildly teased tresses fell around her shoulders. She'd had a boldly pretty face and the kind of curves found on *Playboy* covers.

"May and December," Sunday commented.

"They probably say that about us."

"Oh, Henry, be quiet. And don't try to pretend that you aren't really upset."

"I am," Henry said softly. "I can't imagine what I'd have done when I found myself sitting in the Oval Office after only one term in the Senate without Tommy at my side. Thanks to him I weathered those first months without falling on my face. When I was all set to have it out with Yeltsin, Tommy in his calm, deliberate way showed me how wrong I'd be to force a confrontation and then somehow conveyed the impression that he was only a sounding board for my own decision. Tommy is a gentleman through and through. He's honest, he's smart, he's loyal."

"But he's also a man who must have been aware that people were joking about his relationship with Arabella and how smitten he was with her. Then when she finally wanted out, he lost it," Sunday observed. "That's pretty much the way you see it, isn't it?"

"Yes. Temporary insanity." Henry picked up his breakfast tray and put it on the night table. "Nevertheless he was always there for me and I'm going to be there for him. He's been allowed to post bond. I'm going to see him."

Sunday shoved her tray aside, then managed to catch her half-empty coffee cup before it spilled onto the quilt. "I'm coming too," she said. "Give me ten minutes in the Jacuzzi and I'll be ready."

Henry watched his wife's long legs as she slid out of bed. "The Jacuzzi. What a splendid idea!"

Thomas Acker Shipman tried to ignore the media camped outside his driveway. The lawyer at his side had just forced his way from the car into the house. The events of the day finally hit him and he visibly slumped. "I think a scotch is in order," he said quietly.

Defense attorney Leonard Hart looked at him sympathetically. "I'd say you deserved one. I just want to reassure you that if you insist we'll go ahead with a plea bargain, but I do think we could put together a very strong temporary-insanity defense and I wish you'd agree to go to trial. You went through the agony of losing a beloved wife, then fell in love with a young woman who accepted many gifts from you and then spurned you."

Hart's voice became passionate as though he were addressing a jury. "You asked her to come here and talk it over and then when she arrived you lost your head and killed her. The gun was out only because you planned to kill yourself."

The former secretary of state looked puzzled. "That's how you see it?"

Hart seemed surprised at the question. "Of course. It will be a little hard to explain how you could simply leave Miss Young bleeding on the floor, go upstairs to bed, and sleep so soundly that the next morning you didn't even hear your housekeeper scream when she saw the body; but at a trial we'd contend that you were in shock."

"Would you?" Shipman asked wearily. "I wasn't in shock. In fact after that martini I barely remember what Arabella and I said to each other, never mind recall shooting her."

Leonard Hart looked pained. "I think, sir, that I must beg

you not to make statements like that to anyone. Will you promise? And may I suggest that from now on you go easy on the scotch?"

From behind the drapery, Thomas Shipman watched as his rotund attorney was charged by the media. Rather like the lions released on the solitary Christian, he thought. Only it wasn't Hart's blood they wanted.

He had sent word to Lillian West, his daily housekeeper, to stay home today. He knew last evening when the indictment was handed down that television cameras would witness every step of his leaving the house in handcuffs, the arraignment, fingerprinting, plea of innocence, and less-than-triumphant return. He didn't want her subjected to their attention.

The house felt quiet and lonely. For some unfathomable reason his mind began to slip back to the day he and Constance had bought it thirty years ago. They'd driven up to have lunch at the Bird and Bottle near Bear Mountain and taken a leisurely drive back to Manhattan. It was when they impulsively wandered through local streets in Tarrytown that they'd come across the FOR SALE sign in front of the turn-of-the-century residence overlooking the Hudson River and the Palisades.

And for the next twenty-eight years, two months, and ten days we lived here happily ever after, Shipman thought as—deciding against the scotch—he wandered into the kitchen and reached for the percolator.

Even when he served as Secretary of State they managed occasional weekends here, enough of them to restore their souls. Until one morning two years ago when Constance said, "Tom, I don't feel so well." And a moment later she was gone.

Working twenty hours a day helped to numb the pain. I became known as the Flying Secretary, Shipman thought with a slight smile. But Henry and I did a lot of good. We left Washington and the country in better shape than it's been in years.

He measured coffee into the filter, snapped on the switch, and poured water enough for four cups. Enter Arabella, he thought. So ready with comfort, so alluring. And now so dead.

What had they said to each other in the library? He vaguely remembered how angry he had become. How had he been driven to such an act of violence? How could he have left her bleeding and stumbled up to bed?

The phone rang. Shipman didn't answer it. Instead he walked over to it, turned the ringer to "off," and disconnected the answering device.

When the coffee was ready he poured a cup and with slightly trembling hands carried it into the living room. Normally he'd have settled in his big leather chair in the library, but now he wondered if he'd ever be able to enter that room again.

From outside he heard shouting. He knew the media were still there but what was the point of all the racket? Yet even before he looked out the window, Thomas Shipman guessed which visitor had created such a furor.

The former president of the United States was on the scene to offer aid and comfort.

The Secret Service men tried to hold the media back. His arm protectively around his wife, Henry voluntarily made a statement. "As always in this great country, a man is innocent until proven guilty. Thomas Shipman was a truly great Secretary of State and remains a close friend. Sunday and I are here in friendship."

As the former president reached the porch, Shipman unlocked and opened the door. It was only when it had closed behind the Britlands and he felt himself embraced in a warm bear hug that Thomas Shipman began to sob.

* * *

Sunday insisted on preparing lunch for the three of them. "You'll feel a lot better when you have something hot in your stomach, Tom," she said as she sliced tomatoes, peppers, scallions and ham for a western omelette.

Shipman had regained his composure. Somehow the presence of Henry gave him, at least for the moment, the sense that he could handle whatever he had to face. Sunday's brisk, sure movements at the chopping board brought back a more recent memory of Palm Beach and watching someone else prepare a salad and dreaming dreams about a future that now could never be.

Glancing out the window, he realized that the shade was raised and, if somebody managed to sneak around to the back of the house, there was a perfect opportunity to take a picture of the three of them. Shipman got up and drew the shade to the windowsill.

"You know," he said, "pulling down this shade made me think of how last year some salesman talked me into putting an electric setup on the draperies in all the other rooms. They did something wrong in the library and when you click to open or close the draperies, you'd swear someone had fired a gun. You've heard about coming events casting their shadows before? Ah, well."

He sat across the table from Henry, thinking of the many times they'd faced each other across the desk in the Oval Office. Now he found the courage to say steadily, "Mr. President . . ."

"Tommy, knock it off."

"All right, Henry. We're both lawyers."

"So is Sunday," Henry reminded him. "And she worked as a public defender before she ran for office."

Shipman smiled wanly. "Then I suggest she's our resident expert. Sunday, did you ever launch a defense where your client was dead drunk and not only shot his . . . friend . . . three times but left her to bleed to death while he slept off a hangover?"

"I defended a number of people who were so high on drugs they didn't remember committing a crime."

"They were found guilty, of course."

"They had the book thrown at them," she admitted.

"Exactly. My attorney, Len Hart, is a capable fellow, but as I see it, my only course is to plea-bargain in the hope that in exchange for a guilty plea the state will not seek the death penalty."

Henry and Sunday watched as their friend stared unseeingly ahead. "You understand," Shipman continued, "that I took the life of a young woman who ought to have enjoyed perhaps fifty more years on this planet. If I go to prison I probably won't last more than five or ten years. The confinement, however long it lasts, may help to expiate this awful guilt before I am called to meet my Maker."

They were all silent as Sunday finished tossing a salad, then poured beaten eggs into a heated skillet, added the tomatoes, peppers, scallions and ham, folded the ends of the eggs into flaps, and flipped the omelette over. The toast popped up as she slid the first omelette onto a heated plate and placed it in front of Shipman. "Eat," she commanded.

Twenty minutes later, when Shipman pushed the last bit of salad onto a crust of toast and looked at the empty plates on the table, he observed, "It is an embarrassment of riches, Henry, that with a French chef in your kitchen you are also blessed with a wife who is a culinary delight."

"That's because I was a short-order cook when I was working my way through Fordham," Sunday explained. Then she said quietly, "Tommy, there have got to be some extenuating circumstances that will help you. We understand that Arabella had broken up with you, but why was she here that night?"

Shipman did not answer immediately. "She dropped in," he said evasively.

"You weren't expecting her?" Sunday asked quickly.

"Er, no, I wasn't."

Henry leaned forward. "Tom, as Will Rogers said, 'All I know is just what I read in the papers.' According to the media, you had phoned Arabella and begged her to talk to you. She came over that evening around nine."

"That's right. She came over around nine."

Henry and Sunday exchanged glances. Clearly there was something Tom was not telling them.

"Tom, we want to help you," Henry said gently.

Shipman sighed. "Arabella had been phoning me," he explained. "I returned her last call and we agreed it was important to sit down and talk things out. However, we made no specific date. I did not expect her the night of the tragedy."

"Where did you keep the gun?" Henry asked. "Quite frankly, I was surprised that you had one registered to you. You supported the Brady bill."

"I'd totally forgotten it," Shipman said tonelessly. "It was in the back of the safe for years. Then it came up in conversation that there's going to be another drive to turn in guns for toys. I was clearing out the safe, came across the gun, and decided to contribute it to the drive. I left it out on the library table, the bullets beside it, planning to drop it off at the police station in the morning."

Sunday knew that she and Henry were sharing the same thought. Not only had Tom killed Arabella but he'd loaded the gun after her arrival.

"Tom, what were you doing before Arabella came in?" Henry asked.

They watched as Shipman considered and then answered, "I had been at the annual stockholders' meeting of American Micro. It was an exhausting day. I had a dreadful cold. My housekeeper prepared dinner at seven-thirty. I ate a little and went upstairs immediately afterward. I was suffering from chills and took a long hot shower, then got into bed. I hadn't slept well for several nights and took a sleeping pill. I was in a sound sleep when Lillian knocked at the door and said Arabella was downstairs. Lillian, I might add, was just about to leave."

"You came back downstairs?"

"Yes. Lillian left. Arabella was in the library."

"Were you pleased to see her?"

"No, I was not. I was so groggy from the sleeping pill I could hardly keep my eyes open. I was angry that she had simply come without warning. As you may remember, there's a bar in the library. Arabella had already prepared a martini for each of us."

"Tom, why would you even think of drinking a martini on top of a sleeping pill?"

"Because I'm a fool," Shipman snapped. "Because I was so sick of Arabella's loud voice and cackling laugh that I thought I'd go mad if I didn't drown it out."

Henry and Sunday stared at Shipman. "I thought you were crazy about her," Henry said.

"I was the one who broke it off," Shipman told him. "As a gentleman I thought it proper to tell people it had been her decision. Anyone looking at the disparity in our ages and personalities would certainly have believed that. The truth was that I had finally—temporarily as it turns out—come to my senses."

"Then why were you calling her?"

"Because she was phoning me in the middle of the night, every hour on the hour. I warned her that it could not go on. She pleaded for a meeting and I agreed to see her in the near future but not that night."

"Tom, why haven't you told this to the police? Everyone thinks it was a crime of passion."

"I think in the end it probably was. That last night Arabella told me that she was getting in touch with one of the tabloids and would sell them a story about wild parties during your administration that you and I allegedly gave together."

"That's ridiculous," Henry sputtered.

"Blackmail," Sunday breathed.

"Exactly. Do you think telling that story would help my case? At least there's some dignity to being punished for murdering a woman because I loved her too much to lose her. Dignity for her and, perhaps, even a modicum of dignity for me."

Sunday insisted on cleaning up the kitchen. Henry insisted on escorting Tommy upstairs to rest. "Tommy, I wish there were someone here with you," he said. "I hate to leave you alone."

"I don't feel alone after your visit, Henry."

Nevertheless, Henry worried about his good friend. Constance and Tommy had never had children. So many of their friends from Westchester had moved to Florida. Others were still in Washington. As Shipman went into the bathroom off the master bedroom, Henry's beeper sounded.

It was Jack Collins, the head of his Secret Service detail. "Mr. President, William Osborne, the next-door neighbor, is insisting that Mr. Shipman must be given a message. He says Countess Condazzi is calling from Palm Beach and is distraught trying to reach him. The Countess insists that Mr. Shipman be notified that she is expecting his call."

"Thanks, Jack. I'll tell Secretary Shipman at once. And Sunday and I will be leaving in a few minutes."

"Right, sir."

Countess Condazzi, Henry thought. How interesting. Who can that be?

His interest was further piqued when on being informed of the call, Thomas Acker Shipman's eyes brightened and a smile hovered on his lips. "Betsy phoned. How dear of her!" But then the brightness disappeared from his eyes and the smile vanished and he said, "The Osbornes play golf with Betsy in Florida. That's why she phoned them."

"Are you going to call the Countess back?" Henry asked.

Shipman shook his head. "Absolutely not. Betsy must not be dragged into this mess."

A few minutes later, as Henry and Sunday were being hustled past the media, a Lexus pulled into the driveway beside them. A woman in her fifties, with a coronet of braids, used the diversion caused by the former president to slip up to the front door and let herself in. Henry and Sunday both noticed her.

"That has to be the housekeeper," Sunday decided. "She had a key in her hand. At least Tom won't be alone."

"He must be paying her well," Henry observed. "That car is expensive."

On the drive home he told Sunday about the mysterious phone call from Palm Beach. He could see from the way her head tilted to one side and her forehead puckered that she was both disturbed and thinking deeply.

They were riding in an eight-year-old black Chevy, one of the ten specially equipped secondhand cars Henry delighted in using to avoid recognition. The two Secret Service agents, one driving, one riding shotgun, were separated from overhearing them by a glass divider.

"Henry," Sunday said, "there's something wrong about this case. You can sense that."

Henry nodded. "Oh, that's obvious. I thought it might be that the details are so gruesome that Tommy has to deny them to himself." Then he paused. "But none of this is like him," he exclaimed. "No matter what the provocation I cannot accept that, even laced up on a sleeping pill and a martini, Tommy went so out of control that he killed a woman! Just seeing him today made me realize how extraordinary all this is. Sunday, he was devoted to Constance. But his composure when she died was remarkable. Tommy simply isn't the kind of man who flips out, no matter what the provocation."

"His composure may have been remarkable when his wife died, but falling hook, line, and sinker for Arabella Young when Connie was barely cold in her grave says a lot, doesn't it?"

"Rebound? Denial?"

"Exactly. Sometimes people fall in love immediately and it works, but more often it doesn't."

"You're probably right. The very fact that Tommy never married Arabella after giving her an engagement ring nearly two years ago says to me that all along he knew it was a mistake."

"Henry, all this took place before I came on the scene. I read in the tabloids all about how much in love the staid Secretary of State was with the flashy PR person half his age, but then I saw a picture of him at his wife's funeral side by side with a picture of him snuggling Arabella and I was sure that he was on an emotional roller coaster. No one that grief stricken can be that happy a few months later." Sunday sensed rather than saw her husband's raised eyebrow. "Oh, come on. You read the tabloids cover to cover after I'm finished with them. Tell me the truth. What did you think of Arabella?"

"I thought of her as little as possible."

"You're not answering my question."

"Never speak ill of the dead, but I found her boisterous and vulgar. A shrewd mind but she talked incessantly, and when she laughed I thought the chandelier would shatter."

"That fits in with what I read about her," Sunday commented. "Henry, if Arabella was stooping to blackmail, is it possible that she's tried it before with someone else? Between the sleeping pill and the martini, Tommy passed out. Suppose someone else came in, someone who followed Arabella, and saw an opportunity to get rid of her and let Tommy take the blame?"

"And then carried Tommy upstairs and tucked him into bed?" Henry raised an eyebrow.

The car turned onto the approach to the Garden State Parkway. Sunday stared pensively at the trees with their copper and gold and cardinal-red leaves. "I love autumn," she said. "And it hurts to think that in the late autumn of his life, Tommy should be going through this. Let's try another scenario. Suppose Tommy is angry, even furious, but so groggy he can't think straight. What would you have done if you were in his position that night?"

"What Tommy and I both did when we were at summit meetings. Sense that we're too tired or too angry to think straight and go to bed."

Sunday clasped Henry's hand. "That's exactly my point. Suppose Tommy staggered upstairs to bed and left Arabella there. Suppose someone else she had threatened had followed her over to Tommy's. Nine o'clock's a peculiar time to just show up. We have to find out who Arabella might have been with earlier in the evening. And we should talk to Tommy's housekeeper, Lillian West. She left shortly after Arabella arrived. Maybe there was a car parked on the street that she noticed. And finally the Countess from Palm Beach who so urgently wanted to talk to Tommy. We've got to contact her."

"Agreed," Henry said admiringly. "As usual we're on the same wavelength but you're farther along than I. I wasn't thinking about talking to the Countess." He put his arm around Sunday and pulled her closer. "I have not kissed you since 11:10 this morning," he said.

Sunday caressed his lips with the tip of her index finger. "Then it's more than my steel-trap mind that appeals to you?"

"You've noticed." Henry kissed her fingertips, then pushed his lips insistently against hers.

Sunday pulled back. "Henry, just one thing. You've got to make sure that Tommy doesn't agree to a plea bargain before we can help him."

"How am I supposed to stop that?"

"An executive order, of course."

"Darling, I'm no longer president."

"In Tommy's eyes you are."

"All right, but here's another executive order. Stop talking."

In the front seat, the Secret Service agents glanced in the rearview mirror, then grinned at each other.

The next morning, Henry got up at sunrise for an early-morning ride with the estate manager. At 8:30, Sunday joined him in the charming breakfast room overlooking the classic English garden. A wealth of botanical prints against the background of Belgian linen awning-stripe wall-covering made the room seem joyously, riotously flower-filled and, as Sunday frequently observed, was a long way from the upstairs apartment in the two-family house in Jersey City where she'd been raised and where her parents still lived.

"Congress goes into session next week," she reminded him. "Whatever I can do to help Tommy, I have to start working on right now. My suggestion is that I find out everything I can about Arabella. Did Marvin get a complete background check on her?"

Marvin Klein was in charge of Henry's office, which was located in the former carriage house on the two-thousand-acre property.

"Right here," Henry said. "I just read it. The late Arabella managed to bury her background quite successfully. It took Marvin's people to learn that she had a previous marriage in which she took her ex-husband to the cleaners and that her longtime off-again, on-again boyfriend, Alfred Barker, went to prison for bribing athletes."

"Really! Is he out of prison now?"

"Not only that, dear. He had dinner with Arabella the night she died."

Sunday's jaw dropped. "Darling, how did Marvin ever discover that?"

"How does Marvin ever discover anything? He has his sources. Alfred Barker lives in Yonkers, which as you probably know is not far from Tarrytown. Her ex-husband is remarried happily and not in the area."

"Marvin learned this overnight?" Sunday's eyes snapped with excitement.

Henry nodded as Sims, the butler, hovered the coffeepot over his cup. "Thank you, Sims. Yes," he continued, "and he also learned that Alfred Barker was still very fond of Arabella, improbable as I find that, and had bragged to his friends that now that she was finished with the old fuddy-duddy, she'd be getting together with him."

"What does Alfred Barker do now?" Sunday asked.

"Technically, he owns a plumbing supply store. It's a front for his numbers racket. And the kicker is that he's known to have a violent temper when double-crossed."

"And he had dinner with Arabella the night she barged in on Tommy."

"Exactly."

"I knew this was a crime of passion," Sunday said excitedly. "The thing is that the passion wasn't on Tommy's part. I'll see Barker today as well as Tommy's housekeeper. I keep forgetting her name."

"Dora. No . . . that was the housekeeper who worked for them for years. Great old girl. I think Tommy mentioned that she retired shortly after Constance died. The one we glimpsed yesterday is Lillian West."

"That's right. So I'll take on Barker and the housekeeper, but have you decided what you're going to do?"

"I'm flying down to Palm Beach to meet with the Countess Condazzi. I'll be home for dinner. And remember, this Alfred Barker is obviously an unsavory character. I don't want you giving your Secret Service guys the slip."

"Okay."

"I mean it, Sunday," Henry said in the quiet tone that could make his cabinet members quake in their boots.

"You're one tough hombre." Sunday smiled. "I'll stick to them like glue." She kissed the top of his head and left the breakfast room humming "Hail to the Chief."

Four hours later Henry, having piloted his jet to West Palm Beach airport, was driving up to the Spanish-style mansion that was the home of Countess Condazzi. "Wait outside," he instructed his Secret Service detail.

The Countess was a woman in her mid-sixties. Slender and small with exquisite features and calm gray eyes, she greeted him with cordial warmth. "I was so glad to get your call, Mr. President," she said. "Tommy won't speak to me and I know how much he's suffering. He didn't commit this crime. We've been friends since we were children and there never was a moment that he lost control of himself. Even when at college proms the other boys who drank too much got fresh, Tommy was always a gentleman, drunk or sober."

"That's exactly the way I see it," Henry agreed. "You grew up with him?"

"Across the street from each other in Rye. We dated all through college, but then he met Constance and I married Eduardo Condazzi. A year later, my husband's older brother died. Eduardo inherited the title and the vineyards and we moved to Spain. He passed away three years ago. My son is now the Count and I felt it was time for me to come home. After all these years I bumped into Tommy when he was visiting mutual friends, the Osbornes, for a golfing weekend."

And a young love sparked again, Henry thought. "Countess . . ."

"Betsy."

"All right, Betsy, I have to be blunt. Were you and Tommy starting to pick up where you left off years ago?"

"Yes and no," Betsy said slowly. "You see, Tommy didn't give himself a chance to grieve for Constance. We've talked about that. It's obvious that his involvement with Arabella Young was his way of trying to escape the grieving process. I advised him to drop Arabella, then give himself a period of mourning. But I told him that after six months or a year at the most, he had to call me again and take me to a prom."

Betsy Condazzi's smile was nostalgic, her eyes filled with memories.

"Did he agree?" Henry asked.

"Not completely. He said that he was selling his house and moving down here permanently. He said that he'd be ready long before six months were up to take me to a prom."

Henry studied her, then slowly asked, "If Arabella Young had given a story to a tabloid purporting that during my administration and even before his wife's death, Tommy and I had thrown wild parties in the White House, what would your reaction be?"

"I'd know it wasn't true," she said simply. "And Tommy knows me well enough to be sure of that."

Henry let his pilot fly the jet back to Newark airport. He spent the time deep in thought. Tommy was obviously aware that the future had promised a second chance at happiness and that he didn't have to kill to safeguard that chance. He wondered if Sunday was having any better luck in finding a possible motive for Arabella's death.

Alfred Barker was not a man who invited instinctive liking, Sunday thought as she sat across from him in the office of the plumbing supply store that she knew was a cover-up for nefarious activities.

He appeared to be in his mid-forties, a thick, barrel-chested man with heavy-lidded eyes, a sallow complexion, and salt-and-pepper hair, which he combed across his skull in an effort to hide a bald spot. His open shirt revealed a hairy chest and there was a scar on the back of his right hand.

Sunday had a moment of fleeting gratitude as she thought of Henry's lean, muscular body, the quick smile that showed his firm white teeth, the rugged features that were enhanced by a stubborn jaw, the sable-brown eyes that could convey or, if necessary, conceal emotion. At times she chafed at the presence of her Secret Service men, pointing out that since she'd never been First Lady, she didn't see why she had to have protection now. But at this moment, in this squalid room with this hostile man, she was glad to know they were outside the partially open door.

She had introduced herself as Sandra O'Brien, and it was obvious that Alfred Barker did not have a clue that the rest of her name was Britland.

"Why do ya wanna talk to me about Arabella?" Barker asked her as he lit a cigar.

"I want to start by saying that I'm very sorry about her death," Sunday told him sincerely. "I understand you and she were very close. But I know Mr. Shipman." She paused, then explained, "My husband at one time worked with him. There seems to be a conflicting version of who broke up his relationship with Ms. Young."

"Arabella was sick of the old creep," Barker told her. "Arabella always liked me."

"But she got engaged to Thomas Shipman," Sunday protested.

"Yeah. I knew that would never last. But he had a fat wallet. Ya see, Arabella was married when she was eighteen to some jerk who needed to be introduced to himself every morning. She was smart. I mean, that guy was worth hanging on to 'cause there were big bucks in the family. She hung around for three or four years, went to college, had her teeth fixed, let the guy pay for everything, waited till his rich uncle died, got him to comingle the money, then divorced him."

Alfred Barker lit the tip of his cigar and exhaled noisily. "What a shrewd cookie. A natural."

"And then she started seeing you," Sunday prodded.

"Right. Then I had a little misunderstanding with the government and ended up in the can. She got a job at a fancy public relations firm. The chance to move to their Washington branch came up two years ago and she grabbed it."

Barker inhaled deeply, then coughed noisily. "You couldn't hold Arabella down. I didn't want to. When I got sprung last year she used to call all the time and tell me about that little jerk Shipman, but in the meantime he was giving her fancy jewelry and she was meeting lots of people." Barker leaned over the desk. "Including the President of the United States, Henry Parker Britland the Fourth."

He looked at Sunday accusingly. "How many people in this country ever sat down at the table and traded jokes with the President of the United States? Have you?"

"Not with the President," Sunday said honestly, remembering that first night at the White House when she'd declined Henry's invitation. Instead she and her parents accompanied him on Air Force One back to New Jersey the next day after his successor was sworn in.

"See what I mean?" Barker crowed triumphantly.

"Mr. Barker, according to Secretary Shipman he was the one breaking off the relationship with Arabella."

"Yeah. So what?"

"Then why would he kill her?"

Barker's face flushed. His hand slammed on the desk. "I warned Arabella not to threaten him with the tabloid routine. But she got away with it before and wouldn't listen to me."

"She got away with it before!" Sunday exclaimed, remembering this was exactly what she had suggested to Henry. "Who else did she try to blackmail?"

"Some guy she worked with. I don't know his name. But it's never a good idea to mess around with a guy with the kind of clout Shipman had. Remember how he flushed Castro down the toilet?"

"How much did she talk about blackmailing him?"

"Only to me. She figured it would be worth a coupla bucks." Tears welled in the unlikely pool of Alfred Barker's eyes. "I was just thinking," he said. "I'm nuts about quotations. I read them for laughs and for insight, if you know what I mean."

"My husband is very fond of quotations too," Sunday encouraged. "He said they contain wisdom."

"That's what I mean. Wha'duz your husband do?"

"He's unemployed at the moment."

"That's tough. Does he know anything about plumbing?"

"Not much."

"Can he run numbers?"

Sunday shook her head sadly.

"Arabella had a big mouth. A real big mouth. I came across this quote and showed it to her. I always told her her mouth would get her in trouble."

Barker rummaged through the top drawer of his desk. "Here it is. Read it." He thrust a page that had obviously been torn from a book of quotations. One entry was circled:

Beyond this stone, a lump of clay
Lies Arabella Young
Who on the 24th of May
Began to hold her tongue.

"It was on an old English tombstone. Except for the date, is that a coincidence or is that a coincidence?" Barker sighed heavily. "I'm sure gonna miss Arabella. She was fun."

"You had dinner with her the night she died."

"Yeah."

"Did you drop her off at the Shipman house?"

"I put her in a cab. She was planning to borrow his car to get home." Barker shook his head. "She wasn't planning to return it. She was sure he'd give her anything to keep her from spilling muck to the tabloids. Instead look what he did to her."

Barker stood up. His face turned ugly. "I hope they fry him."

Sunday got to her feet. "The death penalty in New York State is administered by lethal injection. Mr. Barker, what did you do after you put Arabella in a cab?"

"I've been expectin' to be asked that, but the cops didn't even bother to talk to me. They knew they had Arabella's killer. After I put her in the cab, I went to my mother's and took her to the movies. I do that once a month. I was at her house by a quarter of nine and buying tickets at two minutes of nine. The ticket guy knows me. The kid who sells popcorn knows me. The woman who was sitting next to me is Mama's friend and she knows I was there for the whole show."

Barker thumped his fist on the desk. "You wanna help Shipman? Decorate his cell."

Sandra's Secret Service men were suddenly beside her. They stared down at Barker. "I wouldn't pound the desk in this lady's presence," one of them suggested coldly.

* * *

Thomas Acker Shipman had not been pleased to receive the call from Henry's aide, Marvin Klein, ordering him to delay the plea-bargaining process. What was the use? He wanted to get it over with. This house no longer felt like a home but had already become a prison. Once the plea bargain was completed, the media would have their usual field day and then they'd drop interest and move on. A sixty-five-year-old man going to prison for ten or fifteen years didn't stay hot copy for long.

It's only the speculation about whether I'll go to trial that has them camped out there, he thought as once again he peered out from behind a tiny opening in the drawn drapery.

His housekeeper had arrived promptly at eight o'clock. He had put on the safety chain, but when her key did not gain entrance she had firmly pushed the doorbell and called his name until he let her in. "You need taking care of," she'd said sharply, brushing aside the objection he'd voiced yesterday that he didn't want her privacy invaded by the media and actually he'd prefer to be alone.

Lillian West was a handsome woman, an excellent housekeeper and cordon bleu cook, but she had bossy tendencies that made Shipman wistfully remember Dora, his housekeeper of twenty years who sometimes burned the bacon but had been a pleasant fixture in the home.

Also Dora had been of the old school and Lillian clearly believed in equality of employer and employee. Nevertheless, for the short time he'd be in this house before he'd go to prison, Shipman realized that he might as well put up with her takeover attitude and try to enjoy the creature comfort of delicious meals and properly served wine at dinner.

Realizing the necessity of receiving phone calls from his lawyer, Shipman had turned on the answering machine, so that when a call came from Sunday he picked up the phone.

"Tommy, I'm in the car on my way from Yonkers," Sunday explained. "I want to talk to your housekeeper. Is she in today and, if not, where can I reach her?"

"Lillian is here."

"Wonderful. Don't let her go until I have a chance to see her."

"I can't imagine what she'll tell you that the police haven't already heard."

"Tommy, I've just talked to Arabella's boyfriend. He knew of the plan to extort money from you, and from what he said I gathered that Arabella had done that before to at least one other person. We've got to find out who that person was. Maybe someone followed her to your house and when Lillian left she saw a car and didn't think it was important. The police never really investigated any other possible suspects. This ain't over till it's over."

Shipman hung up and turned to see Lillian at the door to his study. Obviously she had been listening to the conversation. Even so he smiled at her pleasantly. "Mrs. Britland is on her way to talk to you," he said. "She and the President apparently think that after all I may not be guilty of Arabella's death. She and the President have a theory that might be very helpful to me."

"That's wonderful," she said coldly. "I can't wait to talk to her."

Sunday's next call was to Henry's plane. They exchanged reports on the Countess and Alfred Barker. After Sunday's revelation about Arabella's habit of blackmailing the men she dated, she added, "The only problem is that no matter who else might have wanted to kill Arabella, proving that person walked into Tommy's home, loaded his gun, and pulled the trigger is going to be quite difficult."

"Difficult but not impossible," Henry tried to reassure her.

"I'll get Marvin to check on Arabella's last places of employment and find out who she might have been involved with at them."

When Henry finished saying good-bye he did not know why sudden uneasiness overcame him. Aside from his concern over Tommy's plight, what could possibly be causing this chilling premonition that something was very wrong?

He sat back in the swivel chair that was his favorite spot on the plane when he wasn't on the flight deck. It was something Sunday had said. What was it? With inch-by-inch precision he reviewed their conversation. Of course. It was her observation about trying to prove that some other person had walked into Tommy's home, loaded the gun, and pulled the trigger.

That was it. And there was one person who could have done that, who knew that Tommy was both sick and overwhelmingly tired, who knew that Arabella was there, who in fact had let her in. *The housekeeper.* She was relatively new. Had anyone checked her out?

Swiftly Henry phoned Countess Condazzi. Let her still be home, he prayed. When her now-familiar voice answered, he wasted no time. "Betsy, did Tommy ever say anything to you about his new housekeeper?"

She hesitated. "Well, jokingly."

"What do you mean?"

"Oh, you know how it is. There are so many women in their fifties and sixties and so few men. When I spoke to Tommy the very day that girl was killed, I said I had a dozen friends who are widows or divorced and would be jealous of me. He said that except for me he intended to steer clear of unattached women, that he'd just had a most unpleasant experience. He'd told his new housekeeper that he was putting his house on the market and moving to Palm Beach. She seemed shocked when he told her that he wouldn't be bringing her with him. He'd confided to her that he was finished with Arabella because someone else had become important to him. He thinks the housekeeper got the crazy idea he meant her."

"Good God," Henry said. "Betsy, I'll get back to you." Swiftly he dialed Marvin Klein. "Marvin," he said, "I've got a hunch about Secretary Shipman's housekeeper, Lillian West. Do a complete check on her immediately."

Marvin Klein did not like to break the law by penetrating the computer records of others, but he knew that when his boss said "immediately," the matter was urgent.

Seven minutes later he had a dossier on fifty-six-year-old Lillian West, including her employment record. Marvin frowned as he began to read. West was a college graduate, had an M.A., had taught home economics at a number of colleges, the last one being Wren College in New Hampshire, and after leaving there six years ago had taken a job as a housekeeper.

To date she'd had four positions. Her references praised her punctuality, work, and cooking. Good but not enthusiastic, Marvin thought. He decided to check on them himself.

Five minutes later he dialed Henry's plane. "Sir, Lillian West had a long history of troubled relationships with her superiors in colleges. After she left the last job, she went to work for a widower in Vermont. He died ten months later, presumably of a heart attack. She then went to work for a divorced executive who unfortunately died within the year. Her third employer was an eighty-year-old millionaire who fired her but gave her a good reference. I spoke to him. While Ms. West was an excellent housekeeper and cook, she was also quite presumptuous and when he realized that she was intent on marrying him he showed her the door."

"Did he ever have any health problems?" Henry asked quietly as he absorbed the possibilities that Lillian West's history opened.

"I knew you'd want to know that, sir. His health is now robust but during the last several weeks of Ms. West's employment, specifically after he had given her notice, he became very ill with fatigue and then pneumonia."

Tommy had talked about a heavy cold and overwhelming fatigue. Henry's hand gripped the phone. "Good job, Marvin."

"Sir, there's more. I spoke to the president of Wren College. Ms. West was forced to resign. She had shown symptoms of being deeply disturbed and absolutely refused counseling."

Sunday was on her way to see Lillian West. She would unwittingly alert West that they were looking into the possibility that someone else had murdered Arabella Young. Henry's hand had never shaken at summit meetings but now his fingers could barely punch the numbers of Sunday's car phone.

Secret Service agent Jack Collins answered. "We're at Secretary Shipman's place, sir. Mrs. Britland is inside."

"Get her," Henry snapped. "Tell her I must speak to her."

"Right away, sir."

Five minutes passed, then Collins was back on the phone. "Sir, there may be a problem. We've rung repeatedly but no one is answering the door."

Sunday and Tommy sat side by side on the leather couch in the den, staring into the muzzle of a revolver. Opposite them, Lillian West sat erect and calm as she held the gun. The pealing of the doorbell did not seem to distract her.

"Your palace guard," she said sarcastically.

The woman's crazy, Sunday thought as she stared into the enlarged pupils of the housekeeper. She's crazy and she's desperate. She knows she has nothing to lose by killing us.

The Secret Service men. Jack Collins and Clint Carr were with her today. What would they do when no one answered the door? They'd force their way in. And when they do, she'll shoot us. I know she will.

"You have everything, Mrs. Britland," Lillian West said suddenly, her voice low and angry. "You're beautiful, you're young, you're in Congress, and you married a rich and attractive man. I hope you've enjoyed your time with him."

"Yes, I have," Sunday said quietly. "And I want more time with him."

"But that's not going to happen and it's your fault. What difference if he"—West's eyes scornfully glanced at Tommy—"if he went to prison. He tricked me. He lied to me. He promised to take me to Florida. He was going to marry me. He wasn't as rich as the others but he has enough. I've gone through his desk, so I know." A smile played on her lips. "And he's nicer than the others. We could have been very happy."

"Lillian, I didn't lie to you," Tommy said quietly. "I think you need help. I want to see that you get it. I promise that both Sunday and I will do everything we can for you."

"Get me another housekeeping job?" West snapped. "Cleaning, cooking, shopping. I traded teaching silly girls for this kind of job because I thought that somebody would finally appreciate me, want to take care of me. And after I waited on all of them, they still treated me like dirt."

The pealing of the doorbell had stopped. Sunday knew that the Secret Service would find a way to get in. Then she froze. When West admitted her, she'd reset the alarm. "Don't want some reporter trying to sneak in," she'd explained.

If Jack or Clint try to open a window, the siren will go off, Sunday thought. She felt Tommy's hand brush hers. He's thinking the same thing. My God, what can we do? She had heard the expression "staring death in the face" and now knew what it meant. Henry, she thought, Henry!

Tommy's hand was closed over hers. His index finger was

insistently racing down the back of her hand. He was trying to signal her. What did he want her to do?

Henry stayed on the line. Collins was speaking from his cellular phone. "Sir, all the draperies are drawn. We've contacted the local police. They're on the way. Clint is climbing a tree in the back that has branches near some windows. We might be able to get in up there. Problem is we have no way of knowing where they are in the house."

My God, Henry thought. It would take at least an hour to get the special cameras and motion detectors over there. Sunday's face loomed in his mind. Sunday. Sunday. He wanted to get out and push the plane. He wanted to order the army out. He had never felt so helpless. Then he heard Jack Collins swear furiously.

"What is it?" he shouted.

"Sir, the draperies of the right front room just opened and there are shots being fired inside."

"That stupid woman gave me my opportunity," Lillian West was saying. "I didn't have time to kill you slowly and this way I not only punished you but that dreadful woman as well."

"You did kill Arabella," Tommy said.

"Of course I did. It was so easy. I didn't leave. I just showed her into this room, woke you up, shut the door, and hid in the study. I heard it all. I knew the gun was there. When you staggered upstairs, I knew it was a matter of minutes before you lost consciousness. My sleeping pills are much better than the ones you were used to. They have special ingredients." West smiled. "Why do you think your cold improved so much in these ten days since that night? Because I'm not giving it a reason to go into pneumonia."

"You were poisoning Tommy?" Sunday exclaimed.

"I was punishing him. I went back into the library. Arabella was just getting ready to leave. She even asked me where your car keys were. She said that you weren't feeling well and she'd be back in the morning. I told her I'd get them for her in a minute. Then I pointed to your gun and said I'd promised to take it with me and turn it in to the police station. The poor fool watched me pick it up and load it. Her last words were 'Isn't it dangerous to load it? I'm sure Mr. Shipman didn't intend that!' "

West began to laugh, a high-pitched hysterical laugh. Tears ran from her eyes but she kept the gun trained on them.

She's working up to killing us, Sunday thought. Tommy's finger was jamming the back of her hand.

" 'Isn't it dangerous to load it?' " West repeated, mimicking a loud, raucous voice. *" 'I'm sure Mr. Shipman didn't intend that!' "*

She rested the gun hand on her left arm, steadying it. The laughter ended.

"Would you consider opening the draperies?" Shipman asked. "I'd like to see the sunlight once more."

West's smile was mirthless. "You're about to see the shining light at the end of the tunnel," she told him.

The draperies, Sunday thought. That was what Tommy was trying to tell her. Yesterday when he'd lowered the shades in the kitchen, he'd mentioned that the electronic device that worked the draperies in this room sounded like a gunshot when it was used. The clicker for it was on the armrest of the couch. It was their only chance.

Sunday pressed Tommy's hand to show him she understood. Then, breathing a silent prayer, with a lightninglike movement she pressed the button that opened the draperies.

The explosive sound made West whirl her head around. In that instant Tommy and Sunday leapt from the couch. Tommy threw himself at West but it was Sunday who slammed her hand upward as the housekeeper began to shoot. A bullet whistled past Tommy's ear. Sunday felt a burning sensation on her left sleeve. She could not force the gun from West, but she threw herself on top of the woman and forced the chair to topple over with both of them on it as shattering glass signaled the welcome sound of her Secret Service detail arriving.

Ten minutes later, the surface wound on her arm wrapped in a handkerchief, Sunday was on the phone with the totally unnerved former president of the United States.

"I'm fine," she said for the fifteenth time. "Tommy is fine. Lillian West is in a straitjacket. Stop worrying."

"You could have been killed." Henry didn't want to let his wife stop talking. He didn't ever want to think that someday he might not be able to hear her voice.

"But I wasn't," Sunday said briskly. "And Henry, darling, we were both right. It was definitely a crime of passion. It was just we were a little slow figuring out *whose* passion was causing the problem."

JAMES CRUMLEY

A significant portion of our cultural life is filled with lists: the year's best movies, top-ranked TV shows, bestsellers, and so on. It's all subjective and often useless, but it's also fun. We all know we should read every book so we can make our own decision about the best books of the year, and we should see every movie so we can decide for ourselves who are the best actors and actresses, and on and on. But in a busy life, this simply isn't possible, and the lists help to give us some direction.

In my own list of the best hard-boiled fiction, I have maintained for the past decade that the single greatest private-eye novel ever written is James Crumley's The Last Good Kiss. *The title alone gives it a running start, and its first sentence is quoted by mystery aficionados more than any line except ''Last night I dreamt I went to Manderley again.''*

When I finally caught up with Abraham Trahearne, he was drinking beer with an alcoholic bulldog named Fireball Roberts in a ramshackle joint just outside of Sonoma, California, drinking the heart right out of a fine spring afternoon.

This is James Crumley's first short story in twenty-three years and it is without question one of the finest crime stories ever written, filled with characters and texture enough for any serious novel.

—O.P.

Hot Springs

BY JAMES CRUMLEY

At night, even in the chill mountain air, Mona Sue insisted on cranking the air conditioner all the way up. Her usual temperature always ran a couple of degrees higher than normal, and she claimed that the baby she carried made her constant fever even worse. She kept the cabin cold enough to hang meat. During the long, sleepless nights Benbow spooned to her naked, burning skin, trying to stay warm.

In the mornings, too, Mona Sue forced him into the cold. The modern cabin sat on a bench in the cool shadow of Mount Nihart, and they broke their fast with a room-service breakfast on the deck, a robe wrapped loosely about her naked body while Benbow bundled into both sweats and a robe. She ate furiously, stoking a furnace, and recounted her dreams as if they were gospel, effortlessly consuming most of the spread of exotic cheeses and expensively unseasonable fruits, a loaf of sourdough toast and four kinds of meat, all the while aimlessly babbling through the events of her internal night, the dreams of a teenage girl, languidly symbolic and vaguely frightening. She dreamt of her mother, young and lovely, devouring her litter of barefoot boys in the dark Ozark hollows. And her father, home from a Tennessee prison, his crooked member dangling against her smooth cheek.

Benbow suspected she left the best parts out and did his best to listen to the soft southern cadences without watching her face. He knew what happened when he watched her talk, watched the soft moving curve of her dark lips, the wise slant of her gray eyes. So he picked at his breakfast and tried to focus his stare downslope at the steam drifting off the large hot-water pool behind the old shagbark lodge.

But then she switched to her daydreams about their dubious future, which were as deadly specific as a .45 slug in the brainpan: after the baby, they could flee to Canada; nobody would follow them up there. He listened and watched with the false patience of a teenage boy involved in his first confrontation with pure lust and hopeless desire.

Mona Sue ate with the precise and delicate greed of a heart surgeon, the pad of her spatulate thumb white on the handle of her spoon as she carved a perfect curled ball from the soft orange meat of her melon. Each bite of meat had to be balanced with an equal weight of toast before being crushed between her tiny white teeth. Then she examined each strawberry poised before her darkly red lips as if it might be a jewel of great omen and she some ancient oracle, then sank her shining teeth into the fleshy fruit as if it were the mortal truth. Benbow's heart rolled in his chest as he tried to fill his lungs with the cold air to fight off the heat of her body.

Fall had come to the mountains, now. The cottonwoods and alders welcomed the change with garish mourning dress, and in the mornings a rime of ice covered the windshield of the gray Taurus he had stolen at the Denver airport. New snow fell each night, moving slowly down the ridges from the high distant peaks of the Hard Rock Range and slipped closer each morning down the steep ridge behind them. Below the bench the old lodge seemed to settle more deeply into the narrow canyon, as if hunkering down for eons of snow, and the steam from the hot springs mixed with wood smoke and lay flat and sinuous among the yellow creek willows.

Benbow suspected, too, that the scenery was wasted on Mona Sue. Her dark eyes seemed turned inward to a dreamscape of her life, her husband, R. L. Dark, the pig farmer, his bull-necked son, Little R.L., and the lumpy Ozark offal of her large worthless family.

"Coach," she'd say—she thought it funny to call him Coach—interrupting the shattered and drifting narrative of her dreams. Then she would sweep back the thick black Indian hair from her face, tilt her narrow head on the slender column of her neck, and laugh. "Coach, that ol' R.L., he's a-comin'. You stole somethin' belonged to him, and you can bet he's on his way. Lit'l R.L., too, prob'ly, 'cause he tol' me once he'd like to string your guts on a bob-wire fence," she recited like a sprightly but not very bright child.

"Sweetheart, R. L. Dark can just barely cipher the numbers on a dollar bill or the spots on a card," Benbow answered, as he had each morning for the six months they'd been on the run, "he can't read a map that he hasn't drawn himself, and by noon he's too drunk to fit his ass in a tractor seat and find his hog pens. . . ."

"You know, Puddin', an ol' boy's got enough a them dollar bills, or stacks a them Franklins like we do," she added, laughing, "he can hire-out that readin' part, and the map part too. So he's a-comin'. You can put that in your momma's piggy bank."

This was a new wrinkle in their morning ritual, and Benbow caught himself glancing down at the parking lot behind the lodge and at the single narrow road up Hidden Springs Canyon, but he shook it off quickly. When he made the fateful decision to take Mona Sue and the money, he vowed to go for it, never glancing over his shoulder, living in the moment.

And this was it. Once more. Leaving his breakfast untouched, again, he slipped his hand through the bulky folds of Mona Sue's terry cloth robe to cradle the warm ripening fullness of her breasts and the long, thick nipples, already rock hard before his touch, and he kissed her mouth, sweet with strawberry and melon. Once again, he marveled at the deep passionate growl from the base of her throat as he pressed his lips into the hollow, then Benbow lifted her small frame—she nestled the baby high under the smooth vault of her rib cage and even at seven months the baby barely showed—and carried her to the bedroom.

Benbow knew, from recent experience, that the horse wrangler who doubled as room-service waiter would be waiting to clear the picnic table when they came out of the house to finish the coffee. The wrangler might have patience with horses but not with guests who spent their mornings in bed. But he would wait for long minutes, silent as an Sioux scout, as Mona Sue searched her robe for his tip, occasionally exposing the rising contour of a breast or the clean scissoring of her long legs. Benbow had given him several hard looks, which the wrangler ignored as if the blunt stares were spoken in a foreign tongue. But nothing helped. Except to take the woman inside and avoid the wrangler altogether.

This morning Benbow laid Mona Sue on the feather bed like a gift, opened her robe, kissed the soft curve of her swollen belly, then blew softly on her feathery pubic hair. Mona Sue sobbed quickly, coughed as if she had a catfish bone caught in her throat, her long body arching. Benbow sobbed, too, his hunger for her more intense than the hunger growling in his empty stomach.

While Mona Sue had swelled through her pregnancy, Benbow had shed twenty-seven pounds from his blocky frame. Sometimes, just after they made love, it seemed as if her burning body had stolen the baby from his own muscled flesh, something stolen during the tangle of love, something growing hard and tight in her smooth, slim body.

As usual, they made love, then finished the coffee, ordered a fresh pot, tipped the wrangler, then made love again before her morning nap.

While Mona Sue slept, usually Benbow would drink the rest of the coffee as he read the day-old Meriwether newspaper, then slip into his sweats and running shoes, and jog down the switchbacks to the lodge to laze in the hot waters of the pools. He loved it there, floating in the water that seemed heavier than normal, thicker but cleaner, clearer. He almost felt whole there, cleansed and healthy and warm, taking the waters like some rich foreign prince, fleeing his failed life.

Occasionally, Benbow wished Mona Sue would interrupt her naps to join him, but she always said it might hurt the baby and she was already plenty hot with her natural fevers. As the weeks passed, Benbow learned to treasure his time alone in the hot pool and stopped asking her.

So their days wound away routinely, spooling like silk ribbons through their fingers, as placid as the deeply still waters of the pool.

But this noon, exhausted from the run and the worry, the lack of sleep and food, Benbow slipped effortlessly into the heated gravity of Mona Sue's sleeping body and slept, only to wake suddenly, sweating in spite of the chill, when the air conditioner was switched off.

R. L. Dark stood at the foot of their bed. Grinning. The old man stretched his crinkled neck, sniffing the air like an ancient snapping turtle, testing the air for food or fun, since he had no natural enemies except for teenage boys with .22's. R.L. had dressed for the occasion. He wore a new Carhart tin coat and clean bib overalls with the old Webley .455 revolver hanging on a string from his neck and bagging the bib pocket.

Two good ol' boys flanked him, one bald and the other wildly hirsute, both huge and dressed in Kmart flannel plaid. The bald one held up a small ballpeen hammer like a trophy. They weren't grinning. A skinny man in a baggy white suit shifted from foot to foot behind them, smiling weakly like a gun-shy pointer pup.

"Well, piss on the fire, boys, and call the dogs," R. L. Dark said, hustling the extra .455 rounds in his pocket as if they were his withered privates, "this hunt's done." The old man's cackle sounded like the sunrise cry of a cannibalistic rooster. "Son, they say you coulda been some kinda football coach, and I know you're one hell of a poker player, but I'd a never thought you'd come to this sorry end—a simpleminded thief and a chicken-fuckin' wife stealer." Then R.L. brayed like one of the old plow mules he kept in the muddy bottoms of the White. "But you can run right smart, son. Gotta say that. Sly as an old boar coon. We might still be a-lookin' if'n Baby Doll there ain't a called her momma. Collect. To brag 'bout the baby."

Jesus, Benbow thought. Her mother. A toothless woman, now, shaped like a potato dumpling, topped with greasy hair, seasoned with moles.

Mona Sue woke, rubbing her eyes like a child, murmuring, "How you been, Daddy Honey?"

And Benbow knew he faced a death even harder than his unlucky life, knew even before the monster on the right popped him behind the ear with the ballpeen hammer and jerked his stunned body out of bed as if he were a child and handed him to his partner, who wrapped him in a full nelson. The bald one flipped the hammer and rapped his nuts smartly with it, then flipped it again and began breaking the small bones of Benbow's right foot with the round knob of the hammerhead.

Before Benbow fainted, harsh laughter raked his throat. Maybe this was the break he had been waiting for all his life.

* * *

Actually, it had all been Little R.L.'s fault. Sort of. Benbow had spotted the hulking bowlegged kid with the tiny ears and the thick neck three years earlier when the downward spiral of his football coaching career had led him to Alabamphilia, a small town on the edge of the Ozarks, a town without hope or dignity or even any convincing religious fervor, a town that smelled of chicken guts, hog manure, and rampant incest, which seemed to be the three main industries.

Benbow first saw Little R.L. in a pickup touch football game played on the hardscrabble playground and knew from the first moment that the boy had the quick grace of a deer, combined with the strength of a wild boar. This kid was one of the best natural running backs he'd ever seen. Benbow also found out just as quickly that Little R.L. was one of the redheaded Dark boys, and the Dark boys didn't play football.

Daddy R.L. thought football was a silly game, a notion with which Benbow agreed, and too much like work not to draw wages, with which once again Benbow agreed, and if'n his boys were going to work for free, they were damn well going to work for him and his hog operation, not some dirt-poor pissant washed-up football bum. Benbow had to agree with that, too, right to R.L.'s face, had to eat the old man's shit to get to the kid. Because this kid could be Benbow's ticket out of this Ozark hell, and he intended to have him. This was the one break Benbow needed to save his life. Once again.

* * *

It had always been that way for Benbow, needing that one break that never seemed to come. During his senior year at the small high school in western Nebraska, after three and a half years of mostly journeyman work as a blocking back in a pass-crazy offense, Benbow's mother had worked double shifts at the truck-stop café—his dad had been dead so long nobody really remembered him—so they could afford to put together a videotape of his best efforts as a running back and pass receiver to send down to the university coaches in Lincoln. Once they had agreed to send a scout up for one game, Benbow had badgered his high school coach into a promise to let him carry the ball at least twenty times that night.

But the weather screwed him. On what should have been a lovely early October Friday night, a storm raced in from Canada, days early, and its icy wind blew Benbow's break right out of the water. Before the game, it rained two hard inches, then the field froze. During the first half it rained again, then hailed, and at the end of the second quarter it became a blinding snow squall.

Benbow had gained sixty yards, sure, but none of it pretty. And at halftime the Nebraska scout came by to apologize but if he was to get home in this weather, he had to start now. The lumpy old man invited Benbow to try a walk-on. Right, Benbow thought. Without a scholarship, he didn't have the money to register for fall semester. *Damn,* Benbow thought as he kicked the water cooler, and *damn it to hell,* he thought as his big toe shattered and his senior season ended.

So he played football for some pissant Christian college in the Dakotas where he didn't bother to take a degree. With his fused toe, he had lost a step in the open-field and his cuts lost their precision, so he haunted the weight room, forced thick muscle over his running back's body, and made himself into a solid if small fullback, but good enough to wrangle an invitation to one of the postseason senior bowl games. Then the first-string fullback, who was sure to be drafted by the pros, strained his knee in practice and refused to play. Oh, God, Benbow thought, another break.

But God foxed this one. The backfield coach was a born-again fundamentalist named Culpepper, and once he caught Benbow neither bowing his head nor even bothering to close his eyes during a lengthy team prayer, the coach became determined to convert the boy. Benbow played along, choking on his anger at the self-righteous bastard until his stomach cramped, swallowing the anger until he was throwing up three times a day, twice during practice and once before lights-out. By game day he'd lost twelve pounds and feared he wouldn't have the strength to play.

But he did. He had a first half to praise the football gods, if not the Christian one: two rushing touchdowns, one three yards dragging a linebacker and a corner, the other thirty-nine yards of fluid grace and power; and one receiving, twenty-two yards. But the quarterback had missed the handoff at the end of the first half, jammed the ball against Benbow's hip, and a blitzing linebacker picked it out of the air, then scored.

In the locker room at halftime, Culpepper was all over him like stink on shit. *Pride goeth before a fall!* he shouted. *We're never as tall as we are on our knees before Jesus!* And all the other soft-brain clichés. Benbow's stomach knotted like a rawhide rope, then rebelled. Benbow caught that bit of vomit and swallowed it. But the second wave was too much. He turned and puked into a nearby sink. Culpepper went mad. Accused him of being out of shape, of drinking, smoking, and fornicating. When Benbow denied the charges, Culpepper added another, screamed *Prevaricator!* his foamy spittle flying into Benbow's face. And that was that.

Culpepper lost an eye from the single punch and nearly died during the operation to rebuild his cheekbone. Everybody said Benbow was lucky not to do time, like his father, who had killed a corrupt weighmaster down in Texas with his tire thumper, and was then killed himself by a bad Houston drug dealer down in the Ellis Unit at Huntsville when Benbow was six. Benbow was lucky, he guessed, but marked "Uncoachable" by the pro scouts and denied tryouts all over the league. Benbow played three years in Canada, then destroyed his knee in a bar fight with a Chinese guy in Vancouver. Then he was out of the game. Forever.

Benbow drifted west, fighting fires in the summers and dealing poker in the winter, taking the occasional college classes until he finally finished a PE teaching degree at Northern Montana and garnered an assistant coach's job at a small town in the Sweetgrass Hills, where he discovered he had an unsuspected gift for coaching, as he did for poker: a quick mind and no fear. A gift, once discovered, that became an addiction to the hard work, long hours, loving the game, and paying the price to win.

Head coach in three years, then two state championships, and a move to a larger school in Washington State. Where his mother came to live with him. Or die with him, as it were. The doctors said it was her heart, but Benbow knew that she died of truck-stop food, cheap whiskey, and long-haul drivers whose souls were as full of stale air as their tires.

But he coached a state championship team the next year and was considering offers from a football power down in northern California when he was struck down by a scandalous lawsuit. His second-string quarterback had become convinced that Benbow was sleeping with his mother, which of course he was. When the kid attacked Benbow at practice with his helmet, Benbow had to hit the kid to keep him off. He knew this part of his life was over when he saw the kid's eye dangling out of its socket on the grayish pink string of the optic nerve.

Downhill, as they say, from there. Drinking and fighting as often as coaching, low-rent poker games and married women, usually married to school-board members or dumb-shit administrators. Downhill all the way to Alabamphilia.

* * *

Benbow came back to this new world propped in a heap on the couch in the cottage's living room with a dull ache behind his ear and a thousand sharp pains in his foot, which was propped in a white cast on the coffee table, the fresh cast the size of a watermelon. Benbow didn't have to ask what purpose it served. The skinny man sat beside him, a syringe in hand. Across the room, R.L.'s bulk stood black against a fiery sunset, Mona Sue sitting curled in a chair in his shadow, slowly filing her nails. Through the window, Benbow could see the Kmart twins walking slow guard tours back and forth across the deck.

"He's comin' out of it, Mr. Dark," the old man said, his voice as sharp as his pale nose.

"Well, give him another dose, Doc," R.L. said without turning. "We don't want that boy a-hurtin' none. Not yet."

Benbow didn't understand what R.L. meant as the doctor stirred beside him, releasing a thin, dry stench like a limestone cavern or an open grave. Benbow had heard that death supposedly hurt no more than having a tooth pulled and he wondered who had brought back that bit of information as the doctor hit him in the shoulder with a blunt needle, then he slipped uneasily into an enforced sleep like a small death.

When he woke again, Benbow found little changed but the light. Mona Sue still curled in her chair, sleeping now, below her husband's hulk against the full dark sky. The doctor slept, too, leaning the fragile bones of his skull against Benbow's sore arm. And Benbow's leg was also asleep, locked in position by the giant cast resting on the coffee table. He sat very still for as long as he could, waiting for his mind to clear, willing his dead leg to awaken, and wondering why he wasn't dead too.

"Don't be gettin' no ideas, son," R.L. said without turning.

Of all the things Benbow had hated during the long Sundays shoveling pig shit or dealing cards for R. L. Dark—that was the trade he and the old man had made for Little R.L.'s football services—he hated the bastard calling him "son."

"I'm not your 'son,' you fucking old bastard."

R.L. ignored him, didn't even bother to turn. "How hot's that there water?" he asked calmly as the doctor stirred.

Benbow answered without thinking. "Somewhere between ninety-eight and one-oh-two. Why?"

"How 'bout half a dose, Doc?" R.L. said, turning now. "And see 'bout makin' that boy's cast waterproof. I'm thinkin' that hot water might take the edge off my rheumatism and I for sure want the coach there to keep me company. . . ."

Once again Benbow found the warm, lazy path back to the darkness at the center of his life, half listening to the old man and Mona Sue squabble over the air conditioner.

* * *

After word of his bargain with R. L. Dark for the gridiron services of his baby son spread throughout every tuck and hollow of the county, Benbow could no longer stop after practice for even a single quiet beer at any one of the rank honky-tonks that surrounded the dry town without hearing snickers as he left. It seemed that whatever he might have gained in sympathy, he surely lost in respect. And the old man treated him worse than a farting joke.

On the Saturdays that first fall, when Benbow began his days exchanging his manual labor for Little R.L.'s rushing talents, the old man dogged him all around the hog farm on a small John Deere tractor, endlessly pointing out Benbow's total ignorance of the details of trading bacon for bread and his general inability to perform hard work, complaining at great length, then cackling wildly and jacking the throttle on the tractor as if this was the funniest thing he'd ever seen. Even knowing that Little R.L. was lying on the couch in front of the television and soothing his sore muscles with a pint jar of 'shine, couldn't make Benbow even begin to resent his bargain, and he never even bothered to look at the old man, knowing that this was his only escape.

Sundays, though, the old man left him alone. Sunday was Poker Day. Land-rich farmers, sly country lawyers with sharp eyes and soft hands, and small-town bankers with the souls of slave traders came from as far away as West Memphis, St. Louis, and Fort Smith to gather in R.L.'s double-wide for a table stakes hold 'em game, a game famous in at least four states, and occasionally in northern Mexico.

On the sabbath he was on his own, except for the surly, lurking presence of Little R.L., who seemed to blame his coach for every ache and pain, and the jittery passage of a slim, petulant teenage girl who slopped past him across the muddy farmyard in a shapeless feed-sack dress and oversized rubber boots, trailing odd, throaty laughter, the same laughter she had when one of the sows decided to dine on her litter. Benbow should have listened.

But these seemed minor difficulties when balanced against the fact that Little R.L. gained nearly a hundred yards a game his freshman year.

The next fall, the shit-shoveling and the old man's attitude seemed easier to bear. Then when Benbow casually let slip that he had once dealt and played poker professionally, R.L.'s watery blue eyes suddenly glistened with greed, and the Sunday portion of Benbow's bargain became both easier and more complicated. Not that the old man needed him to cheat. R. L. Dark always won. The only times the old man signaled him to deal seconds was to give hands to his competitors to keep them in the game so the old man could skin them even deeper.

The brutal and dangerous monotony of Benbow's life continued, controlled and hopeful until the fall of Little R.L.'s junior year when everything came apart. Then back together with a terrible rush. A break, a dislocation, and a connection.

On the Saturday afternoon after Little R.L. broke the state rushing record the night before, the teenage girl stopped chuckling long enough to ask a question. "How long you have to go to college, Coach, to figure out how to scoot pig shit off concrete with a fire hose?"

When she laughed, Benbow finally asked, "Who the fuck are you, honey?"

"Mrs. R. L. Dark, Senior," she replied, the perfect arch of her nose in the air, "that's who." And Benbow looked at her for the first time, watched the thrust of her hard, marvelous body naked beneath the thin fabric of her cheap dress.

Then Benbow tried to make conversation with Mona Sue, made the mistake of asking Mona Sue why she wore rubber boots. "Hookworms," she said, pointing at his sockless feet in old Nikes. *Jesus,* he thought. Then *Jesus wept* that night as he watched the white worms slither through his dark, bloody stool. Now he knew what the old man had been laughing about.

On Sunday a rich Mexican rancher tried to cover one of R.L.'s raises with a Rolex, then the old man insisted on buying the fifteen-thousand-dollar watch with five K cash, and when he opened the small safe set in the floor of the trailer's kitchen, Benbow glimpsed the huge pile of banded stacks of one-hundred-dollar bills that filled the safe.

The next Friday night Little R.L. broke his own rushing record with more than a quarter left in the game, which was good because in the fourth quarter the turf gave way under his right foot, which then slid under a pursuing tackle. Benbow heard the *pop* all the way from the sidelines as the kid's knee dislocated.

Explaining to R.L. that a bargain was a bargain, no matter what happened with the kid's knee, the next day Benbow went about his chores just long enough to lure Mona Sue into a feed shed and out of her dress. But not her rubber boots. Benbow didn't care. He just fucked her. The revenge he planned on R. L. Dark a frozen hell in his heart. But the soft hunger of her mouth and the touch of her astonishing body—diamond-hard nipples, fast-twitch cat muscle slithering under human skin, her cunt like a silken bag of rich, luminous seed pearls suspended in heavenly fucking fire—destroyed his hope of vengeance. Now he simply wanted her. No matter the cost.

Two months later, just as her pregnancy began to show, Benbow cracked the safe with a tablespoon of nitro, took all the money, and they ran.

* * *

Although he was sure Mona Sue still dreamed, she'd lost her audience. Except for the wrangler, who still watched her as if she were some heathen idol. But every time she tried to talk to the dark cowboy, the old man pinched her thigh with horny fingers so hard it left blood blisters.

Their mornings were much different now. They all went to the hot water. The doctor slept on a poolside bench behind Mona Sue who sat on the side of the pool, her feet dangling in the water, her blotched thighs exposed, and her eyes as vacant as her half-smile. R. L. Dark, Curly, and Bald Bill, wearing cutoffs and cheap T-shirts, stood neck-deep in the steamy water, loosely surrounding Benbow, anchored by his plastic-shrouded cast, which loomed like a giant boulder under the heavy water.

A vague sense of threat, like an occasional sharp sniff of sulphur, came off the odd group and kept the other guests at a safe distance, and the number of guests declined every day as the old man rented each cabin and room at the lodge as it came empty. The rich German twins who owned the place didn't seem to care who paid for their cocaine.

During the first few days, nobody had much bothered to speak to Benbow, not even to ask where he had hidden the money. The pain in his foot had retreated to a dull ache, but the itch under the cast had become unbearable. One morning, the doctor had taken pity on him and searched the kitchen drawers for something for Benbow to use to scratch beneath the cast, finally coming up with a cheap shish kebab skewer. Curly and Bald Bill had examined the thin metal stick as if it might be an Arkansas toothpick or a bowie knife, then laughed and let Benbow have it. He kept it holstered in his cast, waiting, scratching the itch. And a deep furrow in the rear of the cast.

Then one morning as they stood silent and safe in the pool, a storm cell drifted slowly down the mountain to fill the canyon with swirling squalls of thick, wet snow, the old man raised his beak into the flakes and finally spoke: "I always meant to come back to this country," he said.

"What?"

Except for the wrangler slowly gathering damp towels and a dark figure in a hooded sweatshirt and sunglasses standing inside the bar, the pool and the deck had emptied when the snow began. Benbow had been watching the snow gather in the dark waves of Mona Sue's hair as she tried to catch a spinning flake on her pink tongue. Even as he faced death, she still stirred the banked embers glowing in Benbow's crotch.

"During WW Two," the old man said softly, "I got in some trouble over at Fort Chaffee—stuck a noncom with a broomstick—so the Army sent me up here to train with the Tenth Mountain. Stupid assholes thought it was some kinda punishment. Always meant to come back someday. . . ."

But Benbow watched the cold wind ripple the stolid surface of the hot water as the snowflakes melted into it. The rising steam became a thick fog.

"I always liked it," Benbow said, glancing up at the mountain as it appeared and disappeared behind the roiling clouds of snow. "Great hunting weather," he added. "There's a little herd of elk bedded just behind that first ridge." As his keepers' eyes followed his upslope, he drifted slowly through the fog toward Mona Sue's feet aimlessly stirring the water. "If you like it so much, you old bastard, maybe you should buy it."

"Watch your tongue, boy," Curly said as he cuffed Benbow on the head. Benbow stumbled closer to Mona Sue.

"I just might do that, son," the old man said, cackling, "just to piss you off. Not that you'll be around to be pissed off."

"So what the fuck are we hanging around here for?" Benbow asked, turning on the old man, which brought him even closer to Mona Sue.

The old man paused as if thinking. "Well, son, we're waitin' for that baby. If'n that baby has red hair and you tell us where you hid the money, we'll just take you home, kill you easy, then feed you to the hogs."

"And if it doesn't have red hair, since I'm not about to tell you where to find the money?"

"We'll just find a hungry sow, son, and feed you to her," the old man said, "startin' with your good toes."

Everybody laughed then: R. L. Dark threw back his head and howled; the hulks exchanged high fives and higher giggles; and Benbow collapsed underwater. Even Mona Sue chuckled deep in her throat. Until Benbow jerked her off the side of the pool. Then she choked. The poor girl had never learned to swim.

Before either the old man or his bodyguards could move, though, the dark figure in the hooded sweatshirt burst through the bar door in a quick, limping dash and dove into the pool, then lifted the struggling girl onto the deck and knelt beside her while enormous amounts of steaming water poured from her nose and mouth before she began breathing. Then the figure swept the hood from the flaming red hair and held Mona Sue close to his chest.

"Holy shit, boy," the old man asked unnecessarily as Bald

Bill helped him out of the pool. "What the fuck you doin' here?"

"Goddammit, baby, lemme go," Mona Sue screamed, "it's a-coming!"

Which roused the doctor from his sleepy rest. And the wrangler from his work. Both of them covered the wide wooden bench with dry towels, upon which Little R.L. gently placed Mona Sue's racked body. Curly scrambled out of the pool, warning Benbow to stay put, and joined the crowd of men around her sudden and violent contractions. Bald Bill helped the old man into his overalls and the pistol's thong as Little R.L. helped the doctor hold Mona Sue's body, arched with sudden pain, on the bench.

"Oh, Lordy me!" she screamed, "it's tearin' me up!"

"Do somethin', you pissant," the old man said to the wiry doctor, then slapped him soundly.

Benbow slipped to the side of the pool, holding on to the edge with one hand as he dug frantically at the cast with the other. Bits of plaster of paris and swirls of blood rose through the hot water. Then it was off, and the skewer in his hand. He planned to roll out of the pool, drive the sliver of metal through the old man's kidney, then grab the Webley. After that, he'd call the shots.

But life should have taught him not to plan.

As Bald Bill helped his boss into the coat, he noticed Benbow at the edge of the pool and stepped over to him. Bald Bill saw the bloody cast floating at Benbow's chest. "What the fuck?" he said, kneeling down to reach for him.

Benbow drove the thin shaft of metal with the strength of a lifetime of disappointment and rage into the bottom of Bald Bill's jaw, up through the root of his tongue, then up through his soft palate, horny brainpan, mushy gray matter, and the thick bones of his skull. Three inches of the skewer poked like a steel finger bone out of the center of his bald head.

Bald Bill didn't make a sound. Just blinked once dreamily, smiled, then stood up. After a moment, swaying, he began to walk in small airless circles at the edge of the deck until Curly noticed his odd behavior.

"Bubba?" he said as he stepped over to his brother.

Benbow leapt out of the water; one hand grabbed an ankle and the other dove up the leg of Curly's trunks to grab his nut sack and jerk the giant toward the pool. Curly's grunt and the soft clunk of his head against the concrete pool edge was lost as Mona Sue delivered the child with a deep sigh, and the old man shouted boldly, "Goddamn, it's a girl! A black-headed girl!"

Benbow had slithered out of the pool and limped halfway to the old man's back as he watched the doctor lay the baby on Mona Sue's heaving chest. "Shit fire and save the matches," the old man said, panting deeply as if the labor had been his.

Little R.L. turned and jerked his father toward him by the front of his coat, hissing, "Shut the fuck up, old man." Then he shoved him violently away, smashing the old man's frail body into Benbow's shoulder. Something cracked inside the old man's body, and he sank to his knees, snapping at the cold air with his bloody beak like a gut-shot turtle. Benbow grabbed the pistol's thong off his neck before the old man tumbled dead into the water.

Benbow cocked the huge pistol with a soft metallic click, then his sharp bark of laughter cut through the snowy air like a gunshot. Everything slowed to a stop. The doctor finished cutting the cord. The wrangler's hands held a folded towel under Mona Sue's head. Little R.L. held his gristled body halfway into a mad charge. Bald Bill stopped his aimless circling long enough to fall into the pool. Even Mona Sue's cooing sighs died. Only the cold wind moved, whipping the steamy fog across the pool as the snowfall thickened.

Then Mona Sue screamed, "No!" and broke the frozen moment.

The bad knee gave Benbow time to get off a round. The heavy slug took Little R.L. in the top of his shoulder, tumbled through his chest, and exited just above his kidney in a shower of blood, bone splinters, and lung tissue, and dropped him like a side of beef on the deck. But the round had already gone on its merry way through the sternum of the doctor as if he weren't there. Which, in moments, he wasn't.

Benbow threw the pistol joyfully behind him, heard it splash in the pool, and hurried to Mona Sue's side. As he kissed her blood-spattered face, she moaned softly. He leaned closer, but only mistook her moans for passion until he understood what she was saying. Over and over. The way she once called his name. And Little R.L.'s. Maybe even the old man's. "Cowboy, Cowboy, Cowboy," she whispered.

Benbow wasn't even mildly surprised when he felt the arm at his throat or the blade tickle his short ribs. "I took you for a backstabber," he said, "the first time I laid eyes on your sorry ass."

"Just tell me where the money is, *old man,*" the wrangler whispered, "and you can die easy."

"You can have the money," Benbow sobbed, trying for one final break, "just leave me the woman." But the flash of scorn in Mona Sue's eyes was the only answer he needed. "Fuck it," Benbow said, almost laughing, "let's do it the hard way."

Then he fell backward onto the hunting knife, driving the blade to the hilt above his short ribs before the wrangler could release the handle. He stepped back in horror as Benbow stumbled toward the hot waters of the pool.

At first, the blade felt cold in Benbow's flesh, but the flowing blood quickly warmed it. Then he eased himself into the hot water and lay back against its compassionate weight like the old man the wrangler had called him. The wrangler stood over Benbow, his eyes like coals glowing through the fog and thick snow.

Mona Sue stepped up beside the wrangler, Benbow's baby whimpering at her chest, snow melting on her shoulders.

"Fuck it," Benbow whispered, drifting now, "it's in the air conditioner."

"Thanks, old man," Mona Sue said, smiling.

"Take care," Benbow whispered, thinking, *This is the easy part,* then leaned farther back into the water, sailing on the pool's wind-riffled, snow-shot surface, eyes closed, happy in the hot, heavy water, moving his hands slightly to stay afloat, his fingers tangled in dark, bloody streams, the wind pushing him toward the cool water at the far end of the pool, blinking against the soft cold snow, until his tired body slipped, unwatched, beneath the hot water to rest.

JOHN GARDNER

Sometimes the price of fame and fortune is high. John Gardner, one of the handful of espionage writers whose best work will endure (I still think his Garden of Weapons *is the greatest spy novel I've read), never quite attained the popular and critical recognition of such contemporaries as John le Carré, Len Deighton, Ken Follett, and Frederick Forsyth. Then, several years after the death of Ian Fleming, he agreed to continue the James Bond series.*

Naturally, those books immediately shot to the bestseller lists, giving him the rewards of vast popularity. Equally predictably, critics blasted him for turning his back on his more serious work, saying the Bond books didn't have the depth and power of his other novels—the same ones they'd ignored in the past. Recently, he has produced novels that rank with his best work, notably Maestro, *which brought Herbie Kruger back to work, and* Confessor.

Gardner wrote (not in this story) that "sex is the glue that holds love together." That may well be the unifying theme of all his best work, which has as much to do with human relations as it does with international skulduggery.

—O.P.

The Loving You Get

BY JOHN GARDNER

Early in the last decade of the Cold War, Godfrey Benyon returned to London unexpectedly from Berlin to find his wife of fifteen years in bed with a senior colleague. For policemen and spies there often can be a high turnover in marriages. Both professions place dreadful strains on the contract between man and woman. The jobs are dangerous and consume a person's time and passion, leaving little space for any normal relationships. Some grains of love and respect can grow into stout and unshakable unions. Others just do not hold up.

Benyon and his wife Susan had married relatively young, and Godfrey had no reason to believe that Susan was anything else but happy and still in love with him. Certainly he still loved her and believed that she had come to terms with the lengthy periods when he was away from home, sometimes not even able to remain in touch.

There used to be a fallacy, commonly believed, that the family of an Intelligence or Security Service officer did not know what the husband or wife did in the way of government work. This, of course, is nonsense. Families always know, just as they know that they are quietly vetted from time to time in order to make sure they have not been suborned by some foreign espionage organization. This regular checking covers all branches of the Foreign Service and those in sensitive situations at the Home Office, not just members of the Secret Intelligence Service.

Ironically, the man with whom Susan Benyon had been committing adultery on a regular basis was the officer detailed to carry out the biannual in-depth examinations of her way of life.

His name was Saunders, commonly known to friends and enemies alike as "Soapy." To begin with, the seduction of Susan Benyon had been a ploy on Soapy's part to ascertain whether she put it about—as the jargon had it—thereby becoming a security risk.

However, after the first time, Saunders had enjoyed the delights of Susan Benyon's body so much that he made certain adjustments in his report and the pair became regular and consistent lovers.

Within a few months, Susan brought up the question of divorce from Godfrey and marriage to Saunders—something old Soapy did not want to happen. He had a decent and loving wife of his own and these extracurricular bouts of sex had livened up his own marriage. Susan had unwittingly assisted in turning Soapy's wilder fantasies into reality, and the result was that he eventually discovered hidden wonders in the sexual behavior of his own wife.

On the afternoon that Godfrey walked in on the lovers, he had naturally been tempted to violence and could easily have killed Saunders with one hand, for he was a born field officer and knew all there was to know about the black arts of death by finger or hand. Happily, he was well disciplined, leaving the room and waiting downstairs for Soapy to leave.

There was no row; no soaring accusations. Godfrey Benyon, being a man with an unforgiving nature, simply told his wife that he would leave that night. She admitted to loving Saunders, yet offered to put him aside and try to make their marriage work. Susan was not a fool and had long realized that, to Saunders, she was merely a bit on the side, to use the common expression of the time.

Even her pleading tears could not move her husband. He was in the business of treachery and knew the price that men and women paid for it within his own sphere of activity. He packed some clothes and a couple of sentimental items, then left the house they had shared for one and a half decades. His last act was to hand her the keys.

On the following morning he contacted his solicitor, set the divorce in motion, then went over to the headquarters of the Secret Intelligence Service—in those days Century House—and put in a report that he knew would get Saunders dismissed from the organization, almost certainly without a pension.

He did not enjoy these tasks, but his deep love for Susan ended at the moment he opened the door and saw, fleetingly, her body entwined with that of a man whom he had, until that second, respected without question.

Oddly, as he reported back for duty, putting his leave off for a few months, he recalled his father once having said to him, "As far as women are concerned, remember one thing: True and all-consuming love can kill. Sometimes it's not worth it." His parents' marriage had been far from ideal, but now he imagined that he knew what his father had been talking about. There was a coarser saying he had heard from junior officers—"The loving you get ain't worth the loving you get." Only, they substituted another word for *loving*. This last summed up his feelings exactly and with it came the anger. He felt a fool not to have detected his wife sooner. Part of his job, his livelihood and survival, had been to sense the danger signals, to put his finger on people and situations that were not quite right.

He did not realize it at the time, but the anger spawned a desire to take his revenge. Automatically he had wreaked havoc on Saunders's life, but the need for vengeance was now aimed at his soon to be ex-wife. While this requirement festered deep within his subconscious, Benyon got on with his professional life—though his colleagues later commented that Godfrey Benyon seemed to change into a hard and uncompromising man, something his superiors applauded. Benyon, they decided, would go a long way in the service.

They sent him back to Berlin, and in the next six months he crossed into the East on five separate occasions, servicing dead letter drops and making contact with the one agent he ran—usually from afar—highly placed in the typing pool of the KGB facility at Karlshorst.

This agent, known as *Brutus,* was a twenty-five-year-old young woman, the daughter of a couple of doctors who lived and worked in the West. Her name was Karen Schmidt—"Such an ordinary name," one of his superiors had said when she first offered herself for active work and cooperation with the Secret Intelligence Service.

Karen's parents were medical P4s for the service: psychiatrists knowledgeable in the ways of what were often known as "deep debriefs"—a term that covered a number of things ranging from counseling of agents who had been through traumas in the field to the kind of interrogations that required the use of certain dangerous drugs allowing inquisitors to reach far into the subconscious of a suspect's mind, trawling for and plundering secrets.

The doctors Schmidt were skilled and respected by the service, their records were squeaky clean, and their work had given Karen her entrée into the world of secrets. She was educated at a private, highly regarded school and went on to Oxford where she read foreign languages at St. Anthony's College—sometimes referred to as the spook prep school. Her parents tipped off the Foreign Office that she was interested in working in Intelligence, so the contact was made and she took the one-year course at the place they kept in Wiltshire for training possible field officers.

Benyon had looked after her when they sent her over the Wall and he had played her, normally at long distance, ever since. Now, at just around the time his divorce was becoming final, there was a reason to see her face-to-face again. A signal had made it plain that a meeting was essential, so he went over one evening in early June of 1986, and following the elaborate choreography necessary to this kind of thing, they wound up at a safe house not far from the Berliner Ensemble Theater.

His first surprise came when they made the initial contact on the street. He had seen her only once since she went over three years before. At that time they had given her the appearance of a mousy little thing, advising her about everything from a severe hairstyle, the kind of low-heeled shoes she should wear, to the nondescript clothes with which to equip her wardrobe. When she had gone over, Karen was a girl that no man would even look at twice. Now, her whole persona had changed. She was still the same girl, but the mouse had gone, leaving the most beautiful willowy young woman in its place.

She had let her hair grow, smooth, black and soft, with such a sheen that Benyon wanted to reach out and run splayed fingers through it. Her face was fuller and you could see that the brown eyes glittered with humor, while her lips seemed to have become fuller and more enticing, the corners bracketed by little laugh lines. She wore a white dress, full skirted so that Benyon was aware of her thighs and body moving under the thin material. In short, the almost ugly duckling had become the most attractive swan on the block.

His look must have been transparent, for Karen picked up

on it immediately. "You've noticed the change." She smiled, showing that one of her front teeth was crooked. "It was inevitable. You know about the promotions over the past couple of years."

"So the Party insists that you become more glamorous as you move up the ladder?"

"You'd be surprised, but yes. Yes, that's about it. I'm a supervisor now, and they expect supervisors to take care of their appearance. That was one of the things I had to see you about." Her voice had altered as well. The English was, of course, perfect, but the voice was more throaty than he remembered it.

They sat across from one another at the little wooden table. Benyon had brought food: bread, cold ham, potato salad, and a bottle of wine, explaining it away at the checkpoint as a picnic that he and his girlfriend were going to eat before the performance at the Berliner Ensemble, who were doing Brecht's *Threepenny Opera* that night. The girlfriend had been his backup—a young woman called Bridget Ransom, of whom the more caustic would say that a king's ransom could not buy the pathway to Bridget's secret garden. Maybe, but she was an incredibly good field officer with immaculate German and a Silesian accent, plus the ability to become invisible almost at will. On this occasion she watched Benyon's back during the sit-down with *Brutus,* and he could not have asked for anyone more professional.

So, in that bedraggled little apartment, not a stone's throw from the theater where Bert Brecht had built his fabled ensemble of actors, Benyon, the agent runner, listened to *Brutus,* his spy.

Over the years he had heard similar stories, but mainly from men. How, in the sensitive position in which they worked, an opportunity had presented itself which, if taken, would lead to a mother lode of hard intelligence. The opportunity always came in the form of a man or woman, depending on the sexual preference of the agent.

It was something Benyon had learned to treat and advise

on with great care. An agent in the field was often the loneliest of people, constantly tested, tried, and a prey to every kind of temptation. The common wisdom on field agents likened them to hermits, monks or nuns, living out their days in a hostile environment and denied a normal way of life.

Karen Schmidt's problem was a senior KGB officer, one of the main liaisons between the East German Intelligence and security forces and Moscow Center. That this man, Colonel Viktor Desnikoff, had access to deeply hidden secrets was not in doubt. Back in London, Benyon had read his dossier many times. It was part of his job to keep an eye on Soviet and East German intelligence officers—their comings and goings, any particular strengths or weaknesses, their general profiles, and all the other litter of life so often used by an opposing intelligence service. Desnikoff was undoubtedly a prime target, and here was Benyon's own agent telling him that the colonel had invited her out to dinner on several occasions and had now proposed that she should become his mistress with a later view to marriage.

Karen provided a wealth of detail about the man, and behind the music of her monologue, it was Benyon's job to see if he could detect gins, traps, or snares being laid for his agent. Equally he listened for sounds that might tell him if there were other facts lying just beneath the surface of what she was telling him. Mainly he weighed what advantage they might make of this man should he tell *Brutus* to go forward, against the possible problems such an operation could cause. He also experienced the constant paranoia of the case officer—had his agent already been quietly turned?

He took his time, keeping the conversation on other matters, ignoring her prods and coaxing for an answer to her main problem—should she commit herself to Desnikoff and the information that would undoubtedly follow? Or should she give the colonel the brush-off?

Benyon, with only one part of his brain on her question,

went through the standard drill. Had she detected any changes in attitude to her? Was she comfortable in the double role she was forced to play? Was she aware of any sudden rivalries that might cause her future chaos? These basic questions were important, as they gave him time to think through the right way to determine if Karen was being totally honest with him.

Finally he could put off the subject no longer.

"You fancy the colonel?" Watch her eyes and hands. Read the body language.

There was nothing to read as she shrugged. "He's a bit of a pig, actually. Not unattractive, but his manners are a little boorish."

"I have to ask you this. Even though he's boorish, are you in love with him?"

She gave a little laugh. "No way. That's an absurd thought."

"But you're willing to sleep with him, feign love for him?"

"Isn't that part of the job? I know what I can get from him with pillow talk. The information he carries in his head is state-of-the-art stuff. He has the ear of the chairman of the KGB. He swaps information with the Stasi and the other heads of Intelligence. I can tap in to that stuff, but there's only one way, and that lies through sexual favors."

"The giving of favors is not your job. We train people in the art of seduction, Karen. It's not part of your brief. Now, are you sure you don't fancy him?"

She smiled, looked into his eyes, held the gaze for a moment, and then dropped her head. One hand reached out and brushed his hand. In a small voice she said, "Not like I fancy some people."

The meaning was perfectly clear to Benyon. She was telling him that she cared for him, and his mind and body reacted in diametrically opposed ways. It had been some time now since he had been with a woman and he felt the hot stirrings in his groin.

Part of him rejected that wink of lust while another part yearned for a young woman as attractive as this one to hold him and tell him she loved him. It was at this moment, in a sudden quick flash, that he wondered if his emotions were motivated by a need for vengeance against his former wife. This he quickly dismissed as irrelevant.

The suspicious, professional side of his mind raised huge doubts. The wiles of women were myriad and complex. There was one of two reasons that Karen Schmidt, *Brutus,* might come on to him like this. One was what the psychiatrists call transference—where a patient begins to see the doctor as a love object. This same phenomenon was not uncommon among field agents and their case officers. The other reason was more ominous. To get her own way, a turned agent would stop at nothing to convince a case officer that she was right for a highly dubious job, and this included an act of seduction.

He thought—should she, shouldn't she? Will she, won't she? Will she join the dance? Aloud he asked her if she thought the colonel was on the level. "Is it, in your opinion, simply a bit of scalp hunting, or do you think he's serious?"

She thought for a moment. Then—"His reputation with the ladies is not good. I can only go by my intuition and *that* tells me he's being honest. Yes, he has a letch for me physically, but I sense it's more than that. He's talked to me about many things. It's a scatter effect, not just drawing a bead on my body. Behind all the boorish behavior, the crude manner, the man has a sensitive side. He's been trying to show me that."

"And you really think you can pull this off?"

"I'm not a virgin. I can fake with the best of them. My first priority is to get my hands—my brain, really—on information. If this is the only way to get the really good stuff, then I'll do it."

"You'll do it willingly?"

"I'll do it because I see it as part of my job. I can give you so much, Charles. Much more than I've been able to supply so far." Charles was Benyon's crypto. She knew him only by that name, and as far as he was aware, she was completely ignorant of his real name.

The telephone rang. Only one person knew the number. It would be Bridget Ransom telling him that the performance at the Berliner Ensemble was about to finish. At the distant end Bridget simply said, "Ten minutes," speaking in German just in case they had some kind of a check on the line.

He had to give Karen some instruction. A yes or a no. He counted to ten, then nodded his head. "Do it," he said, and thought he detected fear in her eyes. Fear and a kind of pleading. A woman who hoped the man would make some move; say that he cared, that he wanted her, or even touch her—fondle her after the ways of men and women who are intimately bound to each other.

Benyon did none of these things. "Do it," he said, then added, "I'll come over again in a few weeks—a couple of months if we're getting good information. I think we should talk after you've set the ball rolling, so to speak." He told her to give him at least ten minutes start before she left the little apartment, which smelled of wood rot, rising damp, and the antiseptic they used in safe houses in the East.

It took only three weeks for her first wedge of material to come in, sent as usual in a cryptic high-speed burst of electronic noise, caught in mid-air by the boys and girls at GCHQ in Cheltenham. GCHQ was Government Communications Headquarters, where they did everything from random frequency sweeps to twenty-four-hour listening, to recording reports sent at ultra-high speed from many places in the world.

Other reports followed and Benyon's senior officers in the SIS were more than pleased with the results. *Brutus* was sending them the pillow talk of Colonel Viktor Desnikoff and the pillow talk was exceptional. Things long hidden were now revealed, and on occasion, they were getting actual conversations between the KGB colonel and his masters in Moscow Center.

"Do we share any of this with the Americans?" Benyon's immediate superior asked of one of their policy-making deputy chiefs.

"Not on your life."

They knew when to share and when to keep quiet. What they were getting back from *Brutus,* while immediately useful, could also be kept in storage for exchange with the American service for some other secret. The heads of intelligence agencies can be like small boys at times, swapping information like kids swap cards.

Six weeks later, Benyon made another trip over the Wall and had a second face-to-face meeting with Karen Schmidt. This time she was more desirable than ever. She even hugged him and held him close for a good minute when they came together. More desirable, yes, but she was already showing the signs of strain.

When Benyon commented on it, she gave a rueful little smile and said something about maybe she had bitten off more than she could chew. "He's insatiable," she said. "But it opens his mouth."

"Can you keep it up?"

She gave a coarse laugh. "Well, he can, so I suppose I'll have to."

On this occasion, when they parted she looked into his eyes longingly and pulled him close, holding him as though she never wanted to let him go.

Back in London, Godfrey Benyon found that Karen the woman lingered too long in his mind. He worried about her and was concerned for her safety as an agent: after all, that was part of his profession. Yet his thoughts strayed to other things. She came to him in dreams, leaned over him naked and sucked his sex drive from his body in a way that was not merely an act of lust, but a ritual of profound love and care. She was present also in daydreams. He would think that he saw her, suddenly, in a crowd. On a few occasions he even hurried after this phantom Karen only to find, as he drew close, that the woman was not like her at all. There were times when he questioned his obsession with her, but finally he came to terms with the fact that he had fallen in love with his agent, who was now giving herself entirely to a Soviet colonel. Benyon began to feel the claws of jealousy cutting into his soul.

Automatically, it seemed, he also began to take more care in his appearance. He bought new clothes, became conscious of things like regular haircuts and unscuffed shoes. Occasionally he would stand in front of the mirror in the little apartment he rented in Chelsea, wondering how a young girl could possibly be interested in him outside his job. At forty-three his hair was showing signs of gray at the temples, yet his face, like his body, remained lean and firm. He was six foot one in height and had a strong bone structure. He would age well, so perhaps a girl of Karen's age might just be interested in him from a physical aspect. Yet she could know nothing of him as a man, for agent runners always held back their true personality, like actors playing the role expected of them.

The high-grade intelligence kept coming, but with it also came an undertow of strain, detectable not only by Benyon but also by those who ruled over him. Together they began to take precautions, setting up a quick route, a black hole through which they could get *Brutus* out should it become necessary.

Benyon knew that, inevitably, it would become necessary. It almost always did, particularly with a high-risk operation like this.

He met her in the following spring and thought she looked tired out, frazzled and jumpy, starting at shadows. Once more they embraced and this time—the first time ever—they kissed, not the air, or lips brushing a cheek, but mouth to mouth, tongue to tongue, body to body, so that each felt the other through their clothing.

Finally he pulled away, scorched with desire, faint with need and love. "There's no time." He sounded out of breath.

"My darling, we have to make time." She pulled him to her again and he drew away.

"This is far too dangerous. Listen, I have things to tell you. . . ." and he began to outline her escape route, which she immediately turned down.

"Charles, if I have to get out, I'm not going to be treated like someone about to face the Inquisition." Her cheeks flushed. "This has been bloody difficult. Hell, in fact. If I do have to run, then I want you to run with me and I want to be left alone, with you, in some nice quiet place for a couple of weeks before they start pounding on my memory and forcing me to give them a blow-by-blow and fuck-by-fuck commentary. . . ."

Benyon knew how she felt. He had seen it in others, the fear of an immediate interrogation—sometimes hostile—when they were still under the trauma of battle fatigue.

"It won't be that bad, my dearest." His heart was not really in it and he did not even believe himself. Interrogation of agents just in from the cold—as they now said, though the term had been filched from a novelist—was anything but amusing.

"No. Tell them from me that if the worst happens, I have to spend a couple of weeks with you before I speak to any of them. If they don't like it, they can forget about me coming over at all. I'll stick around and suffer the consequences." She reached up and twined her arms around his neck, pulled him close to her, and kissed him again, fiercely and with a violence that took his breath away.

"Just the two of us," she said. "A couple of weeks in the sun. It isn't much to ask after all I've done. It's my final offer, darling Charles, so get it for me."

In London they did not like it. This was going against all

the laws of that jungle which is the world of secrets. When you pull someone out, you get at them while they have it all fresh and straight in their minds. Yet, when Benyon laid out her threatened alternative, they finally caved in—if only because the grade A, genuine diamond information kept coming. What she was still giving them confirmed what they believed about certain aspects of the Soviet military, the political leaders, and their future operational plans.

On the next trip over the Wall, Benyon was able to tell her that it was a done deal. He went through all the important moves, which were tricky and needed careful timing. "Once we get you in the West," he smiled and gave her a long squeeze, "once you're over, the pair of us get on a plane and fly to Bermuda. There'll be minders, of course, but you won't even see them. Two weeks in Bermuda can't be bad."

"Right now, two weeks in Bermuda sounds like heaven."

"You're okay to go on at the moment?" he asked, concerned, for she had lost weight and had become more jumpy, while her eyes gave away the truth that she was under even greater strain than ever.

"He may suspect something." She bit her lip. "I don't know. I think I should go on a little longer. The stuff he's giving me . . . ?"

"Yes?"

"Does it still check out? Is it still good?"

"The best."

They kissed again before she left and he could feel her body pulsing urgently. Needing him, wanting him there and then.

The signal that she was in trouble came only two weeks later. A burst of what sounded like static, beamed directly into GCHQ. It contained the one word—*Overcast*.

Immediately a team went into action. Benyon was left out, as it was too dangerous for him to make the trip over the Wall. All he could do was sit and wait in the house they had prepared for Karen's return to the West. Even at this late stage, the people who gave him his orders tried to renege on their agreement. She could do nothing about it, they argued. Once she is in the West we can whisk her out of sight.

Benyon said this was no time to begin playing games with her. "She'll shut up like a clam and you'll never get the full story," he cautioned, knowing that the bureaucratic minds of those at the top of the SIS had to cross all their *T*s and dot all their *I*s.

So it was that Karen Schmidt was smuggled out of East Berlin and deposited in the West. Within an hour of her arrival, she was on a commercial flight to Paris, with Benyon watching over her with all the tender and loving care he could muster.

She had brought nothing with her, but two of the young women from the West Berlin Residents' office had been sent on a shopping spree armed with Karen's measurements—which were current as from the last time Benyon had seen her. It was one of the more pleasurable jobs he had been given: a tying of every thread so that she would not come near naked into her new life.

From Paris they flew direct to Bermuda and there, in a pleasant little villa on the outskirts of St. George's (they all felt that Hamilton was too risky), she overcame her fatigue and made love to Benyon in a way that surpassed any of his fantasies.

"Darling Charles," she whispered again and again as she lay quietly in his arms after the loving.

"Not my real name, my dearest girl," he said.

She gave him a slow and quaint smile, which showed her one crooked tooth. "I know, but I don't like the name Godfrey."

He thought nothing of the last remark and they drifted into a golden sleep, wrapped around one another like a pair of children.

In the days following, they became true lovers. Benyon caught only odd glimpses of the watchers assigned to them. He also took three telephone calls from the officer in charge of the team minding them. Apart from that, they took occasional walks down into St. George's, eating twice in a very good restaurant, doing a little touristy shopping and buying food, which they took turns in cooking for one another. For the balance of the time they were lovers and proved all the pleasures. They even made plans for the future, talked seriously about life out of the service and what they could do once they were both released from the bondage of secrecy.

The island of Bermuda was the perfect place for them after all. Was this not the island of which Shakespeare wrote in *The Tempest*—the isle full of noises and rapture, with the great magician Prospero and the tangle of love lives within that play? Karen and Benyon appeared to be enraptured by the place, in thrall as though Prospero were still in control, weaving a delicious and intoxicating spell around them.

Three nights before they were due to be shipped back to the UK for that long and exhausting time which it would take to clean her out, as the interrogators would phrase it, Karen realized that they had forgotten wine to drink with the dinner she was cooking.

Benyon left the charming little pink villa and walked down to King's Square, glimpsing the full-sized replica of the ship *Deliverance,* built on the island to carry an already shipwrecked group of colonists on to America, standing on Ordnance Island as a piece of living history with the statue of Sir George Somers, ill-fated leader of that expedition, arms raised as if he embraced this magic place. He bought a bottle of Karen's favorite wine and slowly walked back. In all he had been away for less than half an hour, but knew that something was wrong as soon as he saw the villa.

A car stood by the gate leading to the small patch of garden in front of the house, and he recognized one of the watchers, the man's name popping into his head straightaway—Pete Cannon. He had not seen the man for a decade, but knew him instantly, just as he knew something dreadful had occurred.

Inside, standing in the small living room, "Cheezy" Fowles, head of the watchers' unit, stood by the table with another of his men whom Benyon did not recognize.

"What . . . ?" he began.

"We lost her." Fowles, ramrod straight and very angry.

"Lost her? But . . ."

"But me no buts, Mr. Benyon. My people latched on to a couple of likely lads two days ago. I had one man at the back of the house. Now he's dead and she was away before you were ten yards down the street."

"But I don't . . ."

"I've got the island swarming with people, plus the local gendarmes, though I think it was done so quickly and professionally that she may even be far away by now. There are plenty of yachts and small boats off the coast, and we can't cover all of them."

"You mean she's been abducted?"

Slowly Fowles shook his head. "I think not. It would seem that she went of her own accord."

In the midst of the shock an old joke flashed through Benyon's head—"My wife's in the Caribbean." "Jamaica?" "No, she went of her own accord."

"Left you a little billet-doux and a package." He gestured to the table.

The package was neatly wrapped with the kind of paper you buy for wedding presents: all white with golden bells and horseshoes. Against it was a pink envelope.

Benyon hesitated for a moment, hovering between the envelope and the parcel. Finally he opened the parcel. Inside was a white box, around seven inches long and a couple of inches high.

He raised the lid and lifted the contents from a crunch of thin tissue. It was an almost pornographic little statue.

It was fashioned out of that metal so popular as expensive tourist statues: dark and pitted by what appeared to be verdigris. The figures, arched together in the sexual act, were sticklike, elongated and wastingly thin in the style of Giacometti.

There was a card with the gift, which simply read—*We are surely together for eternity now, my darling—Karen.*

With a sense of terrible breathlessness, as though some soot-black shadow had crossed over him, Benyon slowly slit the envelope and unfolded the one sheet of pink paper. Karen had written—

> *I am sorry, my darling Charles, I do care for you. At least that was not a lie, but from the beginning I have worked for KGB. Poor Viktor has been working for the Americans for many years. KGB instructed me to get very close to him, and when I told you the tale, so did you. It is an irony that he was passing the same chicken feed to the Americans, as I was passing to you. In all it looked and sounded authentic because it simply told you what you wanted to hear. What none of us knew then was that Viktor is HIV positive. Now he has full-blown AIDS and I am heading toward it rapidly. You will follow and we will eventually be together. I shall be well cared for until the end, for KGB looks after its own. I hope the same applies in your organization.*
>
> *Much love until death brings us together again.*
>
> *Karen.*

He heard the silent scream deep within him, knew he was a dead man, heard some words from *The Tempest*—"But I would fain die a dry death"—heard his father saying that true love sometimes killed, and lastly, as the truth swept over him, heard the old words—"The loving you get ain't worth the loving you get."

Faye Kellerman

*Hearts and flowers. Moonlight and roses. Passion and obsession. Sometimes love's magical elixir turns suddenly to venom. In Faye Kellerman's haunting tale of romance-*cum*-loathing, a young woman is first swept off her feet, then forced to struggle to regain her balance—all in the name of love.*

Although every lover wears masks, some are more deceptive than others. And sometimes the deception can take an ominous twist that causes the war between the sexes to move past trivial skirmishes onto a bloody battlefield where only a single winner can prevail.

Faye Kellerman, a lovely, charming, apparently gentle woman, has written convincingly of the darkest side of love gone wrong. Sales of her novels have not quite reached the heady levels of her husband Jonathan's (also represented in this volume), but the gap closes a bit with each new publication. They seem to revel in each other's successes and are as proud of each other's as of their own accomplishments. By all accounts, there is no dark side to their *marriage!*

—O.P.

The Stalker

BY FAYE KELLERMAN

It was hard for her to fathom how it all went so sour, because in the beginning the love had been sweet. The roses and candy that had been sent for no occasion, the phone calls at midnight just to say "I love you," the amorous notes left in her mailbox or on the desk at work, his stationery always scented with expensive cologne. The many romantic things that he had done during their courtship were now a thousand years old.

Somewhere buried beneath rage and hatred lay the honied memories. Julian telling her how beautiful and alluring she was, how he loved her lithe body, her soft hazel eyes and silken, chocolate-kissed hair. Bragging to his friends about her rapier wit or whispering in her ear about how her lovemaking had made him weak kneed. The last compliment had always been good for giggles or the playful slap on his chest. How she had blushed whenever he had raised his brows, had given her his famous wolfish leer.

The evening of his proposal had been the pinnacle of their fairy-tale romance, starting off with the Rolls-Royce complete with a uniformed driver. The chauffeur had offered her his arm, escorting her into the back of the white Corniche.

The most fabulous night in her life. And even today, steeped in righteous bitterness and bottomless hostility, she would admit that this sentiment still rang true.

There had been the front-row tickets at the theater. The play, *Fall of the House of Usher,* had been sold out for months. How he had gotten the seats had only added to Julian's aura of mystery and intrigue. Following the drama had been the exclusive backstage party where she had met the leading actors and actresses. They were all renowned stars and she had actually *talked* to them. Well, truth be told, mostly she had gushed and they had murmured polite thank-yous. But just *being* there, being part of the crowd . . .

She had thought herself in a dream.

And the dream had continued. After the play had come the elegant candlelight dinner in the city's most expensive restaurant. Julian had preordered the menu—a peek of what was to come. But, that evening, she had mistaken his controlling nature for élan and confidence. He had arranged everything, starting with the appetizers—beluga caviar accompanied by blinis and crisp, cold vodka. Next came a puree of warmed beets served with a dollop of sour cream and a sprinkle of chives. Then a salad of wild greens, followed by a lemon sorbet to clear the palate. All the courses enhanced with the appropriate wines.

She always remembered the feast clearly. So real. If she thought about it long enough, she'd wind up salivating.

The delectable beef Wellington dressed with pungent, freshly ground horseradish, accompanied by boiled red potatoes and julienne carrots and celery. And the desserts! The most sumptuous pastry cart. To complete the evening's meal—a deep, full-bodied sherry aged over fifty years.

They had eaten and eaten, and afterward their stomachs had bulged to dangerous proportions. So he had suggested a ride to the lake. They had walked the banks in bare feet, small wavelets spilling liquid silver over their toes and onto the shore. How beautiful he had looked that night, his fine, sandy hair slightly disheveled by a rippling breeze, gentle blue eyes full of longing and love. At the perfect moment, he had wrapped his arms around her waist. Strong, muscular arms in perfect proportion with his hard, well-worked body. During the kiss, he had slipped the diamond on her finger.

It had been pure magic.

That night she felt as if she had died and gone to heaven. Looking back on everything that had transpired since, she wished she had.

Subtle changes, barely noticeable at first. The catch in his voice when she came home a few minutes late . . . the questions he had asked.

What happened?

Who were you with?

Why didn't you call, Dana?

She explained herself, but he never seemed satisfied. She brushed off his nosiness and irritation. It was because he cared.

Then there were other things. The lipstick in her purse placed in the wrong zippered compartment, her clothing drawers in disarray even after she distinctly remembered folding her sweaters neatly. Finally came the strange clicks on the extension when she talked to a girlfriend or her mother.

No, it couldn't be, she would tell herself. *Why would Julian want to listen in on her boring conversation?*

Yet the clicks continued—day after day, month after

month. Finally, she summoned her nerve and asked him about it. At first, he had waved her off as imagining things. She took him at his word because the clicks seemed to suddenly stop.

But they returned—occasional at first, then once again at frequent intervals.

He'd been eavesdropping: of that she was sure. She was puzzled by his odd behavior, then angry. He was violating her privacy and that was inexcusable. Another discussion was in order. Despite his initial denials, she knew he was lying. So she pressed him.

Her first mistake. He exploded, raising the phone upward, yanking it out of its jack and heaving it against the wall.

"Goddamn it, Dana! If *you* wouldn't tie up the phone so long, *I* wouldn't have to pick up the extension to see when you finished your conversation."

Tears welled up in her eyes, her ears shocked with disbelief. She stammered, "J-Julian, why didn't you just ask me to get off the phone?"

"I shouldn't have to *ask* you; you should goddamn *know*." He was breathing very hard. Suddenly, he lowered his voice. It became quieter, but not any softer. "A wife should know what her husband wants. And where's your consideration, for God's sake! What kind of a *wife* are you, anyhow?"

Stunned, she turned on her heels to leave. He caught her arm, spun her around. Spittle at the corners of his mouth, red angry blotches upon his face. His fingers clamped around her arm like an iron manacle. And his *eyes*! They had turned into hot pits of violence. She shrank under his scrutiny. His voice so whispery it was sepulchral.

"You don't . . . *ever* . . . walk out on me, you hear?"

Paralyzed with fear, she hadn't been able to respond. When Julian repeated his demand a second time, the threat in his tone even more menacing, she somehow managed a nod.

It was the first of many incidents. The slightest insult—real or imagined—sent him into fits of uncontrollable temper and rage. Though he never actually hit her, his demonic eyes were enough to cause her to cower. She didn't dare tell anyone the truth. Sinking faster and faster into a quicksand pit of despair and loneliness, she knew she had only two options—to die or to escape.

Her defection was quick and complete. One day when he was away at work, Dana simply packed up her meager belongings and left. For six months, she hid under many aliases and assumed identities. As expected, he caught up with her. But six months was a long enough time for her to recover her ground. She boldly marched into the lawyers' offices. A few months later, Julian was served divorce papers along with an official restraining order. She knew that the order had little enforcement or protection power; a weak remedy akin to the Dutch boy plugging up the dike by putting his finger in the hole.

So she took precautions. Every time Dana got into or out of her car, she scanned her surroundings, looking over both shoulders. Keys gripped in her right hand, Mace locked into the fingers of her left hand, she always made it a point to walk quickly from her car to her destination, her head pivoting from side to side, her ears and eyes alert, attuned to the simplest of nuances, perceiving imminent danger out of seemingly innocuous events.

Terrible to live like this, Dana muttered angrily to herself, *but what is the alternative?*

Dana knew Julian was possessed, just too crazy to be dealt with. Maybe it was because the wound was so raw. She hoped that things would get better after the divorce. Julian was no dummy. Surely he'd come to his senses and realize that his obsession was no solution for either of them.

The day their marriage was declared legally over, things became even worse. First came the midnight tapping on her door. Then the rattling of windows and the unexplained jiggling of doorknobs. One night, after weeks of having been mentally tortured by his lunatic hovering, she drew up enough strength to investigate. In a wild burst of energy, she threw open the front door only to witness an eerie dark landscape of streets and trees and houses, all devoid of human intrusion.

A portent of things to come. He always seemed to disappear just out of fingertip's reach.

The sounds continued, so Dana moved—and moved, and moved. But he always seemed to find her. Not that he ever showed his face directly; Julian was too much the coward for that. Still, she was aware of his presence *wherever* she went, *whatever* she did. He appeared as furtive shadows and distant ghosts.

And always at night.

Sometimes she could swear she actually saw him, her fleeting phantom. At these times, she'd run down the street, cursing his name. People thought her crazy.

And Dana felt as if she *was* going crazy. Because no matter how hard she tried, she failed to catch him. Julian seemed to fade into the mist until nothing but air was left behind. Nerves frayed, Dana couldn't eat and her weight dropped dangerously low. Fearful for her sanity, she remained housebound except for essential errands. In desperation, she bought a guard dog, a German shepherd that abruptly died one day from food poisoning. She bought another dog. The second canine, Tiger, was killed by a vicious hit-and-run motorist, the vehicle throwing the dog twenty feet into the air, breaking every bone in her body. The driver, of course, was never caught.

In the animals' martyrdom, Dana finally found an inner strength. Something erupted inside Dana's soul when she carried Tiger's carcass, lovingly wrapped in a warm blanket, to the vet. Nobody should be able to get away with this.

So she began to fight back. At first, she carried a knife in her purse. When she learned that carrying a concealed knife was a felony, she switched over to a gun. Concealing a revolver was just a misdemeanor and she could live with that. With her last spare dollars, she purchased an unregistered .32 Smith & Wesson on the black market. Then she began to learn how to use it. Weekly visits to the shooting range became daily visits. Developing her accuracy, her reflexes, her eye. Six months later, she finally felt as if she had parity with the bastard.

She felt *empowered*!

Just try anything now, Julian. Just try *it!*

If he dared to make a move, so would she.

She was ready.

Frequent moves during the last year did little to enhance Dana's job résumé. After months of rejection in her trained field of social work (who wanted a therapist whose own life was in shambles?), Dana gave up on employment in counseling. Determined to beat her spate of terrible fortune, she managed to land a job as a sales representative for a small family-owned medical supply company. Her job necessitated lots of travel, visits to hundreds of doctors' offices and hospitals scattered over the southern California area.

To Dana's surprise, she loved her work. Her hours were her own and she liked working with people. The unexpected bonus was *Julian*. The son of a bitch had been able to prey upon her when her routine consisted of driving to and from the market. But with her on the road most of the time, traveling from office to office, the bastard just couldn't seem to keep up with her schedule. It was too hard for him to stalk over wide distances.

As a traveling salesperson, Dana was meticulous about the care and upkeep of her car. So she was surprised when her Volvo —usually as reliable as a dray horse—stalled on the freeway.

Of course this had to happen at night.

Quickly, she pulled the car over to the side, shut the motor, shifted back to neutral, and tried again. The engine kicked in but knocked loudly as she drove. Then the motor started smoking.

By her calculations she was still some twenty miles away from home. Immediately, she pulled the car off the freeway, hoping to find a twenty-four-hour service station. But as Dana peered over the deserted ink-washed streets, she decided that getting off the freeway had been a bad idea. Better to be in a trafficked area. She'd phone the AAA from a freeway call box.

Though Dana had only traveled around six blocks, she had abruptly lost her sense of direction. She made a couple of turns, her car bucking at each shift of the wind. Abandoned and fearful, she felt swallowed up by urban decay.

The engine heaved a final hacking cough before dying. Again, Dana tried to breathe life into the machine. Though the motor turned over and over, wheezing like an asthmatic, it refused to kick in.

Suddenly, Dana was aware of her heartbeat.

She had been on the road for over three hours, coming back from San Bernardino. She knew she was somewhere in downtown Los Angeles, but wasn't exactly sure where. She had taken the Los Angeles Street exit from the Santa Monica Freeway. During the day, Los Angeles Street held small shops and open-air stalls of discount apparel. But late at night, as the hands on Dana's watch approached the witching hour, the streets were ugly and desolate.

She didn't panic, though. Her .32 was in her glove compartment. She inserted the key into the box's lock, turned it to the left, and then the door dropped like a drawbridge. She picked up the hard-packed metal. Moonlight struck her eyes as she examined her reflection in the nickel-plated steel. Without thinking, she realized she was fixing her hair.

Well, that makes sense, Dana. Primp and preen so you'll look attractive to all those rapists.

She let the gun drop to her lap and tried the engine for a

final time. The motor spat out rapid clicks that sounded like rounds of muted machine-gun fire.

She yanked the keys out of the ignition and threw them in her purse. Exhaling out loud, she rooted through the glove compartment until she found the box of bullets. Little compact things. For a minute, she fingered them like worry beads, the slender pellets picking up sweat from her hands. Then she loaded the gun. Checking the safety catch, she stowed the revolver inside her jacket.

Dana got out of the car.

She shut the door, securing the car with the beep of a remote. Forget about fixing the damn engine. Just walk back to the freeway, find a roadside phone, call a taxi, and get the hell home. She'd worry about the Volvo in the morning.

If it was still there in the morning. The neighborhood was rich with car thieves and other bad actors.

Don't even think about it.

The sky was foggy, moonlight glowing iridescent through the mist. It was good that there was a moon out tonight, because the streetlights offered little illumination. Just tiny spots of yellow blobs looking like stains of dog piss.

First things first, Dana thought. *Find out where you parked so you can direct the AAA back in the morning.*

She had stalled in the middle of a long, deserted block. Nothing much in the way of immediate landmarks. The street held old two-story buildings fronted with iron bars and grates. As Dana's eyes swept over the street, she noticed a few vacant lots between the stores, breaking up the rows like a giant smile missing a couple of teeth.

Most of the buildings were in disrepair. Some of them had bricks missing from the facades, others had their surface stucco pocked by bullets. All the structures were heavily graffitied. The shops were chockablock retail outlets. Dust-covered windows displayed kitchen supplies and tool chests sitting next to boom boxes, CD players, and television sets. Dresses and jackets were strung on clotheslines across the ceiling, the apparel looking like headless apparitions. Nothing distinct about any of the shops. No names stenciled onto the doors or windows, and the signs above were illegible in the dark.

Just get home and worry about it later.

Warding off the willies, Dana hurried toward the nearest street corner, footsteps echoing behind her. Though wrapped in a wool jacket, Dana realized her legs, encased in thin nylon, were freezing. Her feet, shoved into hard leather pumps, felt like ice blocks. Looking over her shoulders, eyes darting about, she jogged stiffly to the corner, heels clacking against the sidewalk.

No street signs.

Where was she? And where *the hell* was the freeway? She couldn't see in the dark, couldn't make out any elevated roads of concrete. Dana knew she hadn't driven very far from the freeway. Damn thing had to be around here someplace.

A distant shriek made her jump. Who or what had made that noise? A victim's cry for help? Someone whooping for joy? Maybe it was just a night owl.

Heart racing, she realized she was breathing too fast.

Don't panic! Dana instructed herself. *Use your brain!*

No, she couldn't see the freeway. But she could hear it. A soft, distant whooshing of cars passing by at high speeds.

Follow the noise. She turned left at the corner.

Walking toward the sound, making sharp taps on the pavement. Her hands were numb, frigid fingers stuffed into her pockets.

Another turn. She couldn't be far from the on-ramp now.

Her footsteps reverberating, trailing her like Hansel and Gretel's breadcrumbs.

Clack, clack, clack, clack . . .

The blast of a motorcycle shot through the air. Dana stopped, jumped, brought her hand to her chest. She took a deep breath and pressed on. A turn right, then a turn left. Passing one store after another, her stride quick and efficient.

Clack, clack, clack, clack . . .

Another block. More stores. A disquieting sense of sameness . . . stillness.

A ghost town.

Then the strained rumbling of a semi going uphill.

Freeway noises.

Yet the sounds were as distant as before. Was she walking in circles? To the noises? Away from the noise? She was disoriented, lost, and scared.

A chill ran down her spine. She spun around, her eyes catching a glimpse of a shadow.

Or did they?

She was seeing things.

A turn to her left, something darted out of sight.

Her imagination playing head games.

Stop it! she ordered herself.

She began to sweat, clay-cold fingers now slippery wet. She rubbed clammy fingers on her skirt. Looked all around.

Go back to the car!

Where was the car?

Moisture poured off her forehead.

She turned around, heels going clack, clack, clack, clack . . .

Noises followed her.

She stopped cold in her tracks.

Silence.

She continued on, then heard the foreign noises again.

Little pat-pat noises. Rubber-soled shoes—like rodents scurrying in the attic.

Again, she stopped.

And so did the noises.

What to do! What to do!

Julian!

Son of a bitch!

This time, he was going to get her!

Or so he thought!

She willed herself to breathe slowly, rubbed her hands together.

She took a few steps forward.

Clack, clack, clack followed by pat, pat, pat.

She stopped walking.

So did he.

She pivoted around.

Nothing to see. Nothing to hear. A quiet night except for the rapid inhalations of her own breathing. Slowly she made out distant echoes.

A few more steps.

She stopped, jerked her head over her shoulder. Saw nothing but dewy air.

Kept walking.

More footsteps behind her.

She started running.

So did he.

Footsteps keeping pace with her, *stalking* her. Louder, harder, closer. Panic seized her body.

Don't turn around. Don't let the bastard see your fear.

And then the absurdity hit her.

Your fear?!

You're letting the bastard make you feel *fear?!*

Slowly, her right hand reached for her revolver, icicle-hard fingers gripping the butt of the gun.

With shaking hands, she retracted it from her jacket.

This is for you, you *bastard*!

No more!

Trembling so hard, she almost dropped to her knees.

No more, no more, no more!

End it all, Dana!

Right now!

Here!

At this moment!

No more running!

No more hiding!

No more *fear*!

Skidding to a stop, she swung around on her heels, gun grasped in a professional two-handed hold.

Shouting, "Freeze, you filthy *bastard*!"

But he didn't freeze!

Immediately, the air spewed forth hot white lights. Like bursts from firecrackers except it wasn't the Fourth of July. Deafening shots ringing into the air, exploding in her head!

Still, the bastard kept coming at her!

Falling at her!

His mouth open—frozen into a horrific silent scream.

Blood pouring from his gullet.

Crying out as he lunged helplessly toward her, hitting her chest, knocking her backward. A dull thud as he hit the ground facedown. Dana could hear the crunch of facial bones smashing against the hard pavement.

Dana screamed—a helpless siren that was heard by no one. Staggering to keep her balance, her head seeing tiny pinpoints of light.

Don't faint, she pleaded with herself. *Don't faint!*

Breathing hard and deeply, eyes intently focused on the corpse lying at her feet. Her fingers were still gripped around a trigger.

A simple death wasn't enough for the years of abuse he had given her.

Aiming the barrel toward the crumpled body.

Pressing the trigger harder and harder.

Take *that,* you slimy bastard!

Take *that*, and *that*, and *that*!

But the gun refused to spit fire.

Jammed!

But how could that . . .

Then her brain spun into overdrive as her eyes noticed the reason why.

The safety catch was still on.

The gun hadn't jammed.

The gun never went off!

Then how did she . . . how could . . .

Eyes drifting upward from the body to the erect figure in front of her.

Julian!

A smoking gun at his side. An evil smirk on his face.

In the still midnight mist, his soft-spoken words screamed derision inside her head.

"Just can't survive without me, can you, Dana?"

He started walking toward her.

"Gun can't help you, if you don't have the guts to use it. And you don't have the guts, do you?"

His mocking smile widening as he came closer.

"Lucky for you, I was around. Otherwise, you'd have been turned into hamburger by Mister Shit over there."

Julian kicked the body, moved another step closer to her.

"Speak, my love," Julian crooned. "A simple thank-you would be sufficient."

Tears pouring from her eyes, streaming down her face. Dana whispered out a sob-choked thank-you.

Julian's expression softened, but his smug smile remained.

"I'll always be around for you, Dana," he whispered. "Always. Because I love you. I can't escape you, Dana. And you can't escape me either."

She nodded.

Julian fell to his knees. "It's never too late, my beautiful lover. Come back to me. Come back to where you belong."

He stood, then raised his arms, ready to accept her embrace.

She raised her arms.

Unlocking the safety, she pumped six rounds of fiery lead into his body.

He died with the smirk still on his face.

At the eulogy, Dana spoke of his extraordinary valor. How he had saved her from a sick and deranged man with evil on his mind. Through molten gunshots and powder-choked air, in a moment's flash of unthinking selflessness, he had risked his life to save hers. Managing to squeeze off enough rounds to end her attacker's life before succumbing to his own mortal wounds. And because of his superhuman act, her life was spared while his own life had ended. His years . . . cut short . . . in his prime . . . just because of one man's treacherous deeds.

His mother cried bitterly. His sisters wept and wept. The funeral was crowded. It seemed that all the neighbors had come out to pay their last respects. Everyone attending the ceremony knew his history. Yet they were all more than a little puzzled by Dana's flowery words, her effusive commendations and praises.

And so it came to pass that Eugene Hart, a twenty-two-year-old felon with a long and illustrious history of brutal violence and rape, was put to rest with a hero's burial.

JONATHAN KELLERMAN

Love isn't always about hearts and flowers: sometimes it's also about smushed carrots and dirty diapers. An infant, in fact, often tugs at the tenderer emotions even more deeply than the most adoring paramour, because the passion felt for a child is about innocence and vulnerability as well as the ineluctable ties of blood.

In suspense maestro Jonathan Kellerman's confounding tale, mother love certainly seems to be the focus as young mom Karen indulges cute little Zoe in a nearly empty restaurant at lunchtime. Gurgling in her high chair while cleverly pitching peas to the floor, Zoe is oblivious of the table of sinister-looking gents in the corner. Karen, however, is not and, somehow, within the space of a few confused moments, a quick exit is the move she's forced to make.

Jonathan Kellerman is that great rarity—an author who enjoyed enormous success with his first book (When the Bough Breaks, *which won an Edgar Allan Poe award from the Mystery Writers of America), and who manages to increase both the high quality of the work and its success, as each subsequent novel has immediately leapt onto the bestseller list.*

—O.P.

The Things We Do for Love

BY JONATHAN KELLERMAN

Mashed spaghetti. Some things you could never prepare for.

It wasn't as if she and Doug were mega-yuppies but they both liked their pasta al dente and they both liked to sleep late.

Then along came Zoe, God bless her.

The *sculptress.*

Karen smiled as Zoe plunged her tiny hands into the sticky, cheesy mound. Three peas sat on top like tiny bits of topiary. The peas promptly rolled off the high chair and landed on the restaurant floor. Zoe looked down and cracked up. Then she pointed and began to fuss.

"Eh-eh! Eh-eh!"

"Okay, sweetie." Karen bent, retrieved the green balls, and put them in front of her own plate.

"Eh-*eh!*"

"No, they're dirty, honey."

"Eh-eh!"

From behind the bar, the fat dark waiter looked over at them. When they'd come in, he hadn't exactly greeted them with open arms. But the place had been empty, so who was he to be choosy? Even now, fifteen minutes later, the only other lunchers were three men in the booth at the far end. First they'd slurped soup loud enough for Karen to hear. Now they were hunched over platters of spaghetti, each one guarding his food as if afraid someone would steal it. *Theirs* was probably al dente. And from the briny aroma drifting over, with clam sauce.

"Eh!"

"No, Zoe, Mommy can't have you eating dirty peas, okay?"

"Eh!"

"C'mon, Zoe-puss, yucko-grosso—no, no, honey, don't cry—here, try some carrots, aren't they pretty, nice pretty *orange* carrots—orange is *such* a pretty color, much prettier than those yucky peas—here, look, the carrot is dancing. I'm a dancing carrot, my name is Charlie. . . ."

Karen saw the waiter shake his head and go back through the swinging doors into the kitchen. Let him think she was an idiot, the carrot ploy was working: Zoe's gigantic blue eyes had enlarged and a chubby hand reached out.

Touching the carrot. Fingers the size of thimbles closed over it.

Victory! Let's hear it for distraction.

"Eat it, honey, it's soft."

Zoe turned the carrot and studied it. Then she grinned.

Raised it over her head.

Windup and the pitch: fastball straight to the floor.

"Eh-*eh!*"

"Oh, Zoe."

"Eh!"

"Okay, okay."

Time for Mommy to do her four thousandth bend of the morning. Thank God her back was strong but she hoped Zoe got over the hurl-and-whine stage soon. Some of the other mothers at Group complained of serious pain. So far, Karen felt surprisingly fine, despite the lack of sleep. Probably all the years of taking care of herself, aerobics, running with Doug. Now he ran by himself. . . .

"Eh!"

"Try some more spaghetti, honey."

"Eh!"

The waiter came out like a man with a mission, bearing plates heaped with meat. He brought them to the three men at the back, bowed, and served. Karen saw one of the three—the thin lizardy one in the center—nod and slip him a bill. The waiter poured wine and bowed again. As he straightened he glanced across the room at Karen and Zoe. Karen smiled but got a glare in return.

Bad attitude, especially for a dinky little place this dead at the height of the lunch hour. Not to mention the musty smell and what passed for decor: worn lace curtains drawn back carelessly from flyspecked windows, dark, dingy wood varnished so many times it looked like plastic. The booths that lined the mustard-colored walls were cracked black leather, the tables covered with your basic cliché checkered oilcloth. Ditto Chianti bottles in straw hanging from the ceiling and those little hexagonal floor tiles that would never be white again. Call *Architectural Digest*.

When she and Zoe had stepped in, the waiter hadn't even come forward, just kept wiping the bartop like some religious rite. When he'd finally looked up, he'd stared at the high-chair Karen had dragged along as if he'd never seen one before. Stared at Zoe, too, but not with any kindness. Which told you where he was at, because *everyone* adored Zoe, every single person who laid eyes on her said she she was the most adorable little thing they'd ever encountered.

The milky skin—Karen's contribution. The dimples and black curls from Doug.

And not just family. Strangers. People were always stopping Karen on the street just to tell her what a peach Zoe was.

But that was back home. This city was a lot less friendly. She'd be happy to get back.

Let's hear it for business trips. God bless Doug, he did try to be liberated. Agreeing to have all three of them travel together. He'd made a commitment and stuck to it; how many men could you say that about?

The things you do for love.

They'd been together four years. Met on the job, both of them free-lancing, and right away she'd thought he was gorgeous. Maybe too gorgeous, because that type was often unbearably vain. Then to find out he was nice. And bright. *And* a good listener. Pinch me, I'm dreaming.

Within a week they were living together, married a month later. When they'd finally decided to build a family, Doug showed his true colors: true blue. Agreeing to an equal partnership, splitting parenthood right down the middle so they could both take on projects.

It hadn't worked out that way but that was her doing, not his. Karen was a firm believer in the value of careful research and during her pregnancy she read everything she could find about child development. But despite all the books and magazine articles, there was no way she could have known how demanding motherhood would turn out to be. And how it would change her.

Even with that, Doug had done more than his share: convincing her to express milk so he could get up for middle-of-the-night feedings, changing diapers. *Lots* of diapers; Zoe had a healthy digestive system, God bless her, but Doug wasn't one to worry about getting his hands dirty.

He'd even offered to cut back on projects and stay home so Karen could get out more but she found herself wanting to spend less time on the job, more with Zoe.

What a homebody I've become. Go know.

She touched Zoe's hair, thought of the feel of Zoe's soft little body, stretched out wiggling and kicking and pink on the changing table. Then Doug's body, long and muscled . . .

The restaurant had grown quiet.

She realized Zoe was quiet. Elbow-deep in the spaghetti now, kneading. Little Ms. Rodin. Maybe it was a sign of talent. Karen considered herself artistic, though sculpture wasn't her medium.

Watching Zoe's little hands work the mess of what had once been linguine with just a little butter and cheese, she laughed to herself. *Pasta*. It meant paste and now it really was.

Zoe scooped up a gob, looked at it, threw it onto the floor, laughing.

"*Eh*-eh."

Bend and stretch, bend and stretch . . . she did miss running with Doug. The two of them shared so much, had such a special rapport. Working in the same field helped, of course, but Karen liked to think the bond went deeper. That their union had produced something greater than the sum of its parts.

And baby makes three . . . Motherhood was much tougher than anything she'd ever done, but also more rewarding in ways she'd never expected. Nubby fingers caressing her cheek as she rocked Zoe to sleep. The first cries of "Mama!" from the remote-control speaker each morning. Such incredible *need*. Thinking about it almost made her cry. How could she go back to working full-time with this little peach needing her so intensely?

Thank God money was no problem. Doug was doing great

and how many people could say that during these hard times. Karen had learned long ago not to believe in the concept of deservedness, but if anyone deserved success it was Doug. He was terrific at what he did, a rock. Once you got a reputation for reliability, clients came to you.

"Eh-eh!"

"Now what, hon?"

Karen's voice rose and one of the three men in the corner glanced over. The thin one, the one who seemed to be the leader. Definitely saurian. Mr. Salamander. He wore a light gray suit and a black shirt open at the neck, the long-point collars spread over wide jacket lapels. His dirty blond hair was slicked back and he wasn't bad looking, if you went for reptiles. Now he was smiling.

But not at Zoe. Zoe's back was to him.

At Karen and not a what-a-cute-baby smile.

Karen turned away, catching the waiter's eye and looking down at her plate. The thin man waved and the waiter went over and disappeared into the kitchen again. The thin man was still looking at her.

Amused. Confident.

Mr. Stud. And her with a baby! Classy place. Time to finish up and get out of there.

But Zoe was busy with something new, little face turning beet-red, hands clenched, eyes bulging.

"Great," said Karen, ignoring the thin man but certain he was still giving her the once-over. Then she softened her tone, not wanting to give Zoe any complexes. "That's fine, honey. Poop to your heart's content, make a nice big one for Mommy."

Moments later the deed was done and Zoe was scooping up pasta again and hurling it.

"That's it, young lady, time to clean you up and go meet Daddy."

"Eh-eh."

"No more eh-eh, change-change." Standing, Karen undid the straps of the high chair and lifted Zoe out, sniffing. "*Definitely* time to change you."

But Zoe had other ideas and she began to kick and fuss. Holding the baby under one arm, like an oversized football, Karen lifted the gigantic denim bag that now took the place of the calf-leather purse Doug had given her, and walked over to the bar where the waiter stood polishing glasses and sucking his teeth.

He continued to ignore them even when Karen and Zoe were two feet away.

"Excuse me, sir."

One heavy black eyebrow cocked.

"Where's your ladies' room?"

Wet brown eyes ran over Karen's body like dirty oil, then Zoe's. *Definitely* a creep.

He licked his lips. A crooked thumb indicated the back of the restaurant.

Right past the booth with Lizard and his pals.

Taking a deep breath and staring straight ahead, Karen marched, swinging the big bag. God, it was heavy. All the stuff you had to carry.

The three men stopped talking as she walked by. Someone chuckled.

Lizard cleared his throat and said, "Cute kid," in a nasal voice full of locker-room glee.

More laughter.

Karen pushed through the door.

She emerged a few minutes later, having wrestled Zoe to a three-round decision. In one of Zoe's hands was the cow-rattle Karen employed to take Zoe's mind off diaper-changing.

Let's hear it for distraction.

Forced to pass the three men, Karen stared straight ahead but managed to see what they were eating. Double-cut veal chops, bone and gristle and meat spread out over huge plates. Some poor calf had been confined and force-fed and butchered so these three creeps could stuff their faces.

Lizard said, "*Very* cute." The other two laughed and Karen knew he hadn't meant Zoe.

Feeling herself flush, she kept going.

The men started talking.

Zoe shook the rattle.

Karen said, "Eh-eh, huh, Zoe?" and the baby grinned and drew back her hand.

Windup and the pitch.

The rattle sailed toward the back of the restaurant.

Rolling on the tile floor toward the back booth.

Karen ran back, startling the three men. The rattle had landed next to a shiny black loafer.

As she picked it up, the tail end of a sentence faded into silence. A word. A name.

A name from the evening news.

A man, not a nice one, who'd talked about his friends and had been murdered in jail, yesterday, despite police protection.

The man who'd uttered the name was staring at her.

Fear—ice-cube terror—spread across Karen's face, paralyzing it.

Lizard put his knife down. His eyes narrowed to hyphens.

He was still smiling, but differently, very differently.

One of the other men cursed. Lizard shut him up with a blink.

The rattle was in Karen's hand now. Shaking, making ridiculous rattle sounds. Her hand *couldn't* stop shaking.

She began backing away.

"Hey," said Lizard. "Cutie."

Karen kept going.

Lizard looked at Zoe and his smile died.

Karen clutched her baby tight and ran. Past the waiter, forgetting about the high chair, then remembering, but who cared, it was a cheap one, she needed to get out of this place.

She heard chairs scrape the tile floor. "Hey, Cutie, hold on."

She kept going.

The waiter started to move around from behind the bar. Lizard was coming at her too. Moving fast. Taller than he looked sitting down, the gray suit billowing around his lanky frame.

"Hold on!" he shouted.

Karen gripped the door, swung it open, and dashed out hearing his curses.

Quiet neighborhood, a few people on the sidewalk who looked just like the creeps in the restaurant.

Karen turned right at the corner and ran. Rattling, the heavy denim bag knocking against her thigh.

Zoe was crying.

"It's okay, baby, it's okay, Mommy will keep you safe."

She heard a shout and looked back to see Lizard coming after her, people moving away from him, giving him room. Fear in their faces. He pointed at Karen, went after her.

She picked up her pace. Let's hear it for jogging. But this wasn't like running in shorts and a T-shirt; between Zoe and the heavy bag she felt like a plow horse.

Okay, keep a rhythm, the creep was skinny but he probably wasn't in good shape. Nice and easy with the breathing, pretend this is a ten-k and you've carbo-loaded the night before, slept a peaceful eight hours, gotten up when you wanted to. . . .

She made it to another corner. Red light. A taxi sped by and she had to wait. Lizard was gaining on her—running loosely on long legs, his face sharp and pale—not a lizard, a snake. A venomous snake.

Ugly words came out of the snake's mouth. He was pointing at her.

She stepped off the curb. A truck was approaching halfway down the block. She waited until it got closer, bolted, made it stop short. Blocking the snake.

Another block, this one shorter, lined with shabby storefronts. But no corner at the end of this one. Green dead end. A hedge behind high, graffitied stone walls.

A park. The entrance a hundred yards left.

Karen went for it, running even faster, hearing Zoe's cries and the raspy sound of her own breathing.

Plow horse . . .

Steep, cracked steps took her down into the park. A bronze statue besmirched by pigeon dirt, poorly maintained grass, big trees.

She placed a hand behind Zoe's head, making sure not to jolt the supple neck—she'd read that babies could get whiplash without anyone knowing and then years later they'd show signs of brain damage. . . .

Clap clap behind her as Snake's footsteps slapped the steps. Mr. Viper . . . stop thinking stupid thoughts, he was just a man, a creep. Just keep going, she'd find a place to be safe.

The park was empty, the stone path shaded almost black by huge spreading elms.

"Hey!" shouted the snake. "Stop, awready . . . what . . . the . . . *fuck!"*

Panting between words. The creep probably never did anything aerobic.

"What . . . fuck . . . problem . . . wanna talk!"

Karen pumped her legs. The path took on an upward slope.

Good, make the creep work harder, she could handle it, though Zoe's cries in her ear were starting to get to her—poor thing, what kind of mother was she, getting her baby into something like this—

"Jesus!" From behind. Huff, huff. "Stupid . . . *bitch!"*

More trees, bigger, the pathway even darker. Along the side, occasional benches, graffitied, too, no one on them.

No one to help.

Karen ran even faster. Her chest began to hurt and Zoe hadn't stopped wailing.

"Easy, honey," she managed to gasp. "Easy, Zoe-puff."

The slope grew steeper.

"Fucking bitch!"

Then something appeared on the path. A metal-mesh garbage can. Low enough for her to jump in her jogging days, but not with Zoe. She had to sidestep it and the snake saw her lose footing, stumble, veer off onto the grass, and twist her ankle.

She cried out in pain. Tried to run, stopped.

Zoe's chubby cheeks were soaked with tears.

The snake smiled and walked around the can and toward her.

"Fucking city," he said, kicking the can and whipping out a handkerchief and wiping the sweat from his face. Up close he smelled of too-sweet cologne and raw meat. "No maintenance. No one takes any fucking pride anymore."

Karen started to edge away, looked sharply at her ankle, and winced.

"Poor baby," said the snake. "The big one, I mean. With the little one making all that fucking noise—does she ever shut up?"

"Listen, I—"

"No, *you* listen." A long-fingered hand took hold of Karen's arm. The one she held Zoe with. "You listen, what the fuck you running away like some idiot make-me-chase-you-sweat-up-my-suit?"

"I—my baby."

"Your baby should shut the fuck *up,* understand? Your

baby should learn a little discipline, know what I mean? No one learns discipline how's it gonna be?"

Karen didn't answer.

"You know?" said the snake. "How's it gonna be the puppy learns discipline when the bitch don't know it? You tell me that, huh?"

"That's—"

He slapped her face. Not hard enough to sting, just a touch really. Worse than pain.

"You and me," he said, squeezing her arm. "We got things to talk about."

"What?" Panic tightened Karen's voice. "I'm just visiting from—"

"Shut up. And shut the goddamn baby up too—"

"I can't help it if—"

A hard slap rocked Karen's head. "No, bitch. Don't argue. You notice what we were eating back there?"

Karen shook her head.

"Sure you did, I saw you look. What was it?"

"Meat."

"Veal. You know what veal is, sweet-cheeks?"

"Calf."

" 'Zactly. Baby cow." Winking. "Something can be young and cute, go bah-bah, moo-moo, but it don't matter shit when people's *needs* are involved, you know what I'm saying?"

He licked his lips. The hand on her arm moved to Zoe's arm. Pulling.

Karen pulled back and managed to free Zoe. He laughed.

Tripping backward, Karen said, "Leave me alone," in a too-weak voice.

"Yeah, sure," said the snake. "All alone."

The long-fingered hands became fists and he inched toward her. Slowly, enjoying it. The park so silent. No one here, dangerous part of town.

Karen kept retreating, Zoe wailing.

The snake advanced.

Raising a fist. Touching his knuckles with the other hand.

Suddenly, Karen was moving faster, as if her ankle had never been injured.

Moving with an athlete's grace. Placing Zoe on the grass gently, she stepped to the left while reaching into the big, heavy denim bag.

All the things you had to carry.

Zoe cried louder, screaming, and the snake's eyes snapped to the baby.

Let's hear it for distraction.

The snake looked back at Karen.

Karen brought something out of the bag, small and shiny.

Reversing direction abruptly, she walked right up to the snake.

His eyes got very wide.

Three handclaps, not that different from the sound of his feet on the steps. Three small black holes appeared on his forehead, like stigmata.

He gaped at her, turned white, fell.

She fired five more shots into him as he lay there. Three in the chest, two in the groin. Per the client's request.

Placing the gun back in the bag, she rushed toward Zoe. But the baby was already up, in Doug's arms. And quiet. Doug always had that effect upon Zoe. The books said that was common, fathers often did.

"Hey," he said, kissing Zoe, then Karen. "You let him hit you. I was almost going to move in."

"It's fine," said Karen, touching her cheek. The skin felt hot and welts were starting to rise. "Nothing some makeup won't handle."

"Still," said Doug. "You know how I love your skin."

"I'm okay, honey."

He kissed her again, nuzzled Zoe. "That was a little intense, no? And poor little kiddie—I really don't think we should take her along on business."

He picked up the denim bag. Karen felt light—not just because her hands were empty. That special sense of lightness that marked the end of a project.

"You're right," said Karen as the three of them began walking out of the park. "She is getting older, we don't want to traumatize her. But I don't think this'll freak her out too bad. The stuff kids see on TV nowadays, right? If she ever asks we'll say it was TV."

"Guess so," said Doug. "You're the mom, but I never liked it."

A bit of sun came down through the thick trees, highlighting his black curls. And Zoe's. One beautiful tiny head tucked into a beautiful big one.

"It worked," said Karen.

Doug laughed. "That it did. Everything go smoothly?"

"As silk." Karen kissed them both again. "Little Peach was great. The only reason she was crying is she was having so much fun throwing food in the restaurant and didn't want to leave. And the eh-eh worked perfectly. She threw the rattle, gave me a perfect chance to get close to the jerk."

Doug nodded and looked over his shoulder at the body lying across the pathway.

"The Viper," he said, laughing softly. "Not exactly big game."

"More like a worm," said Karen.

Doug laughed again, then turned serious. "You're sure he didn't hit you hard? I love your skin."

"I'm fine, baby. Not to worry."

"I always worry, babe. That's why I'm alive."

"Me too. You know that."

"Sometimes I wonder."

"Some gratitude."

"Hey," said Doug. "It's just that I love your skin, right?" A moment passed. "Love you."

"Love you too."

A few steps later, he said, "When I saw him hit you, babe—the second time—I could actually hear it from the bushes. Your head swiveled hard and I thought uh-oh. I was ready to come out and finish it myself. Came this close. But I knew it would tick you off. Still, it was a little . . . anxiety-provoking."

"You did the right thing."

He shrugged. Karen felt so much love for him she wanted to shout it to the world.

"Thanks, babe," she said, touching his earlobe. "For being there and for *not* doing anything."

He nodded again. Then he said it:

"The things we do for love."

"Oh, yeah."

His beautiful face relaxed.

A rock. Thank God he'd let her go all the way by herself. First project since the baby and she'd needed to get back into the swing.

Zoe was sleeping now, fat cheeks pillowing out on Doug's broad shoulder, eyes closed, the black lashes long and curving.

They grew up so fast.

Soon, before you knew it, the little pudding would be in preschool and Karen would have more time on her hands.

Maybe one day they'd have another baby.

But not right away. She had her career to consider.

Elmore Leonard

Even with the respect finally granted to the art of the best mystery writers in recent years, it still has been rare for authors who write about violent crimes to be taken seriously by critics and sophisticated readers. Probably no crime or mystery writer in history has received the (deserved) acclaim of his contemporaries accorded Elmore Leonard.

Hammett and Chandler were recognized for their powerful influence on American fiction only after they died. Ross Macdonald tasted it only near the end of his career. But for more than fifteen years, the most distinguished critics and the most popular and powerful cultural media have recognized the singular achievement of Elmore Leonard's unique prose style.

After years as a western writer (Hombre, The Tall T, Last Train to Yuma, *among others), Leonard moved his stories into the present. He didn't change his style, which he describes by saying, "I try to leave out the parts that people skip," but the subject matter, and he has enjoyed a string of more than a dozen consecutive bestsellers, including* Bandits, Glitz, Maximum Bob, Pronto, *and* Riding the Rap.

This is Elmore Leonard's first short story in more than thirty years. (In a special fiction issue of The New Yorker *two years ago, there was a superb piece by him, but it was an excerpt from* Riding the Rap.) *You will like some of the characters you are about to meet; happily, they will show up again in later work.*

—O.P.

Karen Makes Out

BY ELMORE LEONARD

They danced until Karen said she had to be up early tomorrow. No argument, he walked with her through the crowd outside Monaco, then along Ocean Drive in the dark to her car. He said, "Lady, you wore me out." He was in his forties, weathered but young-acting, natural, didn't come on with any singles-bar bullshit buying her a drink, or comment when she said thank you, she'd have Jim Beam on the rocks. They had cooled off by the time they reached her Honda and he took her hand and gave her a peck on the cheek saying he hoped to see her again. In no hurry to make something happen. That was fine with Karen. He said "Ciao," and walked off.

Two nights later they left Monaco, came out of that pounding sound to a sidewalk café and drinks and he became Carl Tillman, skipper of a charter deep-sea fishing boat out of American Marina, Bahia Mar. He was single, married seven years and divorced, no children; he lived in a ground-floor two-bedroom apartment in North Miami—one of the bedrooms full of fishing gear he didn't know where else to store. Carl said his boat was out of the water, getting ready to move it to Haulover Dock, closer to where he lived.

Karen liked his weathered, kind of shaggy look, the crow's-feet when he smiled. She liked his soft brown eyes that looked right at her talking about making his living on the ocean, about hurricanes, the trendy scene here on South Beach, movies. He went to the movies every week and told Karen—raising his eyebrows in a vague, kind of stoned way—his favorite actor was Jack Nicholson. Karen asked him if that was his Nicholson impression or was he doing Christian Slater doing Nicholson? He told her she had a keen eye; but couldn't understand why she thought Dennis Quaid was a hunk. That was okay.

He said, "You're a social worker."

Karen said, "A *social* worker—"

"A teacher."

"What kind of teacher?"

"You teach Psychology. College level."

She shook her head.

"English Lit."

"I'm not a teacher."

"Then why'd you ask what kind I thought you were?"

She said, "You want me to tell you what I do?"

"You're a lawyer. Wait. The Honda—you're a public defender." Karen shook her head and he said, "Don't tell me, I want to guess, even if it takes a while." He said, "If that's okay with you."

Fine. Some guys, she'd tell them what she did and they were turned off by it. Or they'd act surprised and then self-conscious and start asking dumb questions. "But how can a girl do that?" Assholes.

That night in the bathroom brushing her teeth Karen

stared at her reflection. She liked to look at herself in mirrors: touch her short blond hair, check out her fanny in profile, long legs in a straight skirt above her knees, Karen still a size six approaching thirty. She didn't think she looked like a social worker or a schoolteacher, even college level. A lawyer maybe, but not a public defender. Karen was low-key high style. She could wear her favorite Calvin Klein suit, the black one her dad had given her for Christmas, her Sig Sauer .38 for evening wear snug against the small of her back, and no one would think for a moment she was packing.

Her new boyfriend called and stopped by her house in Coral Gables Friday evening in a white BMW convertible. They went to a movie and had supper and when he brought her home they kissed in the doorway, arms slipping around each other, holding, Karen thanking God he was a good kisser, comfortable with him, but not quite ready to take her clothes off. When she turned to the door he said, "I can wait. You think it'll be long?"

Karen said, "What're you doing Sunday?"

They kissed the moment he walked in and made love in the afternoon, sunlight flat on the window shades, the bed stripped down to a fresh white sheet. They made love in a hurry because they couldn't wait, had at each other and lay perspiring after. When they made love again, Karen holding his lean body between her legs and not wanting to let go, it lasted and lasted and got them smiling at each other, saying things like "Wow," and "Oh, my God," it was so good, serious business but really fun. They went out for a while, came back to her yellow stucco bungalow in Coral Gables and made love on the living room floor.

Carl said, "We could try it again in the morning."

"I have to be dressed and out of here by six."

"You're a flight attendant."

She said, "Keep guessing."

* * *

Monday morning Karen Sisco was outside the federal courthouse in Miami with a pump-action shotgun on her hip. Karen's right hand gripped the neck of the stock, the barrel extending above her head. Several more U.S. deputy marshals were out here with her; while inside, three Colombian nationals were being charged in District Court with the possession of cocaine in excess of five hundred kilograms. One of the marshals said he hoped the scudders like Atlanta as they'd be doing thirty to life there pretty soon. He said, "Hey, Karen, you want to go with me, drop 'em off? I know a nice ho-tel we could stay at."

She looked over at the good-ole-boy marshals grinning, shuffling their feet, waiting for her reply. Karen said, "Gary, I'd go with you in a minute if it wasn't a mortal sin." They liked that. It was funny, she'd been standing here thinking she'd gone to bed with four different boyfriends in her life: an Eric at Florida Atlantic, a Bill right after she graduated, then a Greg, three years of going to bed with Greg, and now Carl. Only four in her whole life, but two more than the national average for women in the U.S. according to *Time* magazine, their report of a recent sex survey. The average woman had two partners in her lifetime, the average man, six. Karen had thought everybody was getting laid with a lot more different ones than that.

She saw her boss now, Milt Dancey, an old-time marshal in charge of court support, come out of the building to stand looking around, a pack of cigarettes in his hand. Milt looked this way and gave Karen a nod, but paused to light a cigarette before coming over. A guy from the Miami FBI office was with him.

Milt said, "Karen, you know Daniel Burdon?"

Not Dan, not Danny, Daniel. Karen knew him, one of the younger black guys over there, tall and good looking, confident, known to brag about how many women he'd had of all kinds and color. He'd flashed his smile at Karen one time, hitting on her. Karen turned him down saying, "You have two reasons you want to go out with me." Daniel, smiling, said he knew of one reason, what was the other one? Karen said, "So you can tell your buddies you banged a marshal." Daniel said, "Yeah, but you could use it, too, girl. Brag on getting *me* in the sack." See? That's the kind of guy he was.

Milt said, "He wants to ask you about a Carl Tillman."

No flashing smile this time, Daniel Burdon had on a serious, sort of innocent expression, saying to her, "You know the man, Karen? Guy in his forties, sandy hair, goes about five-ten, one-sixty?"

Karen said, "What's this, a test? Do I *know* him?"

Milt reached for her shotgun. "Here, Karen, lemme take that while you're talking."

She turned a shoulder saying, "It's okay, I'm not gonna shoot him," her fist tight on the neck of the twelve-gauge. She said to Daniel, "You have Carl under surveillance?"

"Since last Monday."

"You've seen us together—so what's this do-I-know-him shit? You playing a game with me?"

"What I meant to ask, Karen, was how long have you known him?"

"We met last week, Tuesday."

"And you saw him Thursday, Friday, spent Sunday with him, went to the beach, came back to your place . . . What's he think about you being with the marshals' service?"

"I haven't told him."

"How come?"

"He wants to guess what I do."

"Still working on it, huh? What you think, he a nice guy? Has a sporty car, has money, huh? He a pretty big spender?"

"Look," Karen said, "why don't you quit dickin' around and tell me what this is about, okay?"

"See, Karen, the situation's so unusual," Daniel said, still with the innocent expression, "I don't know how to put it, you know, delicately. Find out a U.S. marshal's fucking a bank robber."

Milt Dancey thought Karen was going to swing at Daniel with the shotgun. He took it from her this time and told the Bureau man to behave himself, watch his mouth if he wanted cooperation here. Stick to the facts. This Carl Tillman was a *suspect* in a bank robbery, a possible suspect in a half dozen more, all the robberies, judging from the bank videos, committed by the same guy. The FBI referred to him as "Slick," having nicknames for all their perps. They had prints off a teller's counter might be the guy's, but no match in their files and not enough evidence on Carl Edward Tillman—the name on his driver's license and car registration—to bring him in. He appeared to be most recently cherry, just getting into a career of crime. His motivation, pissed off at banks because Florida Southern foreclosed on his note and sold his forty-eight-foot Hatteras for nonpayment.

It stopped Karen for a moment. He might've lied about his boat, telling her he was moving it to Haulover; but that didn't make him a bank robber. She said, "What've you got, a video picture, a teller identified him?"

Daniel said, "Since you mentioned it," taking a Bureau wanted flyer from his inside coat pocket, the sheet folded once down the middle. He opened it and Karen was looking at four photos taken from bank video cameras of robberies in progress, the bandits framed in teller windows, three black guys, one white.

Karen said, "Which one?" and Daniel gave her a look before pointing to the white guy: a man with slicked-back hair, an earring, a full mustache, and dark sunglasses. She said, "That's not Carl Tillman," and felt instant relief. There was no resemblance.

"Look at it good."

"What can I tell you? It's not him."

"Look at the nose."

"You serious?"

"That's your friend Carl's nose."

It was. Carl's slender, rather elegant nose. Or like his. Karen said, "You're going with a nose ID, that's all you've got?"

"A witness," Daniel said, "believes she saw this man—right after what would be the first robbery he pulled—run from the bank to a strip mall up the street and drive off in a white BMW convertible. The witness got a partial on the license number and that brought us to your friend Carl."

Karen said, "You ran his name and date of birth . . ."

"Looked him up in NCIC, FCIC, and Warrant Information, drew a blank. That's why I think he's just getting his feet wet. Managed to pull off a few, two three grand each, and found himself a new profession."

"What do you want me to do," Karen said, "get his prints on a beer can?"

Daniel raised his eyebrows. "That would be a start. Might even be all we need. What I'd like you to do, Karen, is snuggle up to the man and find out his secrets. You know what I'm saying—intimate things, like did he ever use another name. . . ."

"Be your snitch," Karen said, knowing it was a mistake as soon as the words were out of her mouth.

It got Daniel's eyebrows raised again. He said, "That what it sounds like to you? I thought you were a federal agent, Karen. Maybe you're too close to him—is that it? Don't want the man to think ill of you?"

Milt said, "That's enough of that shit," standing up for Karen as he would any of his people, not because she was a woman; he had learned not to open doors for her. The only time she wanted to be first through the door was on a fugitive warrant, this girl who scored higher with a handgun, more times than not, than any marshal in the Southern District of Florida.

Daniel was saying, "Man, I need to use her. Is she on our side or not?"

Milt handed Karen her shotgun. "Here, you want to shoot him, go ahead."

"Look," Daniel said, "Karen can get me a close read on the man, where he's lived before, if he ever went by other names, if he has any identifying marks on his body, scars, maybe a gunshot wound, tattoos, things only lovely Karen would see when the man has his clothes off."

Karen took a moment. She said, "There is one thing I noticed."

"Yeah? What's that?"

"He's got the letters f-u-o-n tattooed on his penis."

Daniel frowned at her. "Foo-on?"

"That's when it's, you might say, limp. When he has a hard-on it says Fuck the Federal Bureau of Investigation."

Daniel Burdon grinned at Karen. He said, "Girl, you and I have to get together. I mean it."

Karen could handle "girl." Go either way. Girl, looking at herself in a mirror applying blush-on. Woman, well, that's what she was. Though until just a few years ago she only thought of women old enough to be her mother as women. Women getting together to form organizations of women, saying, Look, we're different from men. Isolating themselves in these groups instead of mixing it up with men and beating them at their own men's games. Men in general were stronger physically than women. Some men were stronger than other men and Karen was stronger than some too; so what did that prove? If she had to put a man on the ground, no matter how big or strong he was, she'd do it. One way or another. Up front, in his face. What she couldn't see herself playing was this sneaky role. Trying to get the stuff on Carl, a guy she liked, a lot, would think of with tender feelings and miss him during the day and want to be with him. Shit. . . . Okay, she'd play the game, but not undercover. She'd first let him know she was a federal officer and see what he thought about it.

Could Carl be a bank robber?

She'd reserve judgment. Assume almost anyone could at one time or another and go from there.

What Karen did, she came home and put a pot roast in the oven and left her bag on the kitchen table, open, the grip of a Beretta nine sticking out in plain sight.

Carl arrived, they kissed in the living room, Karen feeling it but barely looking at him. When he smelled the pot roast cooking Karen said, "Come on, you can make the drinks while I put the potatoes on." In the kitchen, then, she stood with the refrigerator door open, her back to Carl, giving him time to notice the pistol. Finally he said, "Jesus, you're a cop."

She had rehearsed this moment. The idea: turn saying, "You guessed," sounding surprised; then look at the pistol and say something like "Nuts, I gave it away." But she didn't. He said, "Jesus, you're a cop," and she turned from the refrigerator with an ice tray and said, "Federal. I'm a U.S. marshal."

"I would never've guessed," Carl said, "not in a million years."

Thinking about it before, she didn't know if he'd wig out or what. She looked at him now, and he seemed to be taking it okay, smiling a little.

He said, "But why?"

"Why what?"

"Are you a marshal?"

"Well, first of all, my dad has a company, Marshall Sisco Investigations. . . ."

"You mean because of his name, Marshall?"

"What I am—they're not spelled the same. No, but as soon as I learned to drive I started doing surveillance jobs for him. Like following some guy who was trying to screw his insurance company, a phony claim. I got the idea of going into law enforcement. So after a couple of years at Miami I transferred to Florida Atlantic and got in their Criminal Justice program."

"I mean why not FBI, if you're gonna do it, or DEA?"

"Well, for one thing, I liked to smoke grass when I was younger, so DEA didn't appeal to me at all. Secret Service guys I met were so fucking secretive, you ask them a question, they'd go, 'You'll have to check with Washington on that.' See, different federal agents would come to school to give talks. I got to know a couple of marshals—we'd go out after, have a few beers, and I liked them. They're nice guys, condescending at first, naturally; but after a few years they got over it."

Carl was making drinks now, Early Times for Karen, Dewar's in his glass, both with a splash. Standing at the sink, letting the faucet run, he said, "What do you do?"

"I'm on court security this week. My regular assignment is warrants. We go after fugitives, most of them parole violators."

Carl handed her a drink. "Murderers?"

"If they were involved in a federal crime when they did it. Usually drugs."

"Bank robbery, that's federal, isn't it?"

"Yeah, some guys come out of corrections and go right back to work."

"You catch many?"

"Bank robbers?" Karen said, "Nine out of ten," looking right at him.

Carl raised his glass. "Cheers."

* * *

While they were having dinner at the kitchen table he said, "You're quiet this evening."

"I'm tired, I was on my feet all day, with a shotgun."

"I can't picture that," Carl said. "You don't look like a U.S. marshal, or any kind of cop."

"What do I look like?"

"A knockout. You're the best-looking girl I've ever been this close to. I got a pretty close look at Mary Elizabeth Mastrantonio, when they were here shooting *Scarface?* But you're a lot better looking. I like your freckles."

"I used to be loaded with them."

"You have some gravy on your chin. Right here."

Karen touched it with her napkin. She said, "I'd like to see your boat."

He was chewing pot roast and had to wait before saying, "I told you it was out of the water?"

"Yeah?"

"I don't have the boat anymore. It was repossessed when I fell behind in my payments."

"The bank sold it?"

"Yeah, Florida Southern. I didn't want to tell you when we first met. Get off to a shaky start."

"But now that you can tell me I've got gravy on my chin . . ."

"I didn't want you to think I was some kind of loser."

"What've you been doing since?"

"Working as a mate, up at Haulover."

"You still have your place, your apartment?"

"Yeah, I get paid, I can swing that, no problem."

"I have a friend in the marshals lives in North Miami, on Alamanda off a Hundred and twenty-fifth."

Carl nodded. "That's not far from me."

"You want to go out after?"

"I thought you were tired."

"I am."

"Then why don't we stay home?" Carl smiled. "What do you think?"

"Fine."

They made love in the dark. He wanted to turn the lamp on, but Karen said no, leave it off.

Geraldine Regal, the first teller at Sun Federal on Kendall Drive, watched a man with slicked-back hair and sunglasses fishing in his inside coat pocket as he approached her window. It was 9:40, Tuesday morning. At first she thought the guy was Latin. Kind of cool, except that up close his hair looked shellacked, almost metallic. She wanted to ask him if it hurt. He brought papers, deposit slips, and a blank check from the pocket saying, "I'm gonna make this out for four thousand." Began filling out the check and said, "You hear about the woman trapeze artist, her husband's divorcing her?"

Geraldine said she didn't think so, smiling, because it was a little weird, a customer she'd never seen before telling her a joke.

"They're in court. The husband's lawyer asks her, 'Isn't it true that on Monday, March the fifth, hanging from the trapeze upside down, without a net, you had sex with the ringmaster, the lion tamer, two clowns, and a dwarf?' "

Geraldine waited. The man paused, head down as he finished making out the check. Now he looked up.

"The woman trapeze artist thinks for a minute and says, 'What was that date again?' "

Geraldine was laughing as he handed her the check, smiling as she saw it was a note written on a blank check, neatly printed in block letters, that said:

THIS IS NO JOKE
IT'S A STICKUP!
I WANT $4000 *NOW!*

Geraldine stopped smiling. The guy with the metallic hair was telling her he wanted it in hundreds, fifties, and twenties, loose, no bank straps or rubber bands, no bait money, no dye packs, no bills off the bottom of the drawer, and he wanted his note back. Now.

"The teller didn't have four grand in her drawer," Daniel Burdon said, "so the guy settled for twenty-eight hundred and was out of there. Slick changing his style—we *know* it's the same guy, with the shiny hair? Only now he's the Joker. The trouble is, see, I ain't Batman."

Daniel and Karen Sisco were in the hallway outside the central courtroom on the second floor, Daniel resting his long frame against the railing, where you could look below at the atrium with its fountain and potted palms.

"No witness to see him hop in his BMW this time. The man coming to realize that was dumb, using his own car."

Karen said, "Or it's not Carl Tillman."

"You see him last night?"

"He came over."

"Yeah, how was it?"

Karen looked up at Daniel's deadpan expression. "I told him I was a federal agent and he didn't freak."

"So he's cool, huh?"

"He's a nice guy."

"Cordial. Tells jokes robbing banks. I talked to the people at Florida Southern, where he had his boat loan? Found out he was seeing one of the tellers. Not at the main office, one of their branches, girl named Kathy Lopez. Big brown eyes, cute as a puppy, just started working there. She's out with Tillman she tells him about her job, what she does, how she's counting money all day. I asked was Tillman interested, want to know anything in particular? Oh, yeah, he wanted to know what she was supposed to do if the bank ever got robbed. So she tells him about dye packs, how they work, how she gets a two-hundred-dollar bonus if she's ever robbed and can slip one in with the loot. The next time he's in, cute little Kathy Lopez shows him one, explains how you walk out the door with a pack of fake twenties? A half minute later the tear gas blows and you have that red shit all over you and the money you stole. I checked the reports on the other robberies he pulled? Every one of them he said to the teller, no dye packs or that bait money with the registered serial numbers."

"Making conversation," Karen said, trying hard to maintain her composure. "People like to talk about what they do."

Daniel smiled.

And Karen said, "Carl's not your man."

"Tell me why you're so sure."

"I know him. He's a good guy."

"Karen, you hear yourself? You're telling me what you feel, not what you know. Tell me about *him*—you like the way he dances, what?"

Karen didn't answer that one. She wanted Daniel to leave her alone.

He said, "Okay, you want to put a wager on it, you say Tillman's clean?"

That brought her back, hooked her, and she said, "How much?"

"You lose, you go out dancing with me."

"Great. And if I'm right, what do I get?"

"My undying respect," Daniel said.

* * *

As soon as Karen got home she called her dad at Marshall Sisco Investigations and told him about Carl Tillman, the robbery suspect in her life, and about Daniel Burdon's confident, condescending, smart-ass, irritating attitude.

Her dad said, "Is this guy colored?"

"Daniel?"

"I *know* he is. Friends of mine at Metro-Dade call him the white man's Burdon, on account of he gets on their nerves always being right. I mean your guy. There's a running back in the NFL named Tillman. I forget who he's with."

Karen said, "You're not helping any."

"The Tillman in the pros is colored—the reason I asked. I think he's with the Bears."

"Carl's white."

"Okay, and you say you're crazy about him?"

"I like him, a lot."

"But you aren't sure he isn't doing the banks."

"I said I can't believe he is."

"Why don't you ask him?"

"Come on—if he is he's not gonna tell me."

"How do you know?"

She didn't say anything and after a few moments her dad asked if she was still there.

"He's coming over tonight," Karen said.

"You want me to talk to him?"

"You're not serious."

"Then what'd you call me for?"

"I'm not sure what to do."

"Let the FBI work it."

"I'm supposed to be helping them."

"Yeah, but what good are you? You want to believe the guy's clean. Honey, the only way to find out if he is, you have to assume he isn't. You know what I'm saying? Why does a person rob banks? For money, yeah. But you have to be dumb, too, considering the odds against you, the security, cameras taking your picture. . . . So another reason could be the risk involved, it turns him on. The same reason he's playing around with you. . . ."

"He isn't playing around."

"I'm glad I didn't say, 'Sucking up to get information, see what you know.' "

"He's never mentioned banks." Karen paused. "Well, he might've once."

"You could bring it up, see how he reacts. He gets sweaty, call for backup. Look, whether he's playing around or loves you with all his heart, he's still risking twenty years. He doesn't know if you're on to him or not and that heightens the risk. It's like he thinks he's Cary Grant stealing jewels from the broad's home where he's having dinner, in his tux. But your guy's still dumb if he robs banks. You know all that. Your frame of mind, you just don't want to accept it."

"You think I should draw him out. See if I can set him up."

"Actually," her dad said, "I think you should find another boyfriend."

Karen remembered Christopher Walken in *The Dogs of War* placing his gun on a table in the front hall—the doorbell ringing —and laying a newspaper over the gun before he opened the door. She remembered it because at one time she was in love with Christopher Walken, not even caring that he wore his pants so high.

Carl reminded her some of Christopher Walken, the way he smiled with his eyes. He came a little after seven. Karen had on khaki shorts and a T-shirt, tennis shoes without socks.

"I thought we were going out."

They kissed and she touched his face, moving her hand

lightly over his skin, smelling his after-shave, feeling the spot where his right earlobe was pierced.

"I'm making drinks," Karen said. "Let's have one and then I'll get ready." She started for the kitchen.

"Can I help?"

"You've been working all day. Sit down, relax."

It took her a couple of minutes. Karen returned to the living room with a drink in each hand, her leather bag hanging from her shoulder. "This one's yours." Carl took it and she dipped her shoulder to let the bag slip off and drop to the coffee table. Carl grinned.

"What've you got in there, a gun?"

"Two pounds of heavy metal. How was your day?"

They sat on the sofa and he told how it took almost four hours to land an eight-foot marlin, the leader wound around its bill. Carl said he worked his tail off hauling the fish aboard and the guy decided he didn't want it.

Karen said, "After you got back from Kendall?"

It gave him pause.

"Why do you think I was in Kendall?"

Carl had to wait while she sipped her drink.

"Didn't you stop by Florida Southern and withdraw twenty-eight hundred?"

That got him staring at her, but with no expression to speak of. Karen thinking, Tell me you were somewhere else and can prove it.

But he didn't; he kept staring.

"No dye packs, no bait money. Are you still seeing Kathy Lopez?"

Carl hunched over to put his drink on the coffee table and sat like that, leaning on his thighs, not looking at her now as Karen studied his profile, his elegant nose. She looked at his glass, his prints all over it, and felt sorry for him.

"Carl, you blew it."

He turned his head to look at her past his shoulder. He said, "I'm leaving," pushed up from the sofa and said, "If this is what you think of me . . ."

Karen said, "Carl, cut the shit," and put her drink down. Now, if he picked up her bag, that would cancel out any remaining doubts. She watched him pick up her bag. He got the Beretta out and let the bag drop.

"Carl, sit down. Will you, please?"

"I'm leaving. I'm walking out and you'll never see me again. But first . . . ." He made her get a knife from the kitchen and cut the phone line in there and in the bedroom.

He *was* pretty dumb. In the living room again he said, "You know something? We could've made it."

Jesus. And he had seemed like such a cool guy. Karen watched him go to the front door and open it before turning to her again.

"How about letting me have five minutes? For old times' sake."

It was becoming embarrassing, sad. She said, "Carl, don't you understand? You're under arrest."

He said, "I don't want to hurt you, Karen, so don't try to stop me." He went out the door.

Karen walked over to the chest where she dropped her car keys and mail coming in the house: a bombé chest by the front door, the door still open. She laid aside the folded copy of the *Herald* she'd placed there, over her Sig Sauer .38, picked up the pistol, and went out to the front stoop, into the yellow glow of the porch light. She saw Carl at his car now, its white shape pale against the dark street, only about forty feet away.

"Carl, don't make it hard, okay?"

He had the car door open and half turned to look back. "I said I don't want to hurt you."

Karen said, "Yeah, well . . ." raised the pistol to rack the slide and cupped her left hand under the grip. She said, "You move to get in the car, I'll shoot."

Carl turned his head again with a sad, wistful expression. "No you won't, sweetheart."

Don't say ciao, Karen thought. Please.

Carl said, "Ciao," turned to get in the car, and she shot him. Fired a single round at his left thigh and hit him where she'd aimed, in the fleshy part just below his butt. Carl howled and slumped inside against the seat and the steering wheel, his leg extended straight out, his hand gripping it, his eyes raised with a bewildered frown as Karen approached. The poor dumb guy looking at twenty years, and maybe a limp.

Karen felt she should say something. After all, for a few days there they were as intimate as two people can get. She thought about it for several moments, Carl staring up at her with rheumy eyes. Finally Karen said, "Carl, I want you to know I had a pretty good time, considering."

It was the best she could do.

MICHAEL MALONE

Every small town has its legends. Thermopylae, North Carolina, gave Stella Dora Doyle to the world and then, with little choice in the matter—four husbands, one murder trial, and a European exile later—took her back. For young Buddy Hayes, a boy who has grown into manhood while Stella's fabled beauty has only ripened, his father's assessment of her powerful aura lingers in his mind long past his first glimpse of the woman herself.

Never to have desired Stella, his dad solemnly tells him as they watch her climb the courthouse steps, accused of killing Hugh Doyle, her childhood sweetheart and latest husband, is to have missed out on being alive. Haunted by the memory of this fearful glamor, Buddy is nonetheless equal to the occasion when his path and Stella's later cross.

Acclaimed novelist Michael Malone, no stranger to the mysteries of the human heart, understands that the combination of memory, myth, and sudden violent death is an irresistible one. In addition to his bestselling novels of small-town southern life, he has written two superb mystery novels about Justin Savile and Cuddy Mangum, Uncivil Seasons *and* Time's Witness. *He recently won an Emmy as the writer of the daytime drama* One Life to Live.

—O.P.

Red Clay

BY MICHAEL MALONE

Up on its short slope the columned front of our courthouse was wavy in the August sun, like a courthouse in lake water. The leaves hung from maples, and the flag of North Carolina wilted flat against its metal pole. Heat sat sodden over Devereux County week by relentless week; they called the weather "dog days," after the star, Sirius, but none of us knew that. We thought they meant no dog would leave shade for street on such days—no dog except a mad one. I was ten that late August in 1959; I remembered the summer because of the long heat wave, and because of Stella Doyle.

When they pushed open the doors, the policemen and lawyers flung their arms up to their faces to block the sun and stopped there in the doorway as if the hot light were shoving them back inside. Stella Doyle came out last, a deputy on either side to walk her down to where the patrol car, orange as Halloween candles, waited to take her away until the jury could make up its mind about what had happened two months earlier out at Red Hills. It was the only house in the county big enough to have a name. It was where Stella Doyle had, maybe, shot her husband, Hugh Doyle, to death.

Excitement over Doyle's murder had swarmed through the town and stung us alive. No thrill would replace it until the assassination of John F. Kennedy. Outside the courthouse, sidewalk heat steaming up through our shoes, we stood patiently waiting to hear Mrs. Doyle found guilty. The news stood waiting, too, for she was, after all, not merely the murderer of the wealthiest man we knew; she was Stella Doyle. She was the movie star.

Papa's hand squeezed down on my shoulder and there was a tight line to his mouth as he pulled me into the crowd and said, "Listen now, Buddy, if anybody ever asks you, when you're grown, 'Did you ever see the most beautiful woman God made in your lifetime,' son, you say 'Yes, I had that luck, and her name was Stella Dora Doyle.' " His voice got louder, right there in the crowd for everybody to hear. "You tell them how her beauty was so bright, it burned back the shame they tried to heap on her head, burned it right on back to scorch their faces."

Papa spoke these strange words looking up the steps at the almost plump woman in black the deputies were holding. His arms were folded over his seersucker vest, his fingers tight on the sleeves of his shirt. People around us had turned to stare and somebody snickered.

Embarrassed for him, I whispered, "Oh, Papa, she's nothing but an old murderer. Everybody knows how she got drunk and killed Mr. Doyle. She shot him right through the head with a gun."

Papa frowned. "You don't know that."

I kept on. "Everybody says she was so bad and drunk all

the time, she wouldn't let his folks even live in the same house with her. She made him throw out his own mama and papa."

Papa shook his head at me. "I don't like to hear ugly gossip coming out of your mouth, all right, Buddy?"

"Yes, sir."

"She didn't kill Hugh Doyle."

"Yes, sir."

His frown scared me; it was so rare. I stepped closer and took his hand, took his stand against the rest. I had no loyalty to this woman Papa thought so beautiful. I just could never bear to be cut loose from the safety of his good opinion. I suppose that from that moment on, I felt toward Stella Doyle something of what my father felt, though in the end perhaps she meant less to me, and stood for more. Papa never had my habit of symbolizing.

The courthouse steps were wide, uneven stone slabs. As Mrs. Doyle came down, the buzzing of the crowd hushed. All together, like trained dancers, people stepped back to clear a half-circle around the orange patrol car. Newsmen shoved their cameras to the front. She was rushed down so fast that her shoe caught in the crumbling stone and she fell against one of the deputies.

"She's drunk!" hooted a woman near me, a country woman in a flowered dress belted with a strip of painted rope. She and the child she jiggled against her shoulder were puffy with the fat of poverty. "Look'it her"—the woman pointed—"look at that dress. She thinks she's still out there in Hollywood." The woman beside her nodded, squinting out from under the visor of the kind of hat pier fishermen wear. "I went and killed my husband, wouldn't no rich lawyers come running to weasel me out of the law." She slapped at a fly's buzz.

Then they were quiet and everybody else was quiet and our circle of sun-stunned eyes fixed on the woman in black, stared at the wonder of one as high as Mrs. Doyle about to be brought so low.

Holding to the stiff, tan arm of the young deputy, Mrs. Doyle reached down to check the heel of her shoe. Black shoes, black suit and purse, wide black hat—they all sinned against us by their fashionableness, blazing wealth as well as death. She stood there, arrested a moment in the hot immobility of the air, then she hurried down, rushing the two big deputies down with her, to the open door of the orange patrol car. Papa stepped forward so quickly that the gap filled with people before I could follow him. I squeezed through, fighting with my elbows, and I saw that he was holding his straw hat in one hand, and offering the other hand out to the murderer. "Stella, how are you? Clayton Hayes."

As she turned, I saw the strawberry gold hair beneath the hat; then her hand, bright with a big diamond, took away the dark glasses. I saw what Papa meant. She was beautiful. Her eyes were the color of lilacs, but darker than lilacs. And her skin held the light like the inside of a shell. She was not like other pretty women, because the difference was not one of degree. I have never seen anyone else of her kind.

"Why, Clayton! God Almighty, it's been years."

"Well, yes, a long time now, I guess," he said, and shook her hand.

She took the hand in both of hers. "You look the same as ever. Is this your boy?" she said. The violet eyes turned to me.

"Yes, this is Buddy. Ada and I have six so far, three of each."

"Six? Are we that old, Clayton?" She smiled. "They said you'd married Ada Hackney."

A deputy cleared his throat. "Sorry, Clayton, we're going to have to get going."

"Just a minute, Lonnie. Listen, Stella, I just wanted you to know I'm sorry as I can be about your losing Hugh."

Tears welled in her eyes. "He did it himself, Clayton," she said.

"I know that. I know you didn't do this." Papa nodded slowly again and again, the way he did when he was listening. "I know that. Good luck to you."

She swatted tears away. "Thank you."

"I'm telling everybody I'm sure of that."

"Clayton, thank you."

Papa nodded again, then tilted his head back to give her his slow, peaceful smile. "You call Ada and me if there's ever something we can do to help you, you hear?" She kissed his cheek and he stepped back with me into the crowd of hostile, avid faces as she entered the police car. It moved slow as the sun through the sightseers. Cameras pushed against its windows.

A sallow man biting a pipe skipped down the steps to join some other reporters next to us. "Jury sent out for food," he told them. "No telling with these yokels. Could go either way." He pulled off his jacket and balled it under his arm. "Jesus, it's hot."

A younger reporter with thin, wet hair disagreed. "They all think Hollywood's Babylon and she's the whore. Hugh Doyle was the local prince, his daddy kept the mills open in the bad times, quote unquote half the rednecks in the county. They'll fry her. For that hat if nothing else."

"Could go either way," grinned the man with the pipe. "She was born in a shack six miles from here. Hat or no hat, that makes her one of them. So what if she did shoot the guy, he was dying of cancer anyhow, for Christ's sake. Well, she never could act worth the price of a bag of popcorn, but Jesus damn she was something to look at!"

Now that Stella Doyle was gone, people felt the heat again and went back to where they could sit still in the shade until the evening breeze and wait for the jury's decision. Papa and I walked back down Main Street to our furniture store. Papa owned a butcher shop, too, but he didn't like the meat business and wasn't very good at it, so my oldest brother ran it while Papa sat among the mahogany bedroom suites and red maple dining-room sets in a big rocking chair and read, or talked to friends who dropped by. The rocker was actually for sale but he had sat in it for so long now that it was just Papa's chair. Three ceiling fans stirred against the quiet, shady air while he answered my questions about Stella Doyle.

He said that she grew up Stella Dora Hibble on Route 19, in a three-room, tin-roofed little house propped off the red clay by concrete blocks—the kind of saggy-porched, pinewood house whose owners leave on display in their dirt yard, like sculptures, the broken artifacts of their aspirations and the debris of their unmendable lives: the doorless refrigerator and the rusting car, the pyre of metal and plastic that tells drivers along the highway "Dreams don't last."

Stella's mother, Dora Hibble, had believed in dreams anyhow. Dora had been a pretty girl who'd married a farmer and worked harder than she had the health for, because hard work was necessary just to keep from going under. But in the evenings Mrs. Hibble had looked at movie magazines. She had believed the romance was out there and she wanted it, if not for her, for her children. At twenty-seven, Dora Hibble died during her fifth labor. Stella was eight when she watched from the door of the bedroom as they covered her mother's face with a thin blanket. When Stella was fourteen, her father died when a machine jammed at Doyle Mills. When Stella was sixteen, Hugh Doyle, Jr., who was her age, my father's age, fell in love with her.

"Did you love her, too, Papa?"

"Oh, yes. All us boys in town were crazy about Stella Dora, one time or another. I had my attack of it, same as the rest. We were sweethearts in seventh grade. I bought a big-size Whitman's Sampler on Valentine's. I remember it cost every cent I had."

"Why were y'all crazy about her?"

"I guess you'd have to worry you'd missed out on being alive if you didn't feel that way about Stella, one time or another."

I was feeling a terrible emotion I later defined as jealousy. "But didn't you love Mama?"

"Well, now, this was before it was my luck to meet your mama."

"And you met her coming to town along the railroad track and you told your friends 'That's the girl for me and I'm going to marry her,' didn't you?"

"Yes, sir, and I was right on both counts." Papa rocked back in the big chair, his hands peaceful on the armrests.

"Was Stella Dora still crazy about you after you met Mama?"

His face crinkled into the lines of his ready laughter. "No, sir, she wasn't. She loved Hugh Doyle, minute she laid eyes on him, and he felt the same. But Stella had this notion about going off to get to be somebody in the movies. And Hugh couldn't hold her back, and I guess she couldn't get him to see what it was made her want to go off so bad either."

"What was it made her want to go?"

Papa smiled at me. "Well, I don't know, son. What makes you want to go off so bad? You're always saying you're going here, and there, 'cross the world, up to the moon. I reckon you're more like Stella than I am."

"Do you think she was wrong to want to go be in the movies?"

"No."

"You don't think she killed him?"

"No, sir, I don't."

"Somebody killed him."

"Well, Buddy, sometimes people lose hope and heart, and feel like they can't go on living."

"Yeah, I know. Suicide."

Papa's shoes tapped the floor as the rocker creaked back and forth. "That's right. Now you tell me, why're you sitting in here? Why don't you ride your bike on over to the ballpark and see who's there?"

"I want to hear about Stella Doyle."

"You want to hear. Well. Let's go get us a Coca-Cola, then. I don't guess somebody's planning to show up in this heat to buy a chest of drawers they got to haul home."

"You ought to sell air conditioners, Papa. People would buy air conditioners."

"I guess so."

So Papa told me the story. Or at least his version of it. He said Hugh and Stella were meant for each other. From the beginning it seemed to the whole town a fact as natural as harvest that so much money and so much beauty belonged together, and only Hugh Doyle with his long, free, easy stride was rich enough to match the looks of Stella Dora. But even Hugh Doyle couldn't hold her. He was only halfway through the state university, where his father had told him he'd have to go before he married Stella, if he wanted a home to bring her to, when she quit her job at Coldsteam's beauty parlor and took the bus to California. She was out there for six years before Hugh broke down and went after her.

By then every girl in the county was cutting Stella's pictures out of the movie magazines and reading how she got her lucky break, how she married a big director, and divorced him, and married a big star, and how that marriage broke up even quicker. Photographers traveled all the way to Thermopylae to take pictures of where she was born. People tried to tell them her house was gone, had fallen down and been used for firewood, but they just took photographs of Reverend Ballister's house instead and said Stella had grown up in it. Before long, even local girls would go stand in front of the Ballister house like a shrine, sometimes they'd steal flowers out of the yard. The year that *Fever,* her best movie, came to the Grand Theater on Main Street, Hugh Doyle flew out to Los Angeles and won her back. He took her down to Mexico to divorce the baseball player she'd married after the big star. Then Hugh married her himself and put her on an ocean liner and took her all over the world. For a whole two years, they didn't come home to Thermopylae. Everybody in the county talked about this two-year honeymoon, and Hugh's father confessed to some friends that he was disgusted by his son's way of life.

But when the couple did come home, Hugh walked right into the mills and turned a profit. His father confessed to the same friends that he was flabbergasted Hugh had it in him. But after the father died Hugh started drinking and Stella joined him. The parties got a little wild. The fights got loud. People talked. They said he had other women. They said Stella'd been locked up in a sanitorium. They said the Doyles were breaking up.

And then one June day a maid at Red Hills, walking to work before the morning heat, fell over something that lay across a path to the stables. And it was Hugh Doyle in riding clothes with a hole torn in the side of his head. Not far from his gloved hand, the police found Stella's pistol, already too hot from the sun to touch. The cook testified that the Doyles had been fighting like cats and dogs all night long the night before, and Hugh's mother testified that he wanted to divorce Stella but she wouldn't let him, and so Stella was arrested. She said she was innocent, but it was her gun, she was his heir, and she had no alibi. Her trial lasted almost as long as that August heat wave.

A neighbor strolled past the porch, where we sat out the evening heat, waiting for the air to lift. "Jury's still out," he said. Mama waved her hand at him. She pushed herself and me in the big green wood swing that hung from two chains to the porch roof, and answered my questions about Stella Doyle. She said, "Oh, yes, they all said Stella was specially pretty. I never knew her to talk to myself."

"But if Papa liked her so much, why didn't y'all get invited out to their house and everything?"

"Her and your papa just went to school together, that's all. That was a long time back. The Doyles wouldn't ask folks like us over to Red Hills."

"Why not? Papa's family used to have a *whole* lot of money. That's what you said. And Papa went right up to Mrs. Doyle at the courthouse today, right in front of everybody. He told her, You let us know if there's anything we can do."

Mama chuckled the way she always did about Papa, a low ripple like a pigeon nesting, a little exasperated at having to sit still so long. "You know your papa'd offer to help out anybody he figured might be in trouble, white or black. That's just him; that's not any Stella Dora Doyle. Your papa's just a good man. You remember that, Buddy."

Goodness was Papa's stock-in-trade; it was what he had instead of money or ambition, and Mama often reminded us of it. In him she kept safe all the kindness she had never felt she could afford for herself. She, who could neither read nor write, who had stood all day in a cigarette factory from the age of nine until the morning Papa married her, was a fighter. She wanted her children to go farther than Papa had. Still, for years after he died, she would carry down from the attic the yellow mildewed ledgers where his value was recorded in more than $75,000 of out-of-date bills he had been unwilling to force people in trouble to pay. Running her sun-spotted finger down the brown wisps of names and the money they'd owed, she would sigh that proud, exasperated ripple, and shake her head over foolish, generous Papa.

Through the front parlor window I could hear my sisters

practicing the theme from *The Apartment* on the piano. Someone across the street turned on a light. Then we heard the sound of Papa's shoes coming a little faster than usual down the sidewalk. He turned at the hedge carrying the package of shiny butcher's paper in which he brought meat home every evening. "Verdict just came in!" he called out happily. "Not guilty! Jury came back about forty minutes ago. They already took her home."

Mama took the package and sat Papa down in the swing next to her. "Well, well," she said. "They let her off."

"Never ought to have come up for trial in the first place, Ada, like I told everybody all along. It's like her lawyers showed. Hugh went down to Atlanta, saw that doctor, found out he had cancer, and he took his own life. Stella never even knew he was sick."

Mama patted his knee. "Not guilty; well, well."

Papa made a noise of disgust. "Can you believe some folks out on Main Street tonight are all fired up *because* Stella got off! Adele Simpson acted downright indignant!"

Mama said, "And you're surprised?" And she shook her head with me at Papa's innocence.

Talking of the trial, my parents made one shadow along the wood floor of the porch, while inside my sisters played endless variations of "Chopsticks," the notes handed down by ghostly creators long passed away.

A few weeks later, Papa was invited to Red Hills, and he let me come along; we brought a basket of sausage biscuits Mama had made for Mrs. Doyle.

As soon as Papa drove past the wide white gate, I learned how money could change even weather. It was cooler at Red Hills, and the grass was the greenest grass in the county. A black man in a black suit let us into the house, then led us down a wide hallway of pale yellow wood into a big room shuttered against the heat. She was there in an armchair almost the color of her eyes. She wore loose-legged pants and was pouring whiskey from a bottle into a glass.

"Clayton, thanks for coming. Hello there, little Buddy. Look, I hope I didn't drag you from business."

Papa laughed. "Stella, I could stay gone a week and never miss a customer." It embarrassed me to hear him admit such failure to her.

She said she could tell I liked books, so maybe I wouldn't mind if they left me there to read while she borrowed my daddy for a little bit. There were white shelves in the room, full of books. I said I didn't mind but I did; I wanted to keep on seeing her. Even with the loose shirt soiled and rumpled over a waist she tried to hide, even with her face swollen from heat and drink and grief, she was something you wanted to look at as long as possible.

They left me alone. On the white piano were dozens of photographs of Stella Doyle in silver frames. From a big painting over the mantelpiece her remarkable eyes followed me around the room. I looked at that painting as sun deepened across it, until finally she and Papa came back. She had a tissue to her nose, a new drink in her hand. "I'm sorry, honey," she said to me. "Your daddy's been sweet letting me run on. I just needed somebody to talk to for a while about what happened to me." She kissed the top of my head and I could feel her warm lips at the part in my hair.

We followed her down the wide hall out onto the porch. "Clayton, you'll forgive a fat old souse talking your ear off and bawling like a jackass."

"No such thing, Stella."

"And you *never* thought I killed him, even when you first heard. My God, thank you."

Papa took her hand again. "You take care now," he said.

Then suddenly she was hugging herself, rocking from side to side. Words burst from her like a door flung open by wind. "I could kick him in the ass, that bastard! Why didn't he tell me? To quit, to *quit,* and use *my* gun, and just about get me strapped in the gas chamber, that goddamn bastard, and never say a word!" Her profanity must have shocked Papa as much as it did me. He never used it, much less ever heard it from a woman.

But he nodded and said, "Well, good-bye, I guess, Stella. Probably won't be seeing you again."

"Oh, Lord, Clayton, I'll be back. The world's so goddamn little."

She stood at the top of the porch, tears wet in those violet eyes that the movie magazines had loved to talk about. On her cheek a mosquito bite flamed like a slap. Holding to the big white column, she waved as we drove off into the dusty heat. Ice flew from the glass in her hand like diamonds.

Papa was right; they never met again. Papa lost his legs from diabetes, but he'd never gone much of anywhere even before that. And afterward, he was one of two places—home or the store. He'd sit in his big wood wheelchair in the furniture store, with his hands peaceful on the armrests, talking with whoever came by.

I did see Stella Doyle again; the first time in Belgium, twelve years later. I went farther than Papa.

In Bruges there are small restaurants that lean like elegant elbows on the canals and glance down at passing pleasure boats. Stella Doyle was sitting, one evening, at a table in the crook of the elbow of one of them, against an iron railing that curved its reflection in the water. She was alone there when I saw her. She stood, leaned over the rail, and slipped the ice cubes from her glass into the canal. I was in a motor launch full of tourists passing below. She waved with a smile at us and we waved back. It had been a lot of years since her last picture, but probably she waved out of habit. For the tourists motoring past, Stella in white against the dark restaurant was another snapshot of Bruges. For me, she was home and memory. I craned to look back as long as I could, and leapt from the boat at the next possible stop.

When I found the restaurant, she was yelling at a well-dressed young man who was leaning across the table, trying to soothe her in French. They appeared to be quarreling over his late arrival. All at once she hit him, her diamond flashing into his face. He filled the air with angry gestures, then turned and left, a white napkin to his cheek. I was made very shy by what I'd seen—the young man was scarcely older than I was. I stood unable to speak until her staring at me jarred me forward. I said, "Mrs. Doyle? I'm Buddy Hayes. I came out to see you at Red Hills with my father Clayton Hayes one time. You let me look at your books."

She sat back down and poured herself a glass of wine. "You're *that* little boy? God Almighty, how old am I? Am I a hundred yet?" Her laugh had been loosened by the wine. "Well, a Red Clay rambler, like me. How 'bout that. Sit down. What are *you* doing over here?"

I told her, as nonchalantly as I could manage, that I was traveling on college prize money, a journalism award. I wrote a prize essay about a murder trial.

"Mine?" she asked, and laughed.

A waiter, plump and flushed in his neat black suit, trotted to her side. He shook his head at the untouched plates of food. "Madame, your friend has left, then?"

Stella said, "Mister, I helped him along. And turns out, he was no friend."

The waiter then turned his eyes, sad and reproachful, to the trout on the plate.

"How about another bottle of that wine and a great big bucket of ice?" Stella asked.

The waiter kept flapping his fat quick hands around his head, entreating us to come inside. *"Les moustiques, madame!"*

"I just let them bite," she said. He went away grieved.

She was slender now, and elegantly dressed. And while her hands and throat were older, the eyes hadn't changed, nor the red-gold hair. She was still the most beautiful woman God had made in my lifetime, the woman of whom my father had said that any man who had not desired her had missed out on being alive, the one for whose honor my father had turned his back on the whole town of Thermopylae. Because of Papa, I had entered my adolescence daydreaming about fighting for Stella Doyle's honor; we had starred together in a dozen of her movies: I dazzled her jury; I cured Hugh Doyle while hiding my own noble love for his wife. And now here I sat drinking wine with her on a veranda in Bruges; me, the first Hayes ever to win a college prize, ever to get to college. Here I sat with a movie star.

She finished her cigarette, dropped it spinning down into the black canal. "You look like him," she said. "Your papa. I'm sorry to hear that about the diabetes."

"I look like him, but I don't think like him," I told her.

She tipped the wine bottle upside down in the bucket. "You want the world," she said. "Go get it, honey."

"That's what my father doesn't understand."

"He's a good man," she answered. She stood up slowly. "And I think Clayton would want me to get you to your hotel."

All the fenders of her Mercedes were crushed. She said, "When I've had a few drinks, I need a strong car between me and the rest of the cockeyed world."

The big car bounced over the moon-white street. "You know what, Buddy? Hugh Doyle gave me my first Mercedes, one morning in Paris. At breakfast. He held the keys out in his hand like a damn daffodil he'd picked in the yard. He gave me *this* goddamn thing." She waved her finger with its huge diamond. "This damn thing was tied to my big toe one Christmas morning!" And she smiled up at the stars as if Hugh Doyle were up there tying diamonds on them. "He had a beautiful grin, Buddy, but he was a son of a bitch."

The car bumped to a stop on the curb outside my little hotel. "Don't miss your train tomorrow," she said. "And you listen to me, don't go back home; go on to Rome."

"I'm not sure I have time."

She looked at me. "*Take* time. Just take it. Don't get scared, honey."

Then she put her hand in my jacket pocket and the moon came around her hair, and my heart panicked crazily, thudding against my shirt, thinking she might kiss me. But her hand went away, and all she said was, "Say hi to Clayton when you get home, all right? Even losing his legs and all, your daddy's lucky, you know that?"

I said, "I don't see how."

"Oh, I didn't either till I was a lot older than you. And had my damn in-laws trying to throw me into the gas chamber. Go to bed. So long, Red Clay."

Her silver car floated away. In my pocket, I found a large wad of French money, enough to take me to Rome, and a little ribboned box, clearly a gift she had decided not to give the angry young man in the beautiful suit who'd arrived too late. On black velvet lay a man's wristwatch, reddish gold.

It's an extremely handsome watch, and it still tells me the time.

I only went home to Thermopylae for the funerals. It was the worst of the August dog days when Papa died in the hospital bed they'd set up next to his and Mama's big four poster in their bedroom. At his grave, the clots of red clay had already dried to a dusty dull color by the time we shoveled them down upon him, friend after friend taking a turn at the shovel. The petals that fell from roses fell limp to the red earth, wilted like the crowd who stood by the grave while Reverend Ballister told us that Clayton Hayes was "a good man." Behind a cluster of Mama's family, I saw a woman in black turn away and walk down the grassy incline to a car, a Mercedes.

After the services I went driving, but I couldn't outtravel Papa in Devereux County. The man at the gas pump listed Papa's virtues as he cleaned my windshield. The woman who sold me the bottle of bourbon said she'd owed Papa $215.00 since 1944, and when she'd paid him back in 1966 he'd forgotten all about it. I drove along the highway where the foundations of tin-roofed shacks were covered now by the parking lots of minimalls; beneath the asphalt, somewhere, was Stella Doyle's birthplace. Stella Dora Hibble, Papa's first love.

Past the white gates, the Red Hills lawn was as parched as the rest of the county. Paint blistered and peeled on the big white columns. I waited a long time before the elderly black man I'd met twenty years before opened the door irritably.

I heard her voice from the shadowy hall yelling, "Jonas! Let him in."

On the white shelves the books were the same. The photos on the piano as young as ever. She frowned so strangely when I came into the room, I thought she must have been expecting someone else and didn't recognize me.

"I'm Buddy Hayes, Clayton's—"

"I know who you are."

"I saw you leaving the cemetery. . . ."

"I know you did."

I held out the bottle.

Together we finished the bourbon in memory of Papa, while shutters beat back the sun, hid some of the dirty glasses scattered on the floor, hid Stella Doyle in her lilac armchair. Cigarette burns scarred the armrests, left their marks on the oak floor. Behind her the big portrait showed Time up for the heartless bastard he is. Her hair was cropped short, and gray. Only the color of her eyes had stayed the same; they looked as remarkable as ever in the swollen face.

"I came out here to bring you something."

"What?"

I gave her the thin, cheap, yellowed envelope I'd found in Papa's desk with his special letters and papers. It was addressed in neat, cursive pencil to "Clayton." Inside was a silly Valentine card. Betty Boop popping bonbons in her pouty lips, exclaiming "Ooooh, I'm sweet on you." It was childish and lascivious at the same time, and it was signed with a lipstick blot, now brown with age, and with the name "Stella," surrounded by a heart.

I said, "He must have kept this since the seventh grade."

She nodded. "Clayton was a good man." Her cigarette fell from her ashtray onto the floor. When I came over to pick it up, she said, "Goodness is luck; like money, like looks. Clayton was lucky that way." She went to the piano and took more ice from the bucket there; one piece she rubbed around the back of her neck, then dropped into her glass. She turned, the eyes wet, like lilac stars. "You know, in Hollywood, they said, '*Hibble?!* What kind of hick name is that, we can't use that!' So I said, 'Use Doyle, then.' I mean, I took Hugh's name six years before he ever came out to get me. Because I knew he'd come. The day I left Thermopylae he kept yelling at me, 'You can't have both!' He kept yelling it while the bus was pulling out. 'You can't have me and it both!' He wanted to rip my heart out for leaving, for *wanting* to go." Stella moved along the curve of the white piano to a photograph of Hugh Doyle in a white open shirt, grinning straight out at the sun. She said, "But I could have both. There were only two things I *had* to have in this little world, and one was the lead in a movie called *Fever,* and the other one was Hugh Doyle." She put the photograph down carefully. "I didn't know about the cancer till my lawyers found out he'd been to see that doctor in Atlanta. Then it was easy to get the jury to go for suicide." She smiled at me. "Well, not easy. But we turned them around. I think your papa was the only man in town who *never* thought I was guilty."

It took me a while to take it in. "Well, he sure convinced me," I said.

"I expect he convinced a lot of people. Everybody thought so much of Clayton."

"You killed your husband."

We looked at each other. I shook my head. "Why?"

She shrugged. "We had a fight. We were drunk. He was sleeping with my fucking maid. I was crazy. Lots of reasons, no reason. I sure didn't plan it."

"You sure didn't confess it either."

"What good would that have done? Hugh was dead. I wasn't about to let his snooty-assed mother shove me in the gas chamber and pocket the money."

I shook my head. "Jesus. And you've never felt a day's guilt, have you?"

Her head tilted back, smoothing her throat. The shuttered sun had fallen down the room onto the floor, and evening light did a movie fade and turned Stella Doyle into the star in the painting behind her. "Ah, baby, don't believe it," she said. The room stayed quiet.

I stood up and dropped the empty bottle in the wastebasket. I said, "Papa told me how he was in love with you."

Her laugh came warmly through the shuttered dusk. "Yes, and I guess I was sweet on him, too, boop boop dedoo."

"Yeah, Papa said no man could say he'd been alive if he'd seen you and not felt that way. I just wanted to tell you I know what he meant." I raised my hand to wave good-bye.

"Come over here," she said, and I went to her chair and she reached up and brought my head down to her and kissed me full and long on the mouth. "So long, Buddy." Slowly her hand moved down my face, the huge diamond radiant.

* * *

News came over the wire. The tabloids played with it for a few days on back pages. They had some pictures. They dug up the Hugh Doyle trial photos to put beside the old studio glossies. The dramatic death of an old movie star was worth sending a news camera down to Thermopylae, North Carolina, to get a shot of the charred ruin that had once been Red Hills. A shot of the funeral parlor and the flowers on the casket.

My sister phoned me that there was even a crowd at the coroner's inquest at the courthouse. They said Stella Doyle had died in her sleep after a cigarette set fire to her mattress. But rumors started that her body had been found at the foot of the stairs, as if she'd been trying to escape the fire, but had fallen. They said she was drunk. They buried her beside Hugh Doyle in the family plot, the fanciest tomb in the Methodist cemetery, not far from where my parents were buried. Not long after she died, one of the cable networks did a night of her movies. I stayed up to watch *Fever* again.

My wife said, "Buddy, I'm sorry, but this is the biggest bunch of sentimental slop I ever saw. The whore'll sell her jewels and get the medicine and they'll beat the epidemic but she'll die to pay for her past and then the town'll see she was really a saint. Am I right?"

"You're right."

She sat down to watch awhile. "You know, I can't decide if she's a really lousy actress or a really good one. It's weird."

I said, "Actually, I think she was a much better actress than anyone gave her credit for."

My wife went to bed, but I watched through the night. I sat in Papa's old rocking chair that I'd brought north with me after his death. Finally at dawn I turned off the set, and Stella's face disappeared into a star, and went out. The reception was awful and the screen too small. Besides, the last movie was in black and white; I couldn't see her eyes as well as I could remember the shock of their color, when she first turned toward me at the foot of the courthouse steps, that hot August day when I was ten, when my father stepped forward out of the crowd to take her hand, when her eyes were lilacs turned up to his face, and his straw hat in the summer sun was shining like a knight's helmet.

BOBBIE ANN MASON

Girl detectives are supposed to discover *secrets, not harbor them. No one should know this better than Nancy Drew, whose attic adventures and crumbling castle conundrums were more than a match for any swarthy villain. But what happens when her universe—the River Heights that exists beyond the carefully controlled pages of the series so beloved by generations of women—begins to fray a bit about the edges? Clearly, Nancy's long-proven methods for vanquishing the forces of evil aren't of much use when it comes to protecting her against change and decay and, even worse, revisionism.*

Who is Draco S. Wren? And why does he seem so eerily familiar? In this affectionate parody by acclaimed novelist and short-story writer Bobbie Ann Mason, whose own first published book was a history of America's teenage girl detectives titled The Girl Sleuths, *Nancy Drew is an altogether willing captive of her own myth. But even Nancy eventually must acknowledge that crimes of the heart don't make for open-and-shut cases.*

Once named by Elmore Leonard as his favorite writer, Bobbie Ann Mason has won numerous literary prizes for her insightful fiction about southern life, including the bestselling In Country.

—O.P.

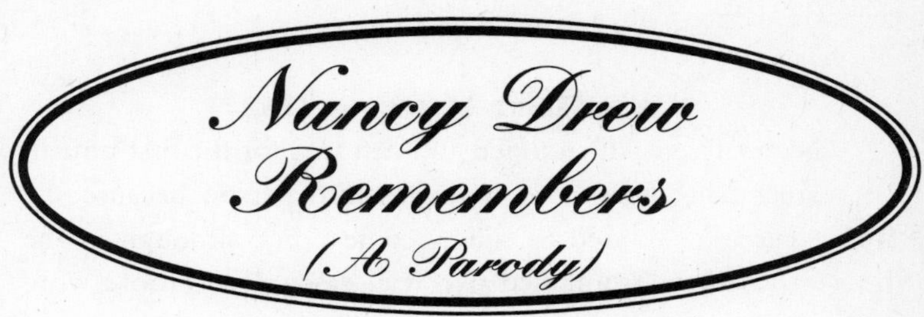

Nancy Drew Remembers (A Parody)

BY BOBBIE ANN MASON

"I shall write my memoirs," Nancy Drew declared. "That should put all those nasty rumors to rest."

As far as Nancy Drew was concerned, she was still the same attractive, golden-haired girl detective she had always been, but not everyone agreed. Chance remarks in River Heights had been troubling her, and her reputation had declined since Draco S. Wren had come to live with her. Nancy knew now that she owed the world an explanation. Besides, her hair wasn't really golden anymore.

"I will begin at the turning point of my career," she thought. "It was many years ago, but I remember it as well as I remember that picnic when Bess Marvin got ptomaine from the pear tart."

She sat at her carved-oak escritoire with the secret clue drawer and began to write the story of what happened many years ago when she was only thirty-nine or so and still had flawless skin.

A Pleasant Afternoon Tea

Nancy Drew felt troubled and defeated for the first time in her career (she decided to write in third person because she wasn't sure she wanted to sign a confession), although in the books she always triumphed over evil easily. The crooks wore hats pulled down low over their eyes, and they always had shockingly poor manners, making them easy to spot. But lately it seemed that her authoress was straying from the proper plots. As Nancy read about herself engaged in this or that adventure, she felt nostalgic for some of her old mysteries.

"The Mystery of the Ivory Charm, for example," she said to herself. "Now *that* was a satisfactory adventure."

Nancy had watched her roadster change to a convertible, and she read about herself on improbable airplane rides. "I was so much more comfortable in the old days," she said with a sigh. "Most of my best mysteries were within driving distance of River Heights." She missed her blue roadster. She wished she had a mystery like *The Password to Larkspur Lane* to solve, instead of her current problem.

Nancy was sitting by a cheerful fire in the tasteful parlor. It was a rainy afternoon, and she was all alone. Hannah Gruen had been called away to care for her sister, who was ill. This often happened in the books too. Nancy was working on a petit-point design of an Arctic amphibian, but impulsively she flung it into her Jane Austen work basket. "It's useless," she thought. "I will not rest until I solve this mystery! Even though there are no murders in my stories, I will have to face the fact sooner or later —my father was murdered!"

She decided to telephone Bess Marvin, now Mrs. Ned Nickerson, plump mother of four.

"Oh, hello, Nancy!" Bess greeted her. "It's good to hear

from you. River Heights isn't the cozy city it used to be. We never seem to get together."

"Bess, I need your help," Nancy said quickly and firmly.

"Oh, Nancy, you sound like your old self again. Do I suspect another mystery?"

"I have something to discuss with you. It may be the most challenging mystery of my career!"

Nancy, with her usual persuasive and friendly manner, so well documented in dozens of her sleuthing tales, soon won Bess's promise to engage a baby-sitter and drive over from the Seascape Towers subdivision of River Heights.

Nancy took her worn copy of *The Clue in the Old Album* from the shelf. She remembered picnicking with Ned Nickerson in that book. Ned had been so devoted to her, but as it turned out, he preferred Bess's cooking. Bess had married him when he finally graduated from Emerson College. He was now a football coach, and Nancy was still good friends with him and Bess. Nancy never held a grudge.

Nancy had been the most attractive and popular girl River Heights had ever seen, as well as the most independent and resourceful. That was because she had lost her mother at an early age and had had to manage the household by herself, as the books always reported faithfully. And Nancy was expert at anything she tried—digging fence-post holes, parsing sentences, skinning rabbits, fixing radios, making lace. She made straight A's and had the loveliest fingernails in her class. She would have been a cheerleader if she could have taken time from her sleuthing.

"But from the time I got involved in that sorority smuggling ring, nothing has been the same," Nancy remembered. She prepared a cup of tea and then began to examine a small ivory igloo on the table beside her. When she apparently pressed a concealed spring, a blank-faced figure in a tiny fur-trimmed parka popped out of the igloo—much like a cuckoo from a clock. His right hand clutched a miniature harpoon dangling on a string. Nancy was so nervous—a fact that surprised her—that she almost spilled the tea, and as she juggled the cup in its saucer, the tiny harpoon fell from the figure's grasp and pricked the back of her left hand.

"Here any regular reader would expect that I have been poisoned," laughed Nancy to herself as she reassembled harpoon and hunter. However, she fell asleep instantly and was awakened two hours later by Bess Nickerson, sounding the door chimes.

"What happened, Nancy? You look as if you've been drugged." Bess was wearing a parka with a fur edge, River Heights fashion that season. "Did I awaken you?"

"Yes, I was probably drugged." Nancy was so used to that familiar trick that it hardly bothered her. "Here's the culprit." She produced the hunter in his igloo. "It reminds me of that Confederate soldier doll whose sword pricked me in old Mrs. Struthers' mansion."

"Oh, Nancy, we were so scared when you wouldn't wake up! And I thought your father would die!" squealed Bess, who still squealed habitually.

"Well, he did," said Nancy grimly.

"Oh, I'm sorry. I didn't mean literally."

Nancy had been Carson Drew's assistant, his confidante, his fair-haired daughter. She had looked after his ties and handkerchiefs and had arranged his appointments. He gave her his most important mystery cases. To ease her grief over his death, Nancy had thrown herself into various charitable amusements. She won the River Heights bake-off and captured a silver loving cup in a bowling tournament. During one week she had assumed a dramatic stage role when the leading lady became ill. Nancy learned her lines in an afternoon. She had similarly substituted in a trapeze act when a circus stopped in town. But none of these pastimes satisfied her. Recently she had gotten out her silver badge, resolving to return to her detective work with renewed energy.

"Shouldn't we sit down and talk?" said Bess. "I must remove this wet parka."

Nancy parked the parka on the hall tree, and they repaired to the parlor, where the souvenirs of Nancy's cases were lined up on the mantel—the old clock, the Turnbull urn, the Paul Revere bell, the heirloom cameo, and several glossy mink pelts. The room had been the scene of many confidences between Carson Drew and his clients, and between father and daughter. Hannah Gruen had served a lot of cocoa and homemade cookies in that room.

Nancy got straight to the point. "Bess, I have reason to believe my father was murdered."

"Nancy!" Bess seemed shocked. "I thought you had given up mysteries."

"Mysteries are my destiny. And this one leads me into dangerous new territory."

"Nancy," said Bess warmly. "I feel you are much too preoccupied with the loss of your father. It's not good for you. And besides, as you say, it may be too dangerous."

"I think you understand, Bess, that my father meant everything to me. He was responsible for that premature career of mine—the glory of it, the brilliant girl detective following in his footsteps. He set standards that I had to live up to, and the resulting acclaim I received spurred me on. I cannot quit now, Bess. I cannot disappoint my fans, or myself, or my dear father's memory."

"I see what you mean," Bess murmured.

"And the most important mystery of my career is unfolding before me now. It has to do with my parentage."

"Your parentage!" exclaimed Bess, wide eyed.

"You know I never knew my mother," said Nancy.

"She died when you were three. All the books say that."

"All the same I can't remember her. Father told me very little about her. He was always evasive. What if she is still alive? What if some dread secret lurks in my past? She may have been murdered or kidnapped. Anything could have happened. And Father may have wanted to keep it from me. There may be a connection to the immediate mystery of my father's death."

"And you think he was murdered." Bess shivered. "Oh, Nancy!"

"Exactly. And here is my first clue."

Expectantly, Bess examined the ivory igloo. "Where did you get it?"

"It came in a parcel the day of Father's death. No return address. Only a label on the igloo—Nome, Alaska."

Nancy produced the packaging from her secret clue drawer. Big block print letters addressed Carson Drew. Nancy had examined the wrapping inside and out with her magnifying glass and found no clues.

"What connection do you make, Nancy, between this and your father's death?"

"I don't know. You see, I found it beside him when I found him slumped over, dead, right there where you're sitting—in that very spot, Bess. I paid no attention to the figurine until much later, and I was too distressed at first to imagine a connection."

Nancy showed Bess how the whale-hunter fit inside the igloo and popped out like a cuckoo. Bess pointed out the drop of fluid at the point of the harpoon.

"It's only a mild drug," Nancy said dismissively. "But my father may not have been able to survive a mild drug. Or perhaps he died of shock—from some unknown horror! The igloo could have reminded him of something. The doctors merely proclaimed heart failure. A vague diagnosis."

"Are you going to notify the police?"

"No, I prefer not to at present."

Danny Crew, the police chief who had succeeded her old friend McGinnis, was not disposed to listen to girl detectives of any age or reputation, no matter how many copies they sold.

"I should have known," groaned Bess.

"It is more complicated than a mere police case. It is a personal mystery. It has a philosophical dimension, you might say."

Bess produced her knitting and prepared to listen. She had never heard Nancy pursue a mystery from such an odd angle before.

"Bess, you are aware that for some years now my stories have not been faithful to my real-life adventures. You know yourself that your participation in my recent adventures has been dwindling."

"Well, with the children, I hardly have time to go exploring caves and chasing crooks as much."

"Certainly. But even in the early stories you were always more preoccupied with the refreshments than with the mystery, so I hadn't expected you to keep up with the adventures. Actually, I must admit to you that I am scarcely consulted anymore about my adventures. The stories are make-believe, written in the manner of my early achievements. The royalties have been handsome, one cannot deny, but I have hardly deserved them."

At first, Nancy had related, with the help of newspaper clippings and various memorabilia from her stockpile of old clues, the tales of her teenage exploits to her patient authoress, who seldom interfered with Nancy's telling. Later, Nancy's adventures were full of loose ends. Crooks never confessed right away for one thing, and heiresses seldom invited her to tea at their mansions. In Nancy's view, the Hardy Boys got some of the better adventures.

"What is a mystery, Bess?" said Nancy after a long pause during which Bess knitted ninety-nine stitches.

"Why, you always said it was the unrevealed coincidences of life."

In one case, Nancy had met a Mrs. Owen, and when she came home and found her father talking with a Mr. Owen, Nancy at once imagined that they might be a tragically separated husband and wife. Mr. Owen had a sad face, as if he might have lost a wife. And as it turned out at the end, Mr. and Mrs. Owen were happily reunited by Nancy Drew, who utilized coincidence to an uncommon advantage, and who, moreover, expected life to arrange itself in a series of interrelated coincidences. These coincidences were Nancy's favorite features of mystery. They shot chills up and down her spine.

"Quite right, Bess," Nancy said as she remembered Mr. and Mrs. Owen. "But are all coincidences mysteries?"

"I don't think so, Nancy. Are you suggesting this mystery might better be left alone?"

"A suggestion."

"Of course, Nancy, I do feel it might be better to let well enough alone. I usually do feel that way."

"Oh, Bess, you don't understand! The real mystery is why my sleuthing luck has failed. This is why I have my hopes pinned on this new mystery—in spite of its shocking nature." She buried her face in her hands a moment. "It must be age," she said. "I always denied it, but I get into my blue convertible, with my matching blue frock, and I follow leads, undaunted by danger. But nothing turns out correctly. It is all so disorderly. Oh, Bess, my mysteries are trite, unglamorous. Gangsters seldom chase my convertible these days. It was different in the roadster."

"Don't feel bad, Nancy."

"I have been studying my books lately, trying to figure it out. The books show some things very plainly. For one thing, I always felt empty and sad at the end of each mystery because I hadn't begun the next mystery yet. Without a mystery I was nothing. That's how I have been feeling for years now—without the challenge of an old-fashioned mystery. I have been looking at the books to see if there are any clues to my father's death. There may have been a conspiracy from the beginning, a devious plot to throw me off the case with a semblance of a solution."

Bess, uncomfortable with Nancy's profound questionings, now pursued the original mystery.

"What else have you learned about your father's untimely demise?" she inquired tactfully.

"There's this ivory igloo and the mysterious name of Draco S. Wren."

"What a strange name—like a code name. Or a vampire. Who is he?"

"A client of my father's. Dad was working on the case when he died."

"What do you know about him?"

"He lives in Alaska!"

"Oh, do you think he has anything to do with this ivory hunter?" Bess fingered the figurine dangerously, and she would have pricked her finger if Nancy had not rescued her in time.

"His name is in a file of current clients, so I call him a client," Nancy said. "The reverse may be the case, however, for in Father's bank statements there are several large checks made out to Draco S. Wren—a sum of over four thousand dollars paid just this year!"

"Nancy, it sounds like blackmail!"

"If this were a typical Nancy Drew teenage detective story, we would now be at about Chapter Five. Two distinct and separate mysteries have been introduced—the mystery of my father's death and the mystery of Draco S. Wren. There has been one mysterious message, half a dozen puzzling clues strewn my way by fate, one disastrous event, one maddening car chase (I did have trouble getting a parking spot yesterday), one adventure with Bess (saving you from the poison harpoon), and one bout with a rainstorm."

No one had ever explained why there were so many rainstorms in the Nancy Drew books, and so few wintry scenes.

"This Draco S. Wren sounds like a dangerous character," said Bess.

"His address is in the file, but I have not decided what I shall do about it. If I write to him, I may scare him away. It might be best to travel to Nome, Alaska, and do a little sleuthing. Could you and George pack a suitcase by tomorrow?"

"Really, Nancy, you can't still expect me to drop everything and join you on such short notice."

"Oh, I forgot about the offspring." Nancy was crestfallen. She brightened. "Shall we have some tea? Hannah has baked a sponge cake with orange butter frosting."

Bess could hardly conceal the hungry gleam in her eye. During the refreshments, daintily served on an embroidered napkin and a silver tea tray, Nancy was thoughtful. Bess concentrated on several pieces of the sponge cake.

Nancy gazed out the window at the unending rain. It was inconvenient that Bess couldn't drop everything and hop in the convertible to pursue a mystery. She turned from the window.

"Bess, this new mystery must be kept secret from my fan club."

"Of course, Nancy," said Bess, rousing herself from the ecstasy of the sponge cake. She put away her knitting and headed for the hall tree. "I have to get home now, but if I might give you a bit of sisterly advice before I leave—I've never really said this before, but, well, I do think you shouldn't be alone."

"What are you trying to say, Bess?" said Nancy pointedly.

"You know what I mean, Nancy," floundered Bess. "It has been ages since you went to a prom or a barbecue with a handsome young man. You need an admirer."

Nancy had not dated anyone since Ned Nickerson married Bess. Nancy, being generous to a fault, did not allow the union to poison her friendship with Bess. Ned had been helpful on mystery cases at times when Nancy needed someone to fetch a clue from a high crevice, but Ned wanted too little from life.

Nancy did not answer Bess. She continued to gaze out the window. Bess said she must hurry home, for the day was at a close. The children would be rampaging, and Ned would be home with his football, ready to devour a horse or two. Bess hugged Nancy good-bye and whispered a message of cheer.

Nancy Searches the Files

The next day Nancy searched her father's files and found nothing significant. Frustrated, she began to look for hidden compartments in her father's bedroom. She was expert at such quests, having explored many mansions for secret sliding panels and hidey holes. Her favorites were in *The Sign of the Twisted Candles.* Nancy recalled longingly the ecstatic feeling of tugging on the little knob which opened the hidden recess in one old attic she had searched. It surprised her that she might be finding such secrets in her own home.

The task occupied the day, broken by a short interval when she shared an attractive luncheon of crab bisque, fresh peas, and lemon mousse with Hannah Gruen. Hannah was eighty, but she still cooked and ran the vacuum.

"Now, Nancy," she said. "Promise me you won't go running off into danger again." Nancy had not told her the particulars, but Hannah never missed anything.

"I won't," promised Nancy. "I almost wish I could. Nothing exciting seems to happen anymore."

Looking through the mail, Nancy found a copy of her father's death certificate. She decided to store it with important papers in an old album in her father's safe. She opened the album, a worn red plush book with embroidered gold letters. The album reminded her of a coffin. Inside, she found several listings of births and marriages and deaths. She pored over them eagerly. She noticed the births and marriages of long-gone aunts and uncles, marveling that their deaths occurred on the next page. She could find no record of her mother's death. As she searched for clues in the antique album, the telephone rang. Nancy found herself talking to Draco S. Wren.

An Urgent Call

It was nine in the morning when Nancy rang up George Fayne. The telephone rang several times, with a frantic sound. Finally George answered.

"George!" Nancy cried exuberantly. "Oh, George. I thought you had already packed your gym bag for the day and left your room."

"I was bounding down the stairs when I heard the telephone."

"Listen, George, I think I am deliriously happy!"

"Hypers, Nancy, this is great news. Have you solved the mystery?"

"Did Bess tell you about that?"

"Bess can't keep a secret—or whistle," said George. "Are we going to Alaska?"

"No. George. Listen—I'm in love."

"Nancy, you must be dreaming. Who's the dream fellow?"

"Draco S. Wren."

"Your mystery man?"

"Exactly."

"Bess is suspicious of him."

"I can take care of myself," Nancy said blithely. "I've managed to get out of dangerous scrapes before. But there's no danger."

"How did you meet him?"

"He came over yesterday to talk about something in relation to a case of Dad's, and I fell in love with him. It was quite natural and inevitable. He's perfectly handsome, as handsome as Dad, and his manner is somewhat like his—firm and taciturn but twinkling and warm beneath. He wears modest clothing and smiles enchantingly. He loves mysteries. He follows all my cases with devotion."

"That's wonderful, Nancy. What does he look like?"

"Draco S. Wren is of medium height with brown hair. He walks with short, hurried steps."

"You described a pickpocket to the police once in exactly those terms," George said.

"And my vivid description enabled the police to pick up the pickpocket instantly," Nancy pointed out. "But Draco S. Wren has excellent manners and a winning smile—hardly the ways of a pickpocket."

"Great."

"We stayed in the parlor till nearly eleven," Nancy confessed. "Hannah brought steaming cocoa and homemade molasses cookies, which we ate by the fire. It was thrilling."

"Did you solve the mystery?"

"I've learned some things. He does live in Alaska, and he apparently has been getting money from Dad. He wouldn't tell me why, but he says he has no intention of soliciting funds from me."

"Still sounds mysterious."

"He said he would tell me more today. This afternoon we're going for a spin. Isn't that exciting?"

"It's nice that you have no suspicions of him."

"Oh, no. You know that with my sharp eyes and powers of observation, I am an instant judge of character." Suddenly Nancy remembered something. "Oh, George, I think I've seen this handsome man before! He was at Father's funeral!"

"You don't say!" George gave a low whistle.

"I believe I glimpsed him once behind the lilies. He was wearing a black leather jacket, broad-brimmed hat, and a purple bandana—yes, it was he, indeed. I remember his glistening brown hair. Funny he didn't mention he was there. Anyway, he told me that he and Dad had had some private business together and that he wanted to explain it to me, but that he would like to get to know me better so that I would trust him. He has such trusting eyes—not dark, piercing eyes such as criminals have. He was very much interested in my work. Why, I regaled him with Nancy Drew stories until half past ten!"

"Did you ask about the ivory igloo?"

"No. Not yet. I'm sure if he sent it, it wasn't with ill intentions. I did ask him if he knew of any enemies my father might have had, and he knew of none."

"Well, Nancy, as long as he isn't a vampire, I'll be interested to meet your new friend, but he sounds sneaky. And I'm disappointed we're not going to Alaska."

"He is mysterious, I admit," Nancy said. "I'm eager to learn more, but I was my usual shrewd self, preferring to observe rather than hurry. I must confess, however, that I feel as thrilled as I usually do with the first five clues of a new mystery!"

Nancy replaced the telephone receiver and lapsed back into her reverie. George had always been skeptical of love. Nancy, too, had wasted little thought on romance. All Ned had cared about was dancing and—Nancy flushed—stealing a kiss in the moonlight. Bess was welcome to him. Ned hadn't the slightest understanding of her calling.

Now as Hannah and Nancy had breakfast together, Hannah observed Nancy's preoccupation. "You've hardly touched your food, dear," she admonished as Nancy picked at her Omaha omelette with blueberry muffins and homemade strawberry jam and fresh creamery butter. "You aren't going to get carried away by that mystery man, are you? If your dear father were alive—"

"Oh, Hannah, lovely Hannah, I'm not in danger. I must confess that I am in love."

As Nancy dwelt more on the subject, the more rapturous she became. She explained it all to Hannah, who understood and with tears in her eyes said she hoped her foster daughter would find the happiness she deserved since losing her dear parents.

"Hannah," said Nancy soberly. "You have told me about my mother when she was alive. Can you tell me more about her death?"

Hannah seemed startled but she soon composed herself. "I think I've told you all I remember—about the night it happened, about the funeral. You were just a little thing in a romper suit."

"I remember only that she gave me my first magnifying glass. I remember looking at her face through my magnifying glass. Her smile was hideous and large, and it made me laugh."

"Yes. She gave you that just before she died. I remember her saying 'Take this, Nancy, and use it to pursue crooks to justice! Let no footprint escape!' What a glorious deathbed speech!"

"Hannah!" Nancy sobbed. "I'm an orphan!"

"Don't feel bad, Nancy," said Hannah. "I'm an orphan too."

"But you're eighty."

"I think so, Nancy, but there's always a certain emptiness you feel. I've felt it for a long time."

"Have you, Hannah?"

"Oh, for many years."

Revelation

Draco S. Wren arrived that afternoon, wearing his purple bandana and glistening hair. He was a striking figure, dressed like an adventurer out of the Old West. He took Nancy for a drive in a large touring car, a kind Nancy recognized from one of her old books. She sat beside him dreamily. For once she was not at the wheel, skillfully maneuvering her smart machine while notorious gangsters gunned along behind her. The touring car glided through the sleepy countryside. The scenery seemed old and beautiful, as if untouched by trucks or time. Nancy thought she recognized the old Turnbull mansion with the hidden staircase from long, long ago. She drifted along on a cloud, receding into her past. Draco S. Wren's amiable chatter reminded Nancy that she was deeply in love with this gentle-eyed stranger. She drew closer to the stranger, feeling as if a particularly puzzling mystery was about to be solved, with a stimulating climactic flourish.

Eventually the touring car drew up before a country inn.

"This is a surprise for you," smiled Draco S. Wren, straightening his bandana. "I didn't know if you knew there was still a Lilac Inn."

Nancy was thrilled. "It's just like the old Lilac Inn in my mystery! It burned down."

"This is a restoration of the original Lilac Inn," said Draco S. Wren. "I happened to hear about it this morning."

"The lilacs are blooming, too!" There was a lilac grove, with flowers ranging in color from white to deep purple. Nancy told Draco S. Wren some lilac lore she had learned when solving the lilac mystery. "They are not to be confused with larkspurs, which figured in another of my mysteries."

"Lilacs become you," he said as he framed her face against a backdrop of lilac blossoms, damp with a recent light rain.

"Oh, Draco S. Wren!" Nancy gushed, then felt embarrassed. She was Nancy Drew, daring girl detective. She had to be calm and collected.

Inside the inn, Draco S. Wren pinned a lilac sprig from the centerpiece to Nancy's shining golden hair. Tea arrived, with a trolley of jam biscuits, lady fingers, charlotte russe cream puffs, almond torten, walnut meringues, raspberry trifle, and assorted other delectables, in addition to dainty, trimmed cucumber and salmon sandwiches.

"This is just like my books!" Nancy exclaimed, delighted, and barely giving a thought to Bess. "Isn't it a charming and thoughtful gesture when life goes as it should?"

As they gaily consumed the delicacies, Draco S. Wren began to speak of the serious matter he had so far kept from Nancy.

"I have come to consult the great Nancy Drew about a mystery," he said. His zircon ring flashed a reflection on his gleaming teeth.

"You *are* a man of mystery," Nancy said sweetly. She was flattered and giddy.

"Nancy, do you remember anything of your mother?"

Nancy was startled at the question and aroused by the coincidence. "She died when I was three. All the books say so."

"Are you sure?"

Nancy's heart leapt up. "I never beheld a death certificate with my own eyes. But I was told of her magnificent deathbed speech. Father wouldn't allow me to attend the funeral."

"Did you ever wonder about her?"

"Yes! Just this week. Do you bring news of my mother? Is she alive after all?" Nancy clapped her hands gleefully. The gesture was surprisingly out of character.

"No, I don't believe she is, I'm sorry to report. But there is something puzzling about her identity. You must apply your sleuthing abilities to several clues I have."

The mention of clues was as appetizing as the cinnamon tea loaf Nancy buttered. She listened eagerly. The atmosphere of Lilac Inn was almost intoxicating.

"What would you say, Nancy, if I told you that your mother didn't die when you were three, but that she ran away to the Alaskan territory?"

"But that seems unlikely. Why should she run away? She had a small child—myself—to care for. We were a contented household. Hannah Gruen was even then an ever-faithful servant."

"Your mother was in love with another man, I am told."

"But how could that be? She was married to Carson Drew, my father." Nancy was truly puzzled.

"I have proof—from various hotel records—that she went to Alaska for a time. And there is a certain note, written on her own perfumed and monogrammed stationery."

Draco S. Wren produced a frayed letter. The note said, "Dear Carson, I am leaving you for another man. His name is Andy C. Wren. We are going to Alaska. Do not try to catch me. Good-bye forever. Bon-Bon."

Nancy recognized her mother's nickname. She was stunned speechless, a rarity. She reviewed her exploits. Could her mother have met foul play at the hands of Felix Raybolt in disguise? A cold, scheming kidnapper he was. Or Alonzo Rugby and Red Busby? A cowardly pair. Or Tom Stripe. She surveyed her repertoire of crooks. The note had been forged, no doubt. Burglars had often entered the Drew home trying to get their hands on Nancy's clues. They could easily have swiped the monogrammed stationery.

"Nancy, I can see you have put your pretty thinking cap on. I knew you would enjoy this mystery."

Nancy's mind was whirling as she pieced facts together rapidly. She could hardly finish her baked Alaska.

"Eat heartily, Nancy. There is more." Draco S. Wren took a baked Alaska and more tea. "Let me tell you about a woman named Candy Wren. You recognize the name, of course."

Nancy nodded. Who could fail to recognize that famous personality? Candy Wren's face had once been in the newspapers daily. She was photographed with wealthy playboys and noblemen. And Candy Wren was a popular author of children's books, as everyone knew. "Then you are related to the famous late Candy Wren? Or late famous?"

"She was my mother," said Draco S. Wren. "She rarely frequented our Alaskan frontier home. She was always away on personal appearance tours in her furs, and she left me with nursemaids. She sought the bright lights of the cities but sent me souvenir soaps from hotels. My father, too, neglected me. He was rarely there, for reasons you will soon guess. I grew up a virtual prisoner of the nursery, for it was too cold to go out and play. Alaska was a crystal tundra. I so longed for a true family that I resolved to set upon a quest for a long-lost sister I had heard of. When I was very young I was told about her—about how beautiful and brilliant she was. Her golden hair was described to me so often by my Inuit nannies that I began to confuse her with the princesses in the fairy tales. My childhood was so lonely that I promised myself that if I ever found this beautiful sister I would care for her and give her everything I had."

"What is your theory about the disappearance of the sister? Was she kidnapped from the cradle?" Nancy recalled such a case involving twins.

"No. It is more complicated. And I'm surprised you haven't guessed the solution."

"I recall that Candy Wren perished in an unusual accident a few years ago. Was your lost sister in the accident?" Nancy probed for clues and connections.

"No, her daughter was not with her. Candy Wren disappeared off the Mediterranean coast following a mysterious boat explosion. Alas, the bulk of her fortune—and mine—was with her. A small, carved chest of jewels."

Nancy recalled the many lost jewel boxes she had recovered. "Do you suspect that your mother is still alive and that the jewels have fallen into unscrupulous hands?" Nancy thought fleetingly of pirates and deserted islands.

"No, Nancy. I know that she is dead and that the jewels are lost in the briny deep. Fragments of the box found floating along the coast of Corfu proved that long ago."

"Of course, a diamond embedded in a wayward barracuda is not an unfathomable coincidence," Nancy ventured, thinking of a glorious yachting cruise.

"I'm not trying to solve the mystery of the boat explosion.

And the jewels are lost. My search is for the long-lost sister. What do you make of these clues?"

Nancy tried to summon all her wits, but her mind was clouded over. A dangerous blackmailer had once had her cornered like this, but she had aroused herself in the nick of time.

"Think of the name Wren, Nancy," said Draco S. Wren with a meaningful look. For a second, he seemed to leer.

"Candy Wren was your mother, and she must have been related to Andy C. Wren, whom you mentioned earlier in an unlikely attachment." Nancy spoke slowly, a crease on her brow.

"That is partially correct. Think of that clue, Nancy. Your mother ran away to Alaska with Andy C. Wren. Andy C. Wren, I now reveal, was married to my mother, Candy Wren." Draco S. Wren paused, watching Nancy intently. When he saw no flicker of comprehension in her blue eyes, he added, "Wren was her married name. She didn't migrate to Alaska as a Wren." He paused again, seeming to study Nancy. He seemed annoyed with her. In exasperation, he said, "I'll give you another clue. Her nickname was Bon-Bon." He seemed to lunge slightly toward Nancy as he said this.

"But surely you refer to mere coincidence?" Nancy gave an elaborate shrug. "Certainly Mother would not have—It must have been Bushy Trott!" she exclaimed suddenly, remembering a particularly nasty crook. "That criminal was a misfit his whole life. When he imprisoned me in the attic with that tarantula it must have been in revenge for what my father must have done to him for what *he* must have done to my mother. He could have abducted her and planted the note. The deathbed speech was a ruse and a clue! My mother knew I would solve the mystery of her tragic fate!"

Draco S. Wren threw up his hands. "But, Nancy, I have proof that she went to Alaska because she loved another man! I even have the minibar of Ivory stamped Ice Palace Hotel to prove it!"

Nancy could feel the wheels spinning in her mind. "There must have been a secret passage!"

Draco S. Wren seemed stunned by Nancy's remark. "Well, Nancy, *this* will stir your imagination. I have a locket here containing a lock of your own hair. My mother gave it to me on one of her rare trips home. I was thirteen."

The significance of the number thirteen did not escape Nancy. The lock of hair was unmistakably blond. "So?" she queried nonchalantly.

Draco S. Wren stared silently into Nancy's eyes for several long moments. He drummed his fingers on the table. "Bon-Bon. Candy. Bon-Bon. Nancy, don't you understand that *you* are my long-lost sister? Candy Wren was your mother too."

The revelation was unthinkable, not to mention absurd. "But my mother was married to Carson Drew," Nancy said. "And Candy is a common name."

"They are one and the same!" Draco S. Wren declared triumphantly, bouncing a lemon bon bon on the table. "Candy ran away to Alaska with Andy C. Wren and had a second child—me. Hadn't you guessed the meaning of my name?"

Nancy averted her gaze. As she looked around the room, Lilac Inn seemed suddenly antiquated. The lilacs had disappeared.

"How can Candy Wren be my mother as well as yours?" she asked distractedly. "She was a children's author."

"There is even more. Carson Drew, not Andy C. Wren, was my real father."

Nancy tossed her golden top. "But you are relating nothing but coincidences—a whole set of coincidences which, obviously, have no meaning." Rainy tears threatened to burst through the dreamy cloud of her afternoon. The beautiful stranger before her was still a stranger, although perhaps there was a resemblance to her father in the determined set of his jaw.

She remembered that her first impression linked him to her father.

"Dad sent me money all my life for my upbringing," Draco S. Wren continued, lapping at his tea. "I think he felt that you would eventually find out about me, with your uncanny sleuthing skills."

"I was never even suspicious," moaned Nancy, crestfallen. Her sleuthing abilities had lapsed. She had even neglected to bring her magnifying glass with her. But, rallying, she remembered that she had one clue left to refute this stranger's bizarre theory.

"Did you send my father a parcel recently?" she asked accusingly.

"A parcel?" queried Draco S. Wren guardedly. "Yes, if you mean a little ivory igloo?"

"Why did you send it?"

"Because he was my father, and I knew he would admire it. It was an old museum piece, an exquisite carving. I do hope you have kept it." Draco S. Wren crammed his mouth full of strawberry jam biscuits.

Nancy then informed Draco S. Wren—in her most even tones—of her knowledge of the ivory igloo. It was Draco S. Wren's turn to be mortified. He insisted that he never knew about the poison in the harpoon, but he was not surprised, since it was an old piece and might have been used for purposes of iniquity sometime in antiquity.

"Yes," Nancy said. "You realize, of course, that you might be held responsible in some way for Father's death, if the facts were known about that ivory whale-hunter in his igloo." For a few moments she felt she had returned victoriously to her proper role—Nancy Drew, girl detective.

Nancy looked at Draco S. Wren intently.

"You see the resemblance, don't you?" he said, grinning. "Here, look at this." He took a miniature leather album from his leather jacket and removed two faded photographs. "This is a picture of me at age three. And here is a picture of you at age three. They could be the same child except for your curls and lace."

Nancy stared in disbelief at the two pictures. One showed a short, fat, dark-haired boy, the other, a slim, golden-haired girl. The resemblance escaped her, but she could not deny the conviction of Draco S. Wren's words. And there was no questioning the fact that both young noses were cute buttons.

"What is your favorite color?" said Nancy faintly.

"What is yours?" Draco S. Wren countered coyly.

"Blue."

"Blue? Why, that is *my* favorite color!"

Nancy stared long and hard at Draco S. Wren, this clever stranger who had stolen her heart. His stories were preposterous but irrefutable. Her intuition had never failed her, and her intuition still told her that here was a truthful and good man.

Draco S. Wren looked back at Nancy. His eyes were definitely not beady, nor dark and piercing. He said, in heartfelt tones, "I must confess, Nancy, that when I met you, I wished desperately that you were not my sister, for I would have fallen in love with you in a moment."

"And I *did* fall in love with you," said Nancy uncharacteristically.

RESOLUTION

In the end, Nancy Drew bowed to her duty. She pledged to be loyal and true to her brother, to take care of him as she had her father (choosing his bandanas carefully, and giving him new appointment books for Christmas), and to make up for their lost childhood. Nancy promised to protect him from any question that should arise concerning a certain ivory gewgaw. She told Bess that the fluid had been analyzed and found to be whale oil. Nancy let it be known that Draco S. Wren was her long-lost brother but refused to divulge the details, so the affair encouraged prominent newspaper headlines and casual gossip. Some said Draco S. Wren was a fraud, falsely claiming a share in Carson Drew's legacy, like the impostor prince in another story about a jewel box. Others maintained quite a different story.

Draco S. Wren moved into the fashionable three-story brick Drew residence and established a law practice in River Heights. Nancy continued to solve mysteries, helping Draco S. Wren on his cases as she had once assisted her father. Nancy continued as the champion of her fan club, addressing its monthly meetings with her "Eye Openers." Her younger fans were loyal, and she sold lots of copies, but the grown-ups talked behind her back. Nevertheless, Nancy's larkspurs continued to win first prize in the flower show year after year, and she still danced in the River Heights talent show.

"I don't think this will do," Nancy said with a sigh as she finished writing. "I have tried to tell my true life story. But my life didn't turn out as it was supposed to."

She wondered if she should have mentioned the servant girl. And the fact that Draco S. Wren had now disappeared, taking all Nancy's priceless souvenirs from her mysteries. Nancy felt bereft. A real brother would not have acted that way. She thought now that some of his brotherly kisses reminded her somewhat of Ned Nickerson's busses. And recently Draco S. Wren's eyes had started to pierce darkly.

"I suppose with some revision—" She paused in thought. The emptiness she felt was not the same emptiness Nancy Drew, girl detective, usually felt as her story drew to a close and she wondered what mystery was in store for her next.

ED MCBAIN

The story that follows is true. Well, not exactly, but the events described did take place, and the characters are based on real-life people. The time and the places described are real, too, and you'll recognize them from the gangster movies and television programs you've seen over the years.

A period piece is not the story one would have expected from Ed McBain, who is best known for his landmark series about the 87th Precinct, and in more recent years for the bestselling Matthew Hope novels.

But, under his real name of Evan Hunter, the author has a wide range of books to his credit, including The Blackboard Jungle, *written when he was only twenty-eight,* Love, Dad, *a variety of science fiction novels, children's books,* Lizzie, *a superb fictional account of the Lizzie Borden murder case, and the screenplay for Alfred Hitchcock's* The Birds.

What you didn't know is that this hugely versatile and popular writer started his professional life as a jazz musician who dreamed of a different career—he wanted to be a painter. When one is born with talent, it simply finds a way to manifest itself. Evan Hunter was born with more talent than any one person deserves!

—O.P.

Running from Legs

BY ED McBAIN

Mahogany and brass.

Burnished and polished and gleaming under the green-shaded lights over the bar where men and women alike sat on padded stools and drank. Women, yes. In a saloon, yes. Sitting at the bar, and sitting in the black leather booths that lined the dimly lighted room. Women. Drinking alcohol. Discreetly, to be sure, for booze and speakeasies were against the law. Before Prohibition, you rarely saw a woman drinking in a saloon. Now you saw them in speakeasies all over the city. Where once there had been fifteen thousand bars, there were now thirty-two thousand speakeasies. The Prohibitionists hadn't expected these side effects of the Eighteenth Amendment.

The speakeasy was called the Brothers Three, named after Bruno Tataglia and his brothers Angelo and Mickey. It was located just off Third Avenue on 87th Street, in a part of the city named Yorkville after the Duke of York. We were here celebrating. My grandmother owned a chain of lingerie shops she called "Scanties," and today had been the grand opening of the third one. Her boyfriend Vinnie was with us, and so was Dominique Lefèvre, who worked for her in the second of her shops, the one on Lexington Avenue. My parents would have been here, too, but they'd been killed in an automobile accident while I was overseas.

In the other room, the band was playing "Ja-Da," a tune from the war years. We were all drinking from coffee cups. In the coffee cups was something very brown and very vile tasting, but it was not coffee.

Dominique was smiling.

It occurred to me that perhaps she was smiling at *me*.

Dominique was twenty-eight years old, a beautiful, dark-haired, dark-eyed woman, tall and slender and utterly desirable. A native of France, she had come to America as a widow shortly after the war ended; her husband had been killed three days before the guns went silent. One day, alone with her in my grandmother's shop—Dominique was folding silk panties, I was sitting on a stool in front of the counter, watching her—she told me she despaired of ever finding another man as wonderful as her husband had been. "I 'ave been spoil', *n'est-ce pas?*" she said. I adored her French accent. I told her that I, too, had suffered losses in my life. And so, like cautious strangers fearful of allowing even our *glances* to meet, we'd skirted the possibilities inherent in our chance proximity.

But now—her smile.

The Brothers Three was very crowded tonight. Lots of smoke and laughter and the sound of a four-piece band coming from the other room. Piano, drums, alto saxophone, and trumpet. There was a dance floor in the other room. I wondered if I should ask Dominique to dance. I had never danced with her. I tried to remember when last I'd danced with anyone.

I'd been limping, yes. And a French girl whispered in my ear—this was after I'd got out of the hospital, it was shortly after the armistice was signed—a French girl whispered to me in Paris that she found a man with a slight limp very sexy. *"Je trouve très séduisante,"* she said, *"une claudication légère."* She had nice *poitrines,* but I'm not sure I believed her. I think she was just being kind to an American doughboy who'd got shot in the foot during the fighting around the Bois des Loges on a bad day in November. I found that somewhat humiliating, getting shot in the foot. It did not seem very heroic, getting shot in the foot. I no longer limped, but I still had the feeling that some people thought I'd shot *myself* in the goddamn foot. To get out of the 78th Division or something. As if such a thought had ever crossed my mind.

Dominique kept smiling at me.

Boozily.

I figured she'd had too much coffee.

She was wearing basic black tonight. A simple black satin, narrow in silhouette, bare of back, its neckline square and adorned with pearls, its waistline low, its hemline falling to midthigh where a three-inch expanse of white flesh separated the dress from the rolled tops of her blond silk stockings. She was smoking. As were Vinnie and my grandmother. Smoking had something to do with drinking. If you drank, you smoked. That seemed to be the way it worked.

Dominique kept drinking and smoking and smiling at me.

I smiled back.

My grandmother ordered another round.

She was drinking Manhattans. Dominique was drinking Martinis. Vinnie was drinking something called a Between the Sheets, which was one-third brandy, one-third Cointreau, one-third rum, and a dash of lemon juice. I was drinking a Bosom Caresser. These were all cocktails, an American word made popular when drinking became illegal. Cocktails.

In the other room, a double paradiddle and a solid bass-drum shot ended the song. There was a pattering of applause, a slight expectant pause, and then the alto saxophone soared into the opening riff of a slow, sad, and bluesy rendition of "Who's Sorry Now?"

"Richard?" Dominique said, and raised one eyebrow. "Aren't you going to ask me to dance?"

She was easily the most beautiful woman in the room. Eyes lined with black mascara, lips and cheeks painted the color of all those poppies I'd seen growing in fields across the length and breadth of France. Her dark hair bobbed in a shingle cut, the scent of mimosa wafting across the table.

"Richard?"

Her voice a caress.

Alto saxophone calling mournfully from the next room.

Smoke swirling like fog coming in off the docks on the day we landed over there. We were back now because it was *over* over there. And I no longer limped. And Dominique was asking me to dance.

"Go dance with her," my grandmother said.

"Yes, come," Dominique said, and put out her cigarette. Rising, she moved out of the booth past my grandmother, who rescued her Manhattan by holding it close to her protective bosom, and then winked at me as if to say "These are new times, Richie, we have the vote now, we can drink and we can smoke, anything goes nowadays, Richie. Go dance with Dominique."

Is what my grandmother's wink seemed to say.

I took Dominique's hand.

Together, hand in hand, we moved toward the other room.

"I love this song," Dominique said, and squeezed my hand.

There were round tables with white tablecloths in the other room, embracing a half-moon-shaped, highly polished, parquet dance floor. The lights were dimmer in this part of the club, perhaps because the fox-trot was a new dance that encouraged cheeks against cheeks and hands upon asses. A party of three—a handsome man in a dinner jacket and two women in gowns—sat at one of the tables with Bruno Tataglia. Bruno was leaning over the table, in obviously obsequious conversation with the good-looking man whose eyes kept checking out women on the dance floor even though there was one beautiful woman sitting on his left and another on his right. Both women were wearing white satin gowns and they both had purple hair. I had heard of women wearing orange, or red, or green, or even purple wigs when they went out on the town, but this was the first time I'd ever actually *seen* one.

Two, in fact.

I wondered how Dominique would look in a purple wig.

"Dominique?"

Bruno's voice.

He rose as we came abreast of the table, took her elbow, and said to the man in the dinner jacket, "Mr. Noland, I'd like you to meet the beauteous Dominique."

"Pleasure," Mr. Noland said.

Dominique nodded politely.

"And Richie here," Bruno said as an afterthought.

"Nice to meet you," I said.

Mr. Noland's eyes were on Dominique.

"Won't you join us?" he said.

"Thank you, but we're about to dance," Dominique said, and squeezed my hand again, and led me out onto the floor. I held her close. We began swaying in time to the music. The trumpet player was putting in a mute. The piano player eased him into his solo.

Liquid brass.

Dominique's left hand moved up to the back of my neck.

"You dance well," she said.

"Thank you."

"Does it ever ache you? Your foot?"

"When it rains," I said.

"Was it terrible, the war?" she asked.

"Yes," I said.

I did not much feel like talking about it. I gently steered her away from the ring of tables and back toward the bandstand, sweeping her gracefully past the table where Bruno was grinning oleaginously at Mr. Noland and his two blond bimbos.

Mr. Noland's eyes met mine.

A shiver ran up my spine.

I had never seen eyes like that in my life.

Not even on the battlefield.

Not even on men eager to kill me.

Dominique and I glided over the parquet floor.

Drifting, drifting to the sound of the muted horn.

There was a gentle tap on my shoulder.

I turned.

Mr. Noland was standing slightly behind me and slightly to my right, his hand resting on my shoulder.

"I'm cutting in," he said.

And his hand tightened on my shoulder, and he moved me away from Dominique, my left hand still holding her right hand, and then stepped into the open circle his intrusion had created, looping his right arm around Dominique's waist and shouldering me out completely.

I moved clumsily off the dance floor and stood in the middle of the arch separating the two rooms, feeling somehow embarrassed and inadequate, watching helplessly as Mr. Noland pulled Dominique in close to him. At the table he'd just vacated, the two women were laughing it up with Bruno. I went through the arch and back into the lounge with its black leather booths and its black leather barstools. My grandmother raised her Manhattan to me in a toast. I nodded acknowledgment, and smiled, and walked toward where Mickey Tataglia was sitting at the bar, chatting up a redhead, who was wearing a windblown bob and a liquid green dress the color of her eyes. He had his hand on her silk-stockinged knee. She had in her hand, I swear to God, a long cigarette holder that made her look exactly like any of the Held flappers on the covers of *Life.* This was a night for firsts. I had never seen two women with purple wigs, and I had never seen a woman with a cigarette holder like this one. I had never danced with Dominique either; easy come, easy go.

As I took the stool on his left, Mickey was telling the redhead all about his war experiences. His brother Angelo was behind the bar, filling coffee cups with booze. I told him I wanted a Bosom Caresser.

"What's a Bosom Caresser?" he asked.

"I have no idea," I said. "Our waiter asked me if I wanted one, and I said yes, and he brought it to me."

"What's in it?"

"Mickey," I said, "what's in a Bosom Caresser?"

"Talk about *fresh!"* the redhead said, and rolled her eyes.

"Are you asking what I would *put* in a Bosom Caresser?" Mickey said. "If I were making such a drink?"

"Who is this person you're talking to?" the redhead said.

"A friend of mine," Mickey said. "This is Maxie," he said, and squeezed her knee.

"How do you do?" I said.

"This is Richie," he said.

"Familiar for Richard," I said.

"I'm familiar for Maxine," Maxie said.

In the other room, the band started playing "Mexicali Rose."

"If you want a Bosom Treasure, you got to tell me what's in it," Angelo said.

"Bosom *Caresser,"* I said.

"Whatever," Angelo said. "I have to know the ingredients."

"Mother's milk, to begin with," Mickey said.

"You're as fresh as he is," Maxie scolded, rolling her eyes at me and playfully slapping Mickey's hand, which was working higher on her knee.

"Laced with gin and egg white," I said.

"Ick," Maxie said.

"And topped with a cherry," Mickey said.

"*Double*-ick," Maxie said.

"We don't have any mother's milk," Angelo said.

"Then I'll have a Rock 'n' Rye," I said.

"I'll have another one of these, whatever it is," Mickey said.

"Ditto," Maxie said.

"Hold the fort," Mickey said, getting off his stool. "I have to visit the gents."

I watched him as he headed toward the men's room. He stopped at my grandmother's table, planted a noisy kiss on her cheek, and then moved on.

"Was he really a war hero?" Maxie asked me.

"Oh, sure," I said. "He was in the battle of—"

"Just keep your damn hands *off* me!" Dominique shouted from the dance floor.

I was off that stool as if I'd heard an incoming artillery shell whistling toward my head. Off that stool and running toward the silvered arch beyond which were the tables with their white tablecloths and the polished parquet dance floor, and Dominique in her short black dress, trying to free her right hand from—

"Let *go* of me!" she shouted.

"No."

A smile on Mr. Noland's face. His hand clutched around her narrow waist.

Maybe he didn't see her eyes. Maybe he was too busy getting a big charge out of this slender, gorgeous woman trying to extricate herself from his powerful grip.

"Damn you!" she said. "Let go or I'll . . ."

"Yes, baby, what is it you'll do?"

She didn't tell him what she'd do. She simply did it. She twisted her body to the left, her arm swinging all the way back and then forward again with all the power of her shoulder behind it. Her bunched left fist collided with Mr. Noland's right cheek, just below his eye, and he touched his eye, and looked at his fingertips as if expecting blood, and then very softly and menacingly said, "Now you get hurt, baby."

Some people never learn.

He had called her "baby" once, and that had been a bad mistake, so what he'd just done was call her "baby" again, which was an even bigger mistake. Dominique nodded curtly, the nod saying "Okay, fine," and then she went for his face with both hands, her nails raking bloody tracks from just under his eyes—which I think she'd been going for—all the way down to his jawline.

Mr. Noland punched her.

Hard.

I yelled the way I'd yelled going across the Marne.

I was on him in ten seconds flat, the time it took to race through that arch and charge across the dance floor, the time it took to clench my fists and hit him first with the left one and then with the right one, bam-bam, a one-two punch to the gut and the jaw that sent him staggering back from me. He rubbed his jaw in surprise. His hands came away with the blood from Dominique's fingernail-raking. He looked at the blood in surprise too. And then he looked at me in surprise, as if trying to figure out how some madman had got inside this civilized speakeasy. He didn't say a word. He merely looked surprised and sad and bloody, shaking his head as if wondering how the world had turned so rotten all at once. And then, abruptly, he stopped shaking his head and took a gun out of a holster under his dinner jacket.

Just like that.

Zip.

One minute, no gun. The next minute, a gun.

Dominique took off one of her high-heeled shoes.

As she raised her leg, Mr. Noland looked under her skirt at her underwear—black silk panties in my grandmother's "Sirocco" line, $4.98 over the counter in any of her shops. Mr. Noland then realized what Dominique was going to do with the shoe. What she was going to do was hit him on the side of the head with it. Which was possibly why he aimed the gun right at her heart.

I did the only thing I could do.

In reaction, Mr. Noland bellowed in rage and doubled over in pain, his hands clutching for his groin, his knees coming together as if he had to pee very badly, and then he fell to the floor and lay there writhing and moaning while everywhere about him were dancers all aghast. Bruno rushed to him at once and knelt beside him, his hands fluttering. "Oh, God, Mr. Noland," he said, "I'm so sorry, Mr. Noland," and Mr. Noland tried to say something but his face was very red and his eyes were bulging and all that came out was a sort of strangled sputter at which point one of the women with the purple hair came running over and said, "Legs? Shall I call a doctor?"

Which is when I grabbed Dominique's hand and began running.

"A bootlegger, a narcotics smuggler, a hijacker, and a trusted friend of an even *bigger* gangster named Little Augie Orgen, *that's* who Legs *Diamond* is."

All this from Mickey Tataglia, who hurried us through tunnels under the club, pressing buttons that opened doors into other tunnels lined with booze smuggled in from Canada.

"He also owns a second-floor speakeasy called the Hotsy Totsy Club on Broadway, between Fifty-fourth and Fifty-fifth streets, that's who Legs Diamond is. You did a stupid thing, both of you. Do you know who arranged the murder of Jack the Dropper?"

"Who is Jack the Dropper?" Dominique asked.

High heels clicking, long legs flashing through dusty underground tunnels lined with cases and cases of illegal booze. Mickey walked swiftly ahead of us, leading the way, brushing aside cobwebs that hung from rafters along which rats scampered.

"Jack the Dropper," he said impatiently. "Alias Kid Dropper, whose real name is Nathan Kaplan, who all three of him was shot dead by Louis Kushner in a trap the Diamonds set up."

"The Diamonds," I said.

"Legs Diamond," Mickey said. "Alias Jack Diamond, alias John Higgins, alias John Hart, whose real name is John Thomas *Noland*, who all five of him will not like getting kicked in the balls by a fucking dope who shot himself in the foot."

"Richard did not shoot himself in the foot," Dominique said heatedly.

"I'm sure the Diamonds will take that into consideration when he kills you both. Or if not him, then one of his apes. The Diamonds has a lot of such people on his payroll. I wish you both a lot of luck," he said, and pressed another button. A wall swung open. Beyond it was an alleyway.

"You're on 88th Street," Mickey said.

We stepped outside into a dusky evengloam.

Mickey hit the button again.

The door closed behind us.

We began running.

* * *

We got to Penn Station at 8:33 P.M., and learned that a train would be leaving for Chattanooga, Tennessee, in exactly seven minutes. It cost us an additional twelve dollars each for a sleeping compartment, but we figured it was worth it. We did not want to be sitting out in the open should any of Diamond's goons decide to check out the trains leaving the city. A sleeping compartment had windows with curtains and shades on them. A sleeping compartment had a door with a lock on it.

The train was the Crescent Limited, making stops in Philadelphia, Baltimore, Washington, D.C., Charlottesville, Spartanburg, Greenville, and Atlanta, before its scheduled arrival in Chattanooga at 10:10 tomorrow night. We figured Chattanooga was far enough away. The total one-way fare came to $41.29 for each of us. The train was scheduled to leave at 8:40.

A black porter carried our bags into the compartment, told us he'd make up the berths for us whenever we liked, and then inquired as to whether we'd care for any kind of beverage before we retired.

The "any kind of beverage" sounded like a code, but I wanted to make certain.

"What kind of beverage did you have in mind?" I asked.

"Whatever sort of beverage might suit your fancy," he said.

"And what sort of beverage might that be?"

"Well, suh," he said, "we has coffee, tea, and milk . . ."

"Uh-huh."

"And a *wide* variety of soft drinks," he said, and winked so broadly that any Prohibition agent wandering past would have arrested him on the strength of the wink alone. Dominique immediately pulled back her skirt, took a silver flask from where it was tucked into her garter, and asked the porter to fill it with any kind of colorless soft drink, please. I took my flask from my hip pocket and told him I'd have the same. He knew we both wanted gin. Or its vague equivalent.

"That'll be twenty dollars each t'fill dese flasks here," he said.

"We'll need some setups too," I said, and took out my wallet and handed him three twenty-dollar bills. He left the compartment and returned some ten minutes later, carrying a tray on which were a siphon bottle of soda, two tall glasses, a bowl of chipped ice with a spoon in it, a lemon on a small dish, a paring knife, and ten dollars in change from the sixty I'd given him. He put the tray on the table between the two facing seats, removed the two filled flasks from the side pockets of his white jacket, put those on the table as well, asked if there was anything else we might be needing, and then told us again that he would make up the berths for us whenever we were of a mind to retire. Dominique said maybe he ought to make them up now. I looked at her.

"No?" she said.

"No, fine," I said.

"Shall I makes 'em up, den?" the porter asked.

"Please," Dominique said.

The porter grinned; I suspected he wanted to get the bed-making over with so he could get a good night's sleep himself. We went out into the corridor, leaving him to his work. Dominique looked at her watch.

I looked at my watch.

It was already ten minutes to nine.

"I'm very frightened," she said.

"So am I."

"You?" She waved this away with the back of her hand. "You have been in the war."

"Still," I said, and shrugged.

She did not know about wars.

Inside the compartment, the porter worked in silence.

"Why aren't we leaving yet?" Dominique asked.

I looked at my watch again.

"There you go, suh," the porter said, stepping out into the corridor.

"Thank you," I said, and tipped him two dollars.

" 'Night, suh," he said, touching the peak of his hat, "ma'am, sleep well, the boths of you."

We went back into the compartment. He had left the folding table up because he knew we'd be drinking, but the seats on either side of the compartment were now made up as narrow beds with pillows and sheets and blankets. I closed and locked the door behind us.

"Did you lock it?" Dominique asked. She was already spooning ice into both glasses, her back to me.

"I locked it," I said.

"Tell me how much," she said, and began pouring from one of the flasks.

"That's enough," I said.

"I want a very strong one," she said, pouring heavily into the other glass.

"Shall I slice this lemon?"

"Please," she said, and sat on the bed on the forward side of the compartment.

I sat opposite her. She picked up the soda siphon, squirted some into each of the glasses. Her legs were slightly parted. Her skirt was riding high on her thighs. Rolled silk stockings. Garter on her right leg, where the flask had been. I halved the lemon, quartered it, squeezed some juice into her glass, dropped the crushed quarter-lemon into it. I raised my own glass.

"Pas de citron pour toi?" she asked.

"I don't like lemon."

"It will taste vile without lemon," she said.

"I don't want to spoil the flavor of premium gin," I said.

Dominique laughed.

"À votre santé," I said, and clinked my glass against hers. We both drank.

It went down like molten fire.

"Jesus!" I said.

"Whoooo!" she said.

"I think I'm going blind!"

"That is not something to joke about."

The train began huffing and puffing.

"Are we leaving?" she asked.

"Enfin," I said.

"Enfin, d'accord," she said, and heaved a sigh of relief.

The train began moving. I thought of the train that had taken us from Calais to the front.

"Now we can relax," she said.

I nodded.

"Do you think he'll send someone after us?"

"Depends on how crazy he is."

"I think he is very crazy."

"So do I."

"Then he will send someone."

"Maybe."

Dominique drew back the curtains on the outside window, lifted the shade. We were out of the tunnel now, already into the night. There were stars overhead. No moon.

"Best to just *sip* this stuff," I said. "Otherwise . . ."

"Ah, oui, bien sûr," she said.

We sipped at the gin. The train was moving along swiftly now, flashing southward into the night.

"So you learned some French over there," she said.

"A little."

"Well . . . *à votre santé* . . . *enfin* . . . quite a bit of French, no?"

"Only enough to get by on."

I was thinking of the German who had mistaken us for

French troops and who'd pleaded with us in broken French to spare his life. I was thinking of his skull exploding when our patrol sergeant opened fire.

"This grows on you, doesn't it?" I said.

"Actually, I think it's very good," she said. "I think it may even be *real* gin."

"Maybe," I said dubiously.

She looked over her glass at me. "Maybe next time there's a war, you won't have to go," she said.

"Because I was wounded, do you mean?"

"Yes."

"Maybe."

The train raced through the night. The New Jersey countryside flashed by in the darkness. Telephone wires swooped and dipped between poles.

"They say there are thirty telephone poles to every mile," I said.

"Vraiment?"

"Well, that's what they say."

"Turn off the lights," she said. "It will look prettier outside."

I turned off the lights.

"And open the window, please. It will be cooler."

I tried pulling up one of the windows, but it wouldn't budge. I finally got the other one up. Cool air rushed into the compartment. There was the smell of smoke from the engine up ahead, cinders and soot on the night.

"Ahhh, yes," she said, and sighed deeply.

Outside, the world rushed past.

We sat sipping the gin, watching the distant lights.

"Do you think Mr. Diamonds will have us killed?"

"Mr. *Diamond,"* I said. "Singular. Legs *Diamond."*

"I wonder why they call him Legs."

"I don't know."

She fell silent. Staring through the window. Face in profile. Touched only by starshine.

"I love the sound of the wheels," she said, and sighed again. "Trains are so sad."

I was thinking the very same thing.

"I'm getting sleepy, are you?" she asked.

"A little."

"I think I'll get ready for bed."

"I'll step outside," I said, and started to get up.

"No, stay," she said, and then, "It's dark."

She rose, reached up to the overhead rack, and took down her suitcase. She snapped open the locks, and lifted the lid. She reached behind her, then, and unbuttoned the buttons at the back of her dress and pulled the dress up over her head.

I turned away, toward the windows.

We were coming through a stretch of farmland, lights only in the far distance now, nothing close to the tracks. The single closed window reflected Dominique in black lingerie from my grandmother's "Flirty Flapper" line, rolled black seamed silk stockings, black lace-edged bra designed to flatten her breasts, black lace-edged tap pants.

The blackness of the night reflected her.

"Pour me some more gin, please," she said.

Softly.

I spooned ice into her glass, unscrewed the flask's top, poured gin over the ice. Silver spilled from silver onto silver. Behind me, there was the rustle of silk.

"A little lemon, please," she said.

In the reflecting window, she was naked now. Pale as starlight.

She took a nightgown out of the suitcase.

I squeezed another quarter-lemon, dropped it into the glass. I squirted soda into the glass. She dropped the nightgown over her head. It slid down past her breasts and hips and thighs.

I turned to her, she turned to me. In the nightgown, she looked almost medieval. The gown was either silk or rayon, as white as snow, its yoke neck trimmed with white lace. My grandmother's "Sleeptite" line.

I handed Dominique her drink.

"Thank you," she said, and looked at my empty glass on the table. "None for you?" she asked.

"I think I've had enough."

"Just a sip," she said. "To drink a toast. I can't drink a toast all alone."

I dropped some ice into my glass, poured a little gin over it.

She raised her glass.

"To now," she said.

"There's no such thing," I said.

"Tonight, then. There is surely tonight."

"Yes. I suppose."

"Will you drink to tonight, then?"

"To tonight," I said.

"And to us."

I looked at her.

"To us, Richard."

"To us," I said.

We drank.

"Doesn't this table move out of the way?" she asked.

"I think it folds down," I said.

"Can you fold it down?"

"If you like."

"Well, I think it's in the way, don't you?"

"I guess it is."

"Well, then, please fold it down, Richard."

I moved everything from the table to the wide sill just inside the window. I got on my knees then, looked under the table, figured out how the hinge and clasp mechanism worked, and lowered the top.

"Voilà!" Dominique said triumphantly.

I picked up my drink from the windowsill. We both sat, Dominique on one bed, I on the other, facing each other, our knees almost touching. Outside, the countryside rolled by, an occasional light splintering the dark.

"I wish we had music," she said. "We could dance again. There's enough room for dancing now, don't you think? With the table down?"

I looked at her skeptically; the space between the beds was perhaps three feet wide by six feet long.

"Without being interrupted this time," she said, and tossed her head and began swaying from side to side.

"I shouldn't have let him cut in," I said.

"Well, how could you have known?"

"I saw his eyes."

"Behind you? When he was cutting in?"

"Earlier. I should have known. Seeing those eyes."

"Dance with me now," she said, and held out her arms.

"We don't have music," I said.

She moved in close against me.

The soft silken feel of her.

"Ja-Da," she sang.

Slowly.

Very slowly.

"Ja-Da . . ."

Not at all in the proper tempo.

"Ja-Da, Ja-Da . . .

"Jing . . . jing . . . *jing."*

I thought at first . . .

"Ja-Da . . ."

What I thought . . .

"Ja-Da . . ."

Was that . . .

"Ja-Da, Ja-Da . . ."

Was that a fierce thrust of her crotch that accompanied each . . .

"Jing . . . jing . . . *jing.*"

I was flamingly erect in the tick of an instant.

"Oh, *mon Dieu,*" Dominique whispered.

Whispered those words in that rumbling sleeping compartment, on that train hurtling through the night, speeding us southward and away from all possible harm, lurching through the darkness, causing us to lose our balance so that we fell still locked in embrace onto the bed that was Dominique's, holding her tight in my arms, kissing her forehead and her cheeks and her nose and her lips and her neck and her shoulders and her breasts as she whispered over and over again, "Oh, *mon Dieu,* oh, *mon Dieu,* oh, *mon Dieu.*"

We brought to the act of love a steamy clumsiness composed of legs and arms and hips and noses and chins in constant collision. The train, the track, seemed maliciously intent on hurling us out of bed and out of embrace. We jostled and jiggled on that thin mattress, juggling passion, sweating in each other's arms as we struggled to maintain purchase, "Ow!" she said as my elbow poked her in the ribs, "Sorry," I mumbled, and then "Ooops!" because I was sliding out of her. She adjusted her hips, lifting them, deeply enclosing me again but almost knocking me off her in the bargain because the train in that very instant decided to run over an imperfection on the track which together with the motion of her ascending hips sent me soaring ceilingward. The only thing that kept me in her and on her was the cunning interlocking design of our separate parts.

We learned quickly enough.

Although, in retrospect, the train did all the work and we were merely willing accomplices.

Up and down the train went, rocketing through the night, in and out of tunnels the train went, racketing through the night, side to side the train rocked, rattling through the night, up and down, in and out, side to side, the train thrust against the night, tattering the darkness with a single searing eye, scattering all before it helter-skelter. Helpless in the grip of this relentless fucking machine, we screamed at last aloud and together, waking the hall porter in the corridor, who screamed himself as though he'd heard shrieks of bloody murder.

And then we lay enfolded in each other's arms and talked. We scarcely knew each other, except intimately, and had never really talked seriously. So now we talked about things that were enormously important to us. Like our favorite colors. Or our favorite times of the year. Or our favorite ice-cream flavors. Or our favorite songs and movies. Our dreams. Our ambitions.

I told her I loved her.

I told her I would do anything in the world for her.

"Would you kill someone for me?" she asked.

"Yes," I said at once.

She nodded.

"I knew you were watching me undress," she said. "I knew you were looking at my reflection in the window. I found that very exciting."

"So did I."

"And getting bounced all around while you were inside me, that was very exciting too."

"Yes."

"I wish you were inside me now," she said.

"Yes."

"Bouncing around inside me."

"Yes."

"That big thing inside me again," she said, and leaned over me and kissed me on the mouth.

Vinnie had bad news when I called home that Saturday.

On Friday afternoon, while Dominique and I were on the

train heading south, two men accosted my grandmother as she came out of her Fourteenth Street shop.

"In the car, Grandma," the skinny one said.

He was the one with the crazy eyes.

That's the way my grandmother later described him to Vinnie.

"He had crazy eyes," she said. "And a knife."

The fat one was behind the wheel of the car. My grandmother described the car as a two-door blue Jewett coach. All three of them sat up front. The fat one driving, my grandmother in the middle, and the skinny one on her right. What the skinny one did, he put the knife under her chin and told her if You-Know-Who did not come back to face the music, the next time he would be looking in at her tonsils, did she catch his drift?

My grandmother caught his drift, all right.

They let her out of the car on Avenue B and East Fourth Street, right near the Most Holy Redeemer Catholic Church. She ran in terror all the way home. Vinnie grabbed a baseball bat and went looking for Fat and Skinny in the streets. He could not find them, nor did he see a single Jewett coach anywhere in the entire 9th Precinct.

"So what do you think?" he asked me on the phone.

"I think I'll have to kill him," I said.

"Who?"

"Legs Diamond."

There was a long silence.

"Vinnie," I said, "did you hear me?"

"I heard you," he said. "I don't think that's such a good idea, Richie."

The wires between us crackled; we were a long way away from each other.

"Vinnie," I said, "I can't hide from this man forever."

"He'll grow tired of hounding you," he said.

"No, I don't think so. He has a lot of people who can do the hounding for him. It's no trouble at all for him, really."

"Richie, listen to me."

"Yes, Vinnie, I'm listening."

"What do you want from life, Richie?"

"I want to marry Dominique," I said. "And I want to have children with her."

"Ah," he said.

"And I want to live in a house with a white picket fence around it."

"Yes," he said. "And that's why you mustn't kill this man."

"No," I said, "that's why I *must* kill this man. Because otherwise . . ."

"Richie, it's not easy to kill someone."

"I've seen a lot of people killing a lot of people, Vinnie. It looked easy to me."

"In a war, yes. But unless you're in a war, it's not so easy to kill someone. Have you ever killed anyone, Richie?"

"No."

"In a war, it's easy," he said. "Everyone is shooting at everyone else, so if *your* bullet doesn't happen to kill anyone, it doesn't matter. Someone *else's* bullet will. But killing somebody in a war isn't *murder,* Richie. That's the first thing a soldier learns: killing someone in a war isn't murder. Because when *everyone* is killing someone, then *no* one is killing *anyone."*

"Well . . ."

"Don't 'well' me, just listen to me. Killing Legs Diamond will be murder. Are you ready to do murder, Richie?"

"Yes," I said.

"Why?"

"Because I love Dominique. And if I don't kill him, he'll hurt her."

"Look . . . let me ask around, okay?" Vinnie said.

"Ask around?"

"Here and there. Meanwhile, don't do anything foolish."

"Vinnie?" I said. "I know where he is. It's in all the newspapers."

I heard a sigh on the other end of the line.

"He's in Troy, New York. They're putting him on trial for kidnapping some kid up there."

"Richie . . ."

"I think I'd better go up to Troy, Vinnie."

"No, Richie," he said. "Don't."

There was another long silence on the line.

"I didn't think it would end this way, Vinnie," I said.

"It doesn't have to end this way."

"I thought . . ."

"What did you think, Richie?"

"I never thought it would get down to killing him. Running from him was one thing, but killing him . . ."

"It doesn't have to get down to that," Vinnie said.

"It does," I said. "It does."

Five hours and thirty-one minutes after the jury began deliberating the case, Legs Diamond was found innocent of all charges against him.

When he and his entourage came out of the courthouse that night, Dominique and I were waiting in a car parked across the street. We were both dressed identically. Long black men's overcoats, black gloves, pearl-gray fedoras.

It was bitterly cold.

Diamond and his family got into a taxi he had hired to chauffeur him to and from the courthouse during the trial. The rest of his party got into cars behind him. In our own car, a maroon sedan, Dominique and I followed them into Albany and then to a speakeasy at 518 Broadway. We did not go into the club. We sat in the car and waited. We did not talk at all. It was even colder now. The windows became rimed with frost. I kept rubbing at the windshield with my gloved hand.

At a little after one in the morning, Diamond and his wife Alice came out of the club. Diamond was wearing a brown chinchilla coat and a brown fedora. Alice was wearing a dress, high-heeled shoes, no coat. The driver came out of the club a moment later. From where we were parked, we could not hear the conversation between Alice and Diamond, but as he walked with his driver toward where the taxi was parked, he yelled over his shoulder, "Stick around till I get back!" The driver got in behind the wheel. Diamond climbed into the backseat. Alice stood on the sidewalk a moment longer, plumes of vapor trailing from her mouth, and then went back into the club. We gave the taxi a reasonable lead and then pulled out after them.

The taxi took Diamond to a rooming house on the corner of Clinton Avenue and Tenbroeck Street. Diamond got out, said something to the driver, closed the door, and went into the building. We drove past, turned the corner, went completely around the block, and then parked halfway up the street. The cab was still parked right in front of the building. We could not have got by the driver without being seen.

Diamond came out at 4:30 A.M.

I nudged Dominique awake.

We began following the taxi again.

Ten days ago, a man and a woman named "Mr. and Mrs. Kelly" had rented three rooms in a rooming house on Dove Street—for themselves and their relatives, a sister-in-law and her ten-year-old son. I learned this from the owner of the rooming house, a woman named Laura Wood, who gave me the information after she identified some newspaper photographs I showed her. She seemed surprised that Mr. Kelly was in fact the big gangster Legs Diamond who was being tried "over in Troy." She told me he was a respectable gentleman, quiet and well behaved, and she had no real cause for complaint. I gave her fifty dollars and asked her not to mention that a reporter had been there.

The taxi took Diamond there now.

Sixty-seven Dove Street.

Diamond got out of the taxi. It was a quarter to five in the morning. The taxi drove off. The street was silent. Not a light showed in the rooming house. He unlocked the front door with a key, and went inside. The door closed behind him. The street was silent again. We waited. On the second floor of the rooming house, a light came on.

"Do you think the wife is already here?" Dominique asked.

"He told her to stay at the club."

"What will you do if she's there with him?"

"I don't know," I said.

"You will have to kill her, too, no?"

"First let me get in the building, okay?"

"No, I want to know."

"What is it you want to know?"

"What you will do if she is there with him."

"I'll see."

"Well, I think you will have to kill her, no?"

"Dominique, there is killing and there is killing."

"Yes, I know that. But if you go in there, you must be prepared to do what must be done. Otherwise, his people will come after us again and again. You know that."

"Yes. I know that."

"We will have to keep running."

"I know."

"So if the woman is there with him, you will have to kill her too. That is only logical, Richard. You cannot leave her alive to identify you."

I nodded.

"If she is there, you must kill them both, it is as simple as that. If you love me."

"I do love you."

"And I love you," she said.

The light on the second floor went out.

"Bonne chance," she said, and kissed me on the mouth.

I left her sitting behind the wheel of the car, its engine running.

I tried the front door of the rooming house.

Locked.

I leaned hard on the door. The lock seemed almost ready to give. I backed away, lifted my left leg, and kicked at the door flat-footed, just above the knob. The lock snapped, the door sprang inward.

Silently, I climbed the steps to the second floor. Mrs. Wood had innocently told me that Diamond and his wife were staying in the room on the right of the stairway. "Such a quiet couple," she'd said. The steps creaked under me as I went up. A night-light was burning on the second floor. Almost too dim to see by. A shabby carpet underfoot. I turned to the right. The door to Diamond's room was at the end of the hall. I took a gun from each pocket of my overcoat. I had loaded both pistols with soft-nosed bullets. Dum-dums. If I was going to do this, it had to be done right.

I tried the doorknob.

The door was unlocked.

I eased it open.

The room was dark except for the faintest glow of daybreak beyond the drawn window shade. I could hear Diamond's shallow breathing across the room. A leather traveling bag was on the floor. His chinchilla coat lay beside it. So did his hat. His trousers were folded over the back of a chair. I went to the bed. I looked down at him. He was sleeping with his mouth open. He stank of booze. My hands were trembling.

My first bullet went into the wall.

The next one went into the floor.

I finally shot Diamond in the head three times.

I came tearing down the steps. The front door was still ajar. I ran out into a cold gray dawn. A man coming out of the building next door saw me racing across the street to where Dominique was standing outside the car on the passenger side, the engine idling, the exhaust throwing up gray clouds on the gray dawn.

"Was she there?" she asked.

"No," I said.

"Did you kill him?"

"Yes."

"Good."

Across the street the man was staring at us.

We got into the car and began driving north. I was behind the wheel now. Dominique was wiping the guns. Just in case. Wiping, wiping with a white silk handkerchief, polishing those gun butts and barrels in the event that somehow, in spite of the gloves, I'd left fingerprints on them. As we approached St. Paul's Church, a mile and a half from Dove Street, I slowed the car. Dominique rolled down the window on her side, and threw out one of the guns, wrapped in the silk handkerchief. Five minutes later, she tossed out the second gun, wrapped in another handkerchief. We sped through dawn. In Saugerties, a uniformed policeman looked up in surprise as we raced through the deserted main street of the town.

We were free again.

But not because I'd killed Legs Diamond.

"What do you mean?" I asked Vinnie on the phone.

"It's okay," he said. "Somebody talked to the goons who scared your grandmother."

"What do you mean? Who? Talked to them about *what?*"

"About you and Dom."

"*Who* did?"

"Mickey Tataglia. He went to see them and convinced them you're not worth bothering with."

"But Diamond is dead. Why would they. . . ?"

"Yeah, somebody killed him, what a pity."

"So why would they be willing to forget. . . ?"

"Well, I think some money changed hands."

"How much money?"

"I don't know how much."

"You do know, Vinnie."

"I think maybe five thousand."

"Where'd the money come from?"

"I don't know."

"Whose money was it, Vinnie?"

The line went silent.

"Vinnie?"

More silence.

"Vinnie, was it Grandma's money? The money she's been saving for another shop?"

"I don't think it was her money. Let's just say *somebody* gave Mickey the money and he gave it to the goons, and you don't have to worry about anything anymore. Come on home."

"Who gave Mickey the money?"

"I have no idea. Come on home."

"*Whoever's* money it was, Vinnie . . . tell him I'll pay it all back one day."

"I'll tell him. Now come home, you and Dom."

"Vinnie?" I said. "Thank you very much."

"Come on, for what?" he said, and hung up.

When I told Dominique about the phone conversation, she said, "So you killed him for nothing."

I should have picked up on the word *you*.

But, after all, *she* hadn't killed anyone, had she?

"I killed him because I love you," I said.

"Alors, merci beaucoup," she said. "But money would have done it just as well, eh?"

A week after we got back to the city, Dominique told me that what we'd enjoyed together on the way to Chattanooga had been very nice, *bien sûr,* but she could never live with a man who had done murder, eh? However noble the cause. *En tout cas,* it was time she went back to Paris to make her home again in the land she loved.

"Tu comprends, mon chéri?" she said.

No, I wanted to say, I don't understand.

I thought we loved each other, I wanted to say.

That night on the train . . .

I thought it would last forever, you know?

I thought Legs Diamond would be our costar forever. We would run from him through all eternity, locked in embrace as he pursued us relentlessly and in vain. We would marry and we would have children and I would become rich and famous and Dominique would stay young and beautiful forever and our love would remain steadfast and true—but only because we would forever be running from Legs. That would be the steadily unifying force in our lives. Running from Legs.

We kissed good-bye.

We promised to stay in touch.

I never heard from her again.

Joyce Carol Oates

Customarily, the well-known writers of an era achieve their stardom, if you will, by one of two means. One is to be prolific and popular with readers, the other is to create a distinctive prose style that is applauded by critics. It is very rare indeed to be able to satisfy the demands of reviewers and literary aesthetes, who mainly seem to want authors to fail, as well as a large number of readers, who mainly want to be entertained.

Joyce Carol Oates, of course, is one of those rare hybrids whose work is eagerly sought by discerning readers, yet who receive glowing reviews from the most sharp-clawed critics. The great astonishment is that she writes so much so brilliantly, with hundreds of short stories tucked among dozens of novels, with some nonfiction on the side to round out the collection.

Ranging from the clear beauty of Belle-Fleur *to the Gothic intensity of* The Mysteries of Winterthorn *to the psychological suspense novels she writes under the pseudonym Rosamunde Smith, Joyce Carol Oates brings to an extraordinary spectrum of work both originality and professionalism. When you have finished reading ''At the Paradise Motel, Sparks, Nevada,'' for example, try to forget it. You will fail.*

—O.P.

At the Paradise Motel, Sparks, Nevada

BY JOYCE CAROL OATES

How many of you pigs. Emissaries of Satan. Adulterers in your hearts and fornicators. How many rapists and despoilers of the innocent, how many creatures groveling in lust. How many of you deserving of God's wrath "Starr Bright" might have killed had I not been run to earth before my time I cannot know for such knowledge is not given to us in the wisdom of the Lord God. Amen.

In the desert, through planes of shimmering light, the hazy mauve mountains of the Sierra Nevadas in the distance, the light fell vertical, sharp as a razor blade. The sky was a hard ceramic blue that looked painted and without depth. "Starr Bright" woke from her druggy reverie of the past several hours and wondered for a moment where she was, and with who. A familiar-unfamiliar succession of motels, restaurants, gas stations, enormous billboards advertising casinos in Reno and Las Vegas—they were approaching the city limits of Sparks, Billy Ray Cobb behind the wheel of his classy rented steel-gray Infiniti with the red leather interior. "Starr Bright" removed her dark-tinted white-framed sunglasses to see better, but the glare was blinding. She wasn't a girl for the harsh overexposed hours of morning or afternoon, her soul best roused at twilight when neon lights flashed into life. *But why am I here, why now? And with who?*

Not knowing she was awaiting God's sign.

Beside her, proud and perky behind the wheel of the Infiniti, was Mr. Cobb of Elton, California, a manufacturer's representative—as he'd introduced himself the previous evening. Mr. Cobb was a thick-necked man of forty-six who perspired easily, with heavy-lidded frog's eyes and a damp, hungry smile. He wore sporty vacation clothes—this *was* his vacation, after all—an electric-blue crinkled-cotton shirt monogrammed *B.R.C.* on the pocket, checked polyester trousers creased at the thighs, a "Navajo" leather belt with a flashy brass buckle. A black onyx ring on his right hand and a gold wedding band on his left hand, both rings embedded in fatty flesh. Out of the corner of her eye "Starr Bright" saw Mr. Cobb peering at her and she quickly replaced the dark glasses. She was heavily made up, her face a flawless cosmetic mask. She knew she looked good but in this damned white-glaring desert sun she might look, if not her age precisely, for "Starr Bright" never looked her age, but, perhaps, thirty-one or -two, not twenty-eight as she'd led credulous Mr. Cobb of Elton, California, to believe.

She was "Starr Bright"—an "exotic dancer" at the Kings Club, Lake Tahoe, California. An independent woman trying to make a decent living amid the moral confusion of contemporary times. Before Lake Tahoe she'd been living in San Diego, California, or had it been Miami, Florida? And there'd been Houston, Texas.

Before that, memory faded. As a dream, even the most vivid and disturbing of dreams, fades rapidly upon waking.

It was not yet 6:00 P.M. And bright as midday. Yet Billy

Ray Cobb was eager to check into a motel. Pawing and squeezing "Starr Bright" in the front seat of the Infiniti, panting and florid cheeked. The red-leather interior smelled of newness, the air-conditioning hummed like a third presence. "Starr Bright" was flattered by her new friend's sexual attraction to her, or should have been. "I'm crazy about you, baby," Mr. Cobb said, an edge to his voice as if he suspected that "Starr Bright" might not believe him. "Like last night, you'll see."

So they did not drive on to Reno as "Starr Bright" had been led to believe they would. Might it have made a difference if they'd gone on to Reno?

Seemingly by impulse, Billy Ray Cobb turned in to the Paradise Motel on Route 80, one of numberless "bargain-rate" motels along the strip, just inside the Sparks city limits. "Starr Bright" could not have said, half-shutting her aching eyes, if she'd been here before. A salmon-colored imitation-Spanish-stucco single-story motel past its prime advertising BARGAIN ROOMS & HONEYMOON SUITES! and HAPPY HOUR 4–8 P.M.! If "Starr Bright" was bitterly disappointed, smelling beforehand the insecticide-odor of the shabby room, she gave no outward sign; she was not that kind of girl.

With her ashy-blond hair and her strong-boned striking face and her long dancer's legs, "Starr Bright" was accustomed to the close scrutiny of men, and knew to keep her most mutinous thoughts to herself. Never to bare her teeth in a quick incandescent flash of anger, nor to frown, or grimace, bringing the fine white lines of her forehead into sharp visibility. Never to raise her thumbnail to her teeth like a desperately unhappy teenage girl and gnaw at the cuticle until she tasted blood.

While Mr. Cobb checked them into the Paradise Motel, "Starr Bright" strolled restlessly about the poolside area, an interior courtyard flanked by thin drooping palm trees that looked brittle as papier mâché. The kidney-shaped pool, in which several near-naked swimmers splashed, smelled sharply of chlorine. And there was the odor of insecticide pervading all. "Starr Bright" checked swiftly to see if she recognized anyone—if anyone recognized her—for, having been acquainted with so many men, over a period of years, she was always vigilant.

This evening, poolside at the Paradise Motel, Route 80, Sparks, Nevada, there appeared to be no one whom "Starr Bright" had reason to know, nor to be known by.

Thank you, God.

Of the dozen or so guests in the courtyard, several, all but one of them fleshy young women, had placed themselves recklessly in the sun—visitors to the Southwest, obviously. Oily, gleaming bodies in scanty bathing suits, dreamy-shut eyes. Painted finger- and toenails like "Starr Bright's" own. There were pastel-bright drinks with melting ice cubes, empty beer and Perrier bottles accumulated on the wrought iron tables. From overhead amplifiers, rock-Muzak made the air vibrate, the pulse quicken. "Starr Bright" felt a wild impulse to dance. That erotic beat, the percussive rhythm, *look at me, here I am, why are none of you looking at me?—here is "Starr Bright"!* She was wearing a short, tight silky-black skirt that came barely to mid-thigh, and a gold lamé halter top that fitted her breasts tightly, and her long blond smooth-shaven legs were bare, her bare feet in cork platform heels. A thin gold chain around her left ankle, a tiny gold heart dangling. Pierced earrings that fell in glittering cascades nearly to her shoulders, a half-dozen rainbow-colored bracelets tinkling on each arm. Crimson lips moist as if she were quick-breathing, feverish. And the glamorous dark glasses that hid bruises, or the shadow of bruises, beneath her eyes. *Why will you not look at me? I am more beautiful than any of you.*

"Starr Bright's" first celebrity was at the age of thirteen, when she'd won first prize in a young people's talent competition in Buffalo, New York. *How many years ago: don't ask.*

When they stop looking, and their eyes go through you, one of the older dancers at the club in Tahoe had told "Starr

Bright," you're dead meat. So be thankful for the rude stares. Those pigs are money in the bank.

But no one seemed to notice "Starr Bright" at poolside. Which was God's sign, too, in its own way. Though "Starr Bright" could not have known at the time, just as she did not know, but would learn afterward from Nevada newspapers and TV, that Billy Ray Cobb was signing them into the Paradise Motel as "Mr. & Mrs. Elton Flynn" of Los Angeles, California.

Attention was in fact drawn to noisy-splashy activity in the pool. A voluptuous young woman in a tiny yellow bikini was squealing and kicking, hugging an inflated air-mattress striped like an American flag to her breasts, as a tanned muscled young man tickled her; their cries and laughter pierced the air. What exhibitionists! "Starr Bright" stared, a bit envious. But she was disapproving. So close to naked, so vulgar, the young woman and the young man seemed virtually to be making love in the pool. The bright water heaved and rippled about them. Others were staring openly, grinning; the lovers behaved as if they were oblivious, though obviously delighting in being observed. *Look at us, how happy we are, what pleasure our bodies take in one another, aren't you all jealous!* The young woman's arms flailed, her breasts nearly sprang out of her bikini bra, her strong legs thrashed and the young man pushed himself boldly between them, aiming a mock-bite at her throat, as the air-mattress slipped from them and they began, wildly squealing, to sink. "Starr Bright" pursed her lips and looked quickly away.

It was at this point that Billy Ray Cobb caught up with her. A vexed little frown, pouty-sagging lips, his heavy-lidded eyes veined with red as, panting just slightly, he closed his fingers around "Starr Bright's" wrist. He said two things to her but afterward she would not be able to recall which he said first. One was "Wondered where you were, baby!" and the other was "Looks like the fun's already started, eh?"

* * *

Not in her scratched oxblood-leather Gucci overnight case but in her midnight-blue sequined purse with wallet, makeup supplies, designer condoms, and amphetamine and Valium tablets did "Starr Bright" carry her *protection.* A pearl-handled German-made stainless steel knife with a slender five-inch blade. Kept wrapped in tissue at the bottom of the purse, its razor-sharp blade untested. The knife was *protection,* not a *weapon.* Still less a *concealed weapon.* So far as she knew, the knife was not illegal in any of the several states in which "Starr Bright" had been a resident since acquiring it several years before. *Protection* after she'd been falsely arrested in a cocktail lounge of a Hyatt Regency Hotel in Houston, Texas, by two plainclothes vice-squad detectives who'd detained her for five hours during which time they'd forced her to commit upon their persons sex acts of a particularly repulsive nature. *Never again will "Starr Bright" be humiliated, never again made to service pigs on any terms but my own.*

That night, "Starr Bright" dreamt so strangely!—obsessively, with much anguish, of the air-mattress in the motel pool.

She had scarcely seen it, had virtually no impression of it except it was made of plastic, stripes the colors of the American flag red white and blue, about five feet long perhaps, not a child's but a grown-up's float, an object of salvation if one were in water over one's head, in danger of drowning. "Starr Bright" was not a capable swimmer, water frightened her, the eerie buoyancy that cannot be depended upon, the disequilibrium, loss of control. In her dreams she was naked in the water, she was clutching at the air-mattress gasping for breath, her heart pounding as someone, a man, faceless, heavy bodied, tried to pull her from it and into the water to drown. Sometimes the man was Billy Ray Cobb, sometimes he was a stranger—or were there two men, or more?—laughing at her terror, which was a female's ridiculous, contemptible terror, their fingers hard and pitiless as steel yanking at her ankles, her bare legs, arms, gripping the nape of her neck. "Starr Bright" was naked and defenseless in the water, which was a dark choppy water and not the synthetic bright turquoise of the motel pool. If only she could grab hold of the air-mattress and pull herself up onto it she could save herself—but her arm- and shoulder-muscles were weak, flaccid, her feeble strength was rapidly fading, her mouth filled with poisonous water it would be death to swallow. And the jeering laughing, and the hard, hurting male fingers.

Help me! Please help me! Oh, God!

"Starr Bright" thrashed about wildly, flailing her arms, kicking, fighting for her life . . . and woke suddenly to find herself in a strange bed, a damp rumpled bed in a room that hummed loudly with air-conditioning that yet did not dispel the odor of whiskey and cigarette smoke and human sweat and the underlying stench of insecticide. She was not alone but beside a stranger, naked, a fattish man who lay sprawled on his back in the center of the bed, head flung back and mouth ajar, wetly snoring.

Mr. Cobb it was. Who'd been unexpectedly rough, impatient with her. Reddish-veined pig's eyes contracting and his vision going inward *oh! oh! uh!* as he'd grunted grinding himself stubbornly and then desperately into her. Twenty-two solid minutes she'd clocked it as the night before she'd clocked their earlier episodes eight minutes, twelve minutes, sixteen, a part of "Starr Bright's" brain detached and even clinical despite the generous lines of coke she'd snorted with her froggy-eyed friend whose first name, or names, momentarily eluded her. They'd checked into the Paradise Motel in the early evening and had sexual intercourse then gone out again hurriedly not taking time even to shower and cleanse themselves as "Starr Bright" so badly wanted, yes and to shampoo her sticky hair as well, scrub thoroughly between her chafed legs and run the shower as hot as she could bear it but Mr. Cobb had insisted upon going out at once to purchase a bottle of Jack Daniel's whiskey and several grams of cocaine innocently white and powdery-granular as confectioner's sugar and so the night had shut about her like walls pushing inward, threatening suffocation. *C'mon, baby! Loosen up, baby!* Though Mr. Cobb was in fact a stranger to her yet "Starr Bright" seemed to know how necessary it might be to anesthetize herself, she'd only pretended to inhale a line of coke held on a shaky spoon-mirror to her nostrils, in fact in the secrecy of the ill-smelling bathroom she'd hurriedly swallowed not one, nor even two, but three tablets of Valium, the most she allowed herself in even emergency situations, or when alcohol, too, was involved. So she'd been amiably dulled against Mr. Cobb's grinding, grunting, panting, and his hard grasping hands, his red-rimmed frog's eyes, his escalating demands. How many minutes, how many hours, where exactly they were, and why she, "Starr Bright," a top "exotic dancer" admired by the other girls for her Ice Princess glamor and her obvious intelligence, was here she did not know, could not comprehend. And sinking to sleep again, drenched with sweat, shivering, trying to keep as far away as possible from the snoring man in the center of the bed, "Starr Bright" found herself this time in a swimming pool in a distant city, she was eight or nine years old and she'd been brought to Atwater Park by an older girl cousin who lived in the city, little Shirley Lott from Shaheen visiting for the day, shy and excited as always when visiting Yewville which seemed to her a large city, fraught with mystery and adventure. But something had gone wrong, her cousin was not watching her as her mother had requested, but drawn off with her own friends and out of earshot and so Shirley, in her pink-puckered swimsuit and her white rubber bathing cap with the strap that buckled a little too tightly beneath her chin, found herself surrounded in the pool by children she didn't know. Several older, bigger boys stared at her, skinny strangers with hair wetly rat-slick, eyes alert asking who she was, where was she from? and Shirley told them and they smiled at her as if they liked her and invited her to come for a ride in their inner-tube across the pool. Shirley was wary at first trying to see where her cousin Tildy had gone, but she couldn't see Tildy, the boys seemed so friendly, grinning at her so she trusted them, yes she was flattered too. Shirley Lott was a pretty little girl much prettier than her younger sister Gwendolyn and her daddy loved her best, she could see it in his eyes he loved her best, and she had boy cousins her age and older, all of them members of the First Methodist Church in Shaheen where Ephraim Lott was the minister and so Shirley trusted these Yewville boys though they were strangers to her and she'd been warned by her mother not to take up with children she didn't know unless Tildy knew them, many times she'd been warned but in the excitement of the Atwater pool she forgot. *Come with us! Don't be afraid!* the boys said, and there was Shirley allowing herself to be pushed through the opening of the boys' inner-tube that was so slippery and bouncy in the water, she'd squealed with childish excitement paddling and kicking as immediately the boys tugged her toward the farther end of the pool where the water was six feet deep and Shirley began to be frightened but the boys swimming beside her said it was okay, she was okay, nothing would happen to her, she was safe inside the inner-tube. But the bolder boys were ducking beneath her and tugging at her feet, pinching her thighs, poking their fingers between her legs as she thrashed helplessly, panicked, sobbing, *No! No! Let me go!* swallowing water, choking. But the boys wouldn't let their little-girl victim go, they'd captured her in the inner-tube and were tugging her in noisy triumph across the pool into the deep water where only older children and teenagers were allowed to swim, and at last someone intervened, an older girl who knew the boys and shouted at them to leave Shirley alone, what the hell did they think they were doing?—as the boys shoved Shirley out of the inner-tube and into the water and she began to sink and would have drowned had not the girl caught her, and hauled her out of the pool and onto the puddled concrete where she lay sobbing and coughing up water, stricken as a wounded animal. The boys had fled from the pool shrieking with laughter, carrying their inner-tube with them, and Shirley's cousin Tildy at last took notice of her, the circle of onlookers gathered around her, and came running to her, and the nightmare was ended. *Except the nightmares of childhood never end but continue forever beneath the surface of memory so long as memory endures.*

This time, "Starr Bright" woke sobbing and choking out of her drugged sleep. It was 4:46 A.M. There would be no more sleep that night.

Through a cracked venetian blind a fluorescent-pink neon sign flashed rhythmically. PARADISE MOTEL. PARADISE MOTEL. "Starr Bright" slipped stealthily from the damp rumpled pigsty of a bed shivering in the air-conditioned chill though her naked body was covered in sticky sweat. She dared not wake Cobb, had to escape from him, a dangerous man. He had hurt her, bruised her breasts, the insides of her thighs, grinding himself against her *oh! oh! uh!* as if he'd have liked to kill her, eyes bulging and flushed face swelling like a balloon about to burst. Drunk, and high on cocaine, he'd turned into a beast, he'd lied to her, too, promising her she could bathe herself undisturbed, shampoo her hair, like all of them he'd lied to her; he had no mercy.

I must change my life. Help me, God. I'm run to earth.

For God had sent her, sinner though she was, a miraculous dream, a dream of lost childhood. She had had no such dream for a decade, or more. It was a sign of His terrible love.

Quickly and fumblingly "Starr Bright" dressed herself in

the dark. Stepping into the black satin lace panties Cobb had ripped from her, struggling into the tight-fitting skirt, the fake-gold lamé halter. And where were her shoes? and her overnight case? and her sequined purse?

One day they would ask her: why hadn't she simply fled Billy Ray Cobb and the Paradise Motel? For indeed "Starr Bright" might have done so, seeking refuge on foot somewhere in Sparks, Nevada, in the early morning hours of whatever day, whatever month and year scarcely known to her panicked mind. For indeed it would not have been the first time in the more than twenty years since she'd left her home in Shaheen, New York, that she'd fled, on foot, in such haste and desperation. It would not have been the first time she'd known herself, in a fury of self-loathing and disgust, *run to earth.*

But instead there was "Starr Bright" stealthily examining Cobb's clothes flung across a chair. The "Navajo" leather belt with the brass buckle. The monogrammed shirt, polyester trousers. By the dim-flickering pink glow from the window she could see just well enough to go rapidly through the trouser pockets, remove a wallet, car keys. Her hand shook but was unerring. And there, on a table close by, the near-empty bottle of Jack Daniel's, and somehow she had it in her hand and drank impulsively, regretted it at once as she began to cough and Billy Ray Cobb's snoring stopped and he woke muttering, "Eh? What? Who's that?"

There followed then a space of time distended as in a dream never to be recalled precisely by "Starr Bright" except in quick-jumping flashes, images.

She told the angry suspicious man it was just her, "Starr Bright," but already he was fully awake though groggy, swinging his legs out of bed, demanding to know, "Why're you *up*? It's fucking *night.*" And she tried to hide the wallet and the car keys inside her clothes, turned away from Cobb, saying she needed to use the bathroom. And by now Cobb was on his feet. Swaying but belligerent. He was no more than an inch or so taller than "Starr Bright" at five feet eight but he outweighed her by a hundred pounds. "Yeah?" he said, advancing upon her, "—the bathroom's in this direction, babe. Or were you gonna take a leak on the floor?" And, stammering, "Starr Bright" said she needed to take a hot shower, needed to wash her hair, she couldn't sleep smelly and dirty as she was and Cobb said, "Hot water in the middle of the fucking *night*? What's going on here?" and she was about to run for the door but he'd seen the wallet and keys in her hand, and grabbed her, began slapping her, "What the fuck, bitch? Caught you, eh?" shaking and slapping and getting a hammerlock on her head dragging her in the direction of the bathroom, "You want a shower, eh?—your dirty hair washed? How's about in the toilet bowl? Think you can put something over on *me!* Fuck with *me!* Billy Ray Cobb!"

"Starr Bright" fell to her knees. Cobb cursed her and released the hammerlock but slapped and punched her, furious, shamed, "Telling me all that shit last night, and I fell for it. What a sucker! Shoulda known you whores are all alike, don't deserve to live! Going into my wallet! Can't wait till morning to be paid?" and with a grunt picked up his wallet where it lay on the floor, extracted a handful of bills tossing them into the air and pushing "Starr Bright" down on hands and knees amid them where they fell, telling her to crawl for it, pick them up, pick them up with her cunt, and when "Starr Bright" did not he straddled her, his heavy sweating naked body on her back, "Hey, you like it, babe! You know you like it! 'Starr Bright'!—phony name! phony bitch! all of you phony bitches!—whores! Don't deserve to live, you contaminate the world for decent women." He took up his belt with the brass buckle and began to strike her buttocks, laughing, "Giddyup horsey! Giddyup horsey! You like it, eh?—cunt? Sure you do!" and when "Starr Bright" collapsed onto the floor Cobb ground himself into her, penis like a steel rod, until at last he cried out, hooting, and laughing, and collapsed onto her, and lay unmoving, heavily panting, for a beat. When he rose from her, "Starr Bright" lay limp.

"Now get out of here, you. Fast. Before I get serious and do something can't be undone." Prodding her with his foot, seizing her by the hair. "Don't play no more games with me, cunt. This room *I'm* paying for, get *out.*"

Cobb forced "Starr Bright" to crawl on hands and knees through the scattered bills, in the direction of the door, fingers gripping the back of her neck. How triumphant he was, how an angry satisfied joy irradiated from his body, waves of animal-heat! Saying she was real lucky he hadn't broken her jaw, he'd been known to break the jaws of whores, filthy things not deserving to live among decent women, and when "Starr Bright" fumbled for her sequined purse which lay on the floor he said, "Yeah! Take your trash with you! Stinking up the place!" He marched to the door, unbolted and opened it as "Starr Bright" rose shakily to her feet, clothes torn, nose bloodied, Cobb sighted her cork-heeled shoes on the floor and snatched them up and tossed them out the door, "Trash! Stinking! Get *out!*" and when "Starr Bright" did not move quickly enough to suit him he gripped her again by the nape of the neck set to fling her through the doorway after her shoes but in that instant suddenly no longer dazed and fumbling *as if God gave me the strength: guided my hand* "Starr Bright" had the knife out of her purse, held it tightly and drew its razor-sharp blade across Cobb's throat and he cried out in astonishment and horror beginning to bleed at once profusely, clutching at his throat as if to stem the flow, and "Starr Bright" leapt free of him, panting, as he sank to his knees, "What—? My God— Help me—"

"Starr Bright" watched Billy Ray Cobb die. Amid a pool of

blood dark as oil staining the carpet in the dim-flickering pink-fluorescent glow from the window.

"Now you see! Now you see! All of you!"

In the light of early morning, not yet dawn, an eerie calm prevailed. It was the silence of the western desert, the vast western sky. Below, in the courtyard of the Paradise Motel, the kidney-shaped swimming pool was deserted of course, smaller than it had appeared the previous evening. And there was the air-mattress floating at the deep end, not striped like the American flag as "Starr Bright" had believed but only red and blue—inflated plastic, a bit worn. A toy for adults, something sad about it. Almost imperceptibly it floated atop the rippleless turquoise water that was like a skin stretched over something living, invisible, inviolable, unknowable.

It was not yet 6:00 A.M. In no haste, "Starr Bright" left room 22 of the motel, quietly crossed the empty courtyard to the parking lot at the rear; unlocked the steel-gray Infiniti sedan with the rental license plates; placed her scarred Gucci case on the passenger's seat, and her midnight-blue sequined purse atop the case. An observer, had there been one, would have noted a tall, poised, coolly attractive blond woman in white linen trousers, a pale blue silk shirt, flat-heeled shoes. Her ashy-blond hair, still damp from the shower, was brushed back neatly from her face. Her eyes were hidden behind tinted glasses so dark they might have been black. Her flawless cosmetic mask betrayed no sign of alarm, nor even of especial concern. *As if I'd been here before. In His sign. And all yet to come, in His terrible mercy.*

In the eastern sky, beyond the imitation-Spanish facade of a neighboring Holiday Inn, the morning sun was emerging out of a pearl-opalescent darkness of massed clouds. A fiery all-seeing eye. Beneath its scrutiny "Starr Bright" drove the unfamiliar car out of the parking lot of the Paradise Motel and turned left on the near-deserted Route 80 as if this had always been the plan, a fate prescribed for her clear and unerring as a road map. She would drive south and east on Route 95 into Vegas where, amid a sea of cars at Caesars Palace, she would abandon the Infiniti. She meant, for as long as she could, to keep that fiery eye before her.

Sara Paretsky

Whether it's wanted or not, or whether it's fair, or appropriate, or pleasing to the subjects, some authors cannot be mentioned without another coming to mind. Hammett and Chandler. Sayers and Christie. Paretsky and Grafton.

One of those odd confluences of timing and circumstance brought two books to the world in the same year—1982: Indemnity Only *and* "A" Is for Alibi. *Only those few years ago, now seemingly another lifetime, and the strong, independent, female private eye awakened half the readers in America to want books about V. I. Warshawski and Kinsey Milhone and their literary progeny (and the other half to write them, it seems).*

Yes, Marcia Muller created Sharon McCone nearly a decade earlier, and P. D. James demonstrated that Cordelia Gray was the equal (or more) of any male gumshoe, but it was the combination of Grafton and Paretsky that catapulted the female detective into the most popular and widely read character of the 1980s, an appetite that has not diminished to the present day.

This is not a V. I. Warshawski story, but one that reveals a hitherto unknown talent on the part of the much acclaimed mystery writer: had she set her sights in a different direction, she could have been a highly successful writer of Harlequin Romances. (This, in case you didn't get it, is a joke.)

—O.P.

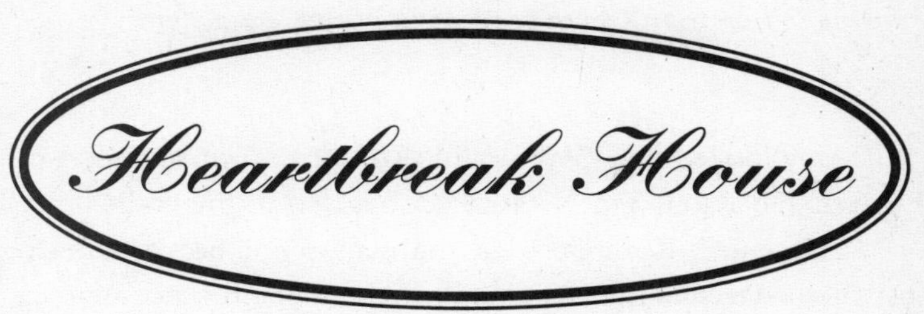

Heartbreak House

BY SARA PARETSKY

Natasha's hair, as sleek and black as a raven's wing, framed the delicate oval of her face. Raoul thought she had never looked more desirable than now, with her dark, doelike eyes filled with tears, and a longing beyond tears.

"It's no good, darling," she whispered, summoning a valiant smile. "Papa has lost all his money. I must go to India with the Crawfords to mind their children."

"Darling—for you to be a nanny—how utterly absurd. And in that climate. You must not!" His square, manly face suffused with color, betraying the strength of his feeling.

"You haven't even mentioned marriage," Natasha whispered, looking at the bracelets on her slender wrists, wondering if they, too, must be sold, along with Mama's diamonds.

Raoul flushed more deeply. "We're engaged. Even if our fam-

ilies don't know about it. But how can I marry you now, when I have no prospects and your papa cannot give you a dowry. . . ."

Amy looked up. "Wonderful, Roxanne. Your strongest effort yet. Do Raoul and Natasha get married in the end?"

"No, no." Roxanne took the manuscript back. "They're just the first generation. Natasha marries a planter, not that she can ever give her heart to him, and Raoul dies of blackwater fever in the jungle during the Boer War, with Natasha's name on his writhen lips. It's their grandchildren who finally get together. That's the significance of the last page."

She turned the manuscript over and read aloud to Amy, *"Natalie had never met Granny Natasha, but she recognized the face smiling at the head of the bed as she embraced Ralph. It seemed to say 'Godspeed and God bless,' and even, in the brief glimpse she caught before surrendering herself to love, to wink."*

"Yes, yes, I see," Amy agreed, wondering if there were another person in New York—in the world—who could use *writhen* with Roxanne's sincere intensity. "Very much in the spirit of Isabel Allende or Laura Esquivel."

Roxanne looked haughtily at her editor. She didn't know the names and didn't care to learn them. If Amy thought the star of Gaudy Press needed to copy someone, it was time for her to have a conversation with Lila Trumbull, Roxanne's agent.

Amy, an expert on Roxanne Craybourne's own doelike glances, leaned forward. "All the South American writers who've been winning Nobel prizes lately have ghosts haunting their work. I thought it was a nice touch, to show *The New York Times* and some of these other snobs in the most delicate way imaginable that you are fully aware of contemporary literary conventions, but you only choose to use them when you can enhance them."

Roxanne smiled. Amy really was quite nice. She'd proved it

the weekend she'd stayed at the Taos house, after all. It was terrible to be so suspicious of everyone that you couldn't trust their lightest comments. But then, when she thought how badly Kenny had betrayed her . . .

Amy, watching the shift from complacency to tragedy on her star's face, wondered what nerve-storm she now had to deflect. "Is everything all right, Roxanne?" she asked in a gentle, caring voice that would have astounded her own children and grandchildren.

Roxanne gave a little sniff, brushing the hint of a tear from her left eye. "I was just thinking of Kenny, and how badly he treated me. And then to see it written up in the *Star* and the *Sun*. It's too much to suffer tragedy, without having it plastered around the supermarkets where all one's friends see it, and badger one forever. Not to mention Mother's insufferable mahjongg club."

"Kenny? What—did his embezzling habits not die at the end of his parole?" Amy was startled out of maternal concern into her normal sardonic speech. She cursed herself as soon as the words were out, but Roxanne, in as full a dramatic flight as one of her own heroines, hadn't noticed.

"I thought he was trying." She fluttered tapered, manicured fingers, muscular from the weight of the rings they held up. "Mother kept telling me he was just taking advantage, but it's the kind of thing she's always saying about my boyfriends, ever since high school, jealous because she never had half as many when she was young. And when he hit me the first time and said he was *truly* sorry of course I believed him. Anyone would have. But when he walked off with a million in bearer bonds it was just too much. What else could I do? And then, well, you know I had to spend *months* in the hospital."

Amy did know. There had been dreadful late-night meetings at Gaudy Press over the news that Roxanne Craybourne might have suffered permanent brain damage when Kenny Coleman beat her up for the last time. Even Roxanne, on checking out of the rehabilitation clinic where she'd spent two months after leaving the hospital, had decided she couldn't forgive Kenny that. She divorced him, changed her security system, and moved the twenty-four-year-old gardener who'd brought her flowers every day into the master suite.

And then, in eleven weeks, gone on to write the thrilling tale of Natasha, the heiress victimized by her papa's trusted henchman, who embezzled all his money. "Poured white-hot from her molten pen" was the copy Gaudy would run in the national ad campaign.

"And I'm terrified that she'll marry that damned gardener next," Amy told her boss the next morning. "First it was the dreadful surgeon who slept with his women patients, then Kenny, and now some gardener who needs a green card."

Clay Rossiter grinned. "Send her a wedding present. She thrives on that kind of situation."

"I'm the one who has to hold her hand through all these trials," Amy snapped. "She doesn't thrive: she trembles on the verge of a nervous breakdown."

"But, Amy, sweetie, don't you see—that's what makes her such a phenomenal success. She's the helpless waif who crops up in *A Clean Wound, Embarrassment of Riches,* and the rest. She believes in the agonies of all those idiotic Glendas and Corinnes and—who did you say the latest was—Natasha? Did you persuade her she couldn't call it *A Passage to India?*"

"It was tough," Amy said. "Of course she'd never heard of E. M. Forster—I finally had to show her the video of *A Passage to India* before she listened to me. And even then she only agreed to a title change when I persuaded her that Forster's estate would make money from her because her fans would buy the video thinking it was her story. And no, I haven't got a clue whether he's got an estate or if it would get royalties, and don't go talking to Lila Trumbull about it, either, for pity's sake. We're calling Natasha's misery *Broken Covenant*. Oh, by the way, *A Clean Wound* hit the paperback list at number two. We're printing another five hundred thousand."

Rossiter smiled. "Just keep feeding her herbal tea. Send her roses. Let her know we're her best friends. See if you can engender some kind of vicious streak in the gardener, assuming he hasn't got one already."

"*You* do that," Amy said, getting to her feet. "I've got a meeting with one of our few real writers—Gary Blanchard has done a beautiful book, a kind of modern-day quest set in the Dakotas. It'll sell around eight thousand, ten if we're lucky. *Broken Covenant* should make it possible to give him an advance."

After Amy left, Clay went back to the fax he'd received from Jambon et Cie PLC, his corporate masters in Brussels. They were very disappointed in Gaudy's third-quarter performance. It's true they'd made a profit, thanks to the strong showing of *Embarrassment of Riches* in hardcover, but Gaudy needed several more bankable stars. They were too dependent on Roxanne Craybourne—if they lost her they'd be dribbling along with the nickel-and-dime stuff, the so-called literary writers which Jambon was doing its best to discard. If Clay Rossiter didn't want to be looking for a new job in six months, Jambon expected a marketing plan and sales numbers to show the list was acquiring market flexibility.

Clay curled his lip. Eighteen pages of numbers followed, a demented outburst of someone's spreadsheet program. Title by title Brussels had gone through Gaudy's list, with projections of sales based on changing the number of copies in Wal-Mart, the amount of bus-side advertising, the weight of paper used in dust jackets, the number of trips each sales rep made to key accounts. And Clay was expected—ordered, really—to give a written response to all these projections by the end of the month.

"The curse of modern business is not tight capital, bad

management, low productivity, or poor education, but the personal computer," he snarled.

His secretary poked her head through the door. "Did you say something, Clay?"

"Yes. Idiotic boys—and girls—who've never held a book think they can run the book industry from three thousand miles away because they have a microchip that lets them conjure up scenarios. If they'd ever ridden a truck from a warehouse into Wal-Mart they'd know you can't even tell how many copies the store took, let alone—oh, well. What's the use. Send a note down to Amy that she cannot give her new literary pet—what's his name? Gary Blanchard?—more than twenty thousand. If he wants to walk, let him. If I see Farrar or Knopf on the spine when the book comes out it will not make me weep with frustration."

* * *

Isabella trembled in his arms. "I must not. You know I must not. Your mama, if she saw me—"

Her raven hair, enhancing the milky purity of her skin, cascaded over his shoulders as Albion pulled her to him more tightly. "She will learn to love you as I do, my beautiful Mexican flower. Ah, how could I ever have thought I was in love before?"

Albion Whittley thought distastefully of all the spoiled debutantes he'd squired around New York City. He wasn't just Albion Whittley—there was that damned "IV" after his name, meaning his parents expected him to marry someone in their set. How could he expect them to believe that the gardener's daughter stood head and shoulders above all the Bennington girls he'd had to date? The purity of her heart, the nobility of her impulses—every penny she earned going back to Guadalupe to her crippled grandmother.

"Albion, darling, are you enjoying your little holiday? Isabella, I left my gloves on my dressing table. Fetch them for me while my son and I have a talk."

Mrs. Albion Whittley the Third had appeared on the terrace. Her tinkling laugh and light sarcastic manner made both young people blush. Albion dropped Isabella's hand as though it had turned to molten lava. The girl fled inside the mansion. . . .

* * *

"Beautiful," Amy gushed, marveling at her own acting ability. "They triumph over every obstacle in the end? Or is it like Natasha, only able to experience happiness through her granddaughter?"

Roxanne looked reproachful. "I never tell the same story twice. My readers wouldn't stand for it. Albion joins the CIA to prove his manliness to Mama. He's sent on a secret mission to Central America, where he has to take on a drug lord. When he's wounded Isabella finds him in the jungle and nurses him back to health, but the drug lord is smitten by her beauty. Since she knows Albion's mother is implacable she agrees to become the drug lord's mistress. This leads her to a jet-setting career in Brazil and Spain, and she meets Mrs. Whittley as an equal in Majorca. In the end the CIA kills the drug lord, and Albion, who's never forgotten her, rescues her from the fortress where she's been incarcerated."

"Wonderful," Amy said. "Only I don't think we can call it *The Trail of Tears.*"

She tried explaining how disrespectful this might seem to the American Indian community, but gave up when her star's eyes flashed fury.

"Everyone knows how good I am to the Indians who live on my estate in Taos. I'm not having them wreck my book because of some hundred-year-old battle they can't forget. And after the way Gerardo treated me—he was half Indian, and always bragging about it—I think they owe me some consideration for a change."

"It's the libraries," Amy said hastily. "*So* ignorant. But we don't want your book shelved with Indian literature, do we? Your loyal fans will want to see it prominently displayed with new fiction."

They agreed in the end on *Fool's Gold,* with a Central American pyramid to be shown in jagged pieces around a single rose. Roxanne settled her jacket around her shoulders and held out her cup for more tea. She wasn't sure she even wanted a Central American pyramid. Wouldn't it always remind her of the misery she'd felt when Gerardo betrayed her? Her mother had warned her, but then Mother was positively lying in wait to watch her misery.

Amy, alert to the quiver in Roxanne's chin, asked if the cover decision troubled her. "We'll get Peter to do a series of layouts. You know we're not tied to what we decide today."

Roxanne held out a hand. Amy tried hard, but she wasn't sensitive—she wasn't an artist, after all—she lived in the world of sales and bottom lines.

"This whole discussion overwhelms me with memories of Gerardo. People said he only wanted me for my money. And to get a green card. But it's not impossible for love to flourish between a man of twenty-four and a woman my age. Just think of Cher. And despite all those ridiculous exercise videos she isn't any better looking than I am."

That much was true. Adolescent passion kept Roxanne young. Her own skin could indeed be described as milky, her dark eyes lustrous, childlike, confiding. Her auburn hair was perhaps hand tinted to keep its youthful shades of color, but if you didn't know she was forty-six you'd assume the rich browns and reds were natural.

"When I found him in bed with my maid I believed Gerardo, that she was homesick and he was comforting her. My mother ridiculed me, but how can you possibly live so cynically and ever be happy?"

Roxanne held her hands out in mute appeal—two poignant doves, Amy thought, murmuring, "Yes, indeed."

"But then, the night I got back from Cannes, I found them together at the swimming pool. He wouldn't come to Cannes with me—he said he shouldn't leave the country until his immigrant status was straightened out, so I raced home a day early just to be with him, but then even I had to realize—and he'd paid for her abortion, with money I'd given him."

"You poor child," Amy said, patting her hand. "You're far too trusting."

Roxanne lifted her doelike eyes in mute gratitude. Amy was so warm, a true friend, unlike the hangers-on who only wanted to sponge off her success.

"Someone in Santa Fe suggested I talk to a psychiatrist. As if I were sick!"

"How dreadful." Amy sounded shocked. "And yet, the right psychiatrist—a sympathetic woman, perhaps—could listen to you impartially. Unlike your mother, or your friends, who are always judging you and scolding you."

"Is that what psychiatrists do?" Roxanne opened her eyes wide. "Listen?"

"The good ones do," Amy said.

* * *

"You did what?" Clay Rossiter screamed. *"You're* the one who needs a psychiatrist. We can't have her getting over her neuroses. They're what drive her books. Look, fifteen weeks after finding Raoul in bed with her maid she produces a bestseller for us. We can do an initial run of a million five. That's our paychecks for the entire year, Amy."

"Raoul was the hero of *Broken Covenant*. Gerardo was her gardener. You're not the one who has to feed her tea and bolster her after the cad has been found out. Not to mention take her to Lutèce and listen to the storm of passion while it's at gale force."

Clay bared his teeth at her. "That's what we pay you to do, Amy. You're the goddamn star's goddamn editor. She likes you. We even had to write it into her last contract that she will only work with you."

"Don't lose sleep over it. The chances are against Roxanne entering therapy. She's more likely to pick some New Age guru and have a deep mystical experience with him." Amy got up. "You know Gary Blanchard signed with Ticknor & Fields? I'm really annoyed, Clay. We could have kept him for twenty-five thousand: he's very humble in his needs and it makes me sick to lose a talented writer."

"He's humble because he knows no one wants to read artistic work. Let Ticknor & Fields have him. They don't have Jambon et Cie breathing down their necks." Clay picked up his latest fax from Brussels and waved it at her.

Amy skimmed it. Jambon was disappointed that Clay had rejected all of their previous marketing proposals, but pleased he had let Gary Blanchard go. All of the scenarios they had run on Quattro showed that every dollar spent on advertising would lose them thirty cents on revenue from Blanchard's work. They definitely did not want anyone on the Gaudy list who sold fewer than twenty-seven thousand in hardcover.

"This isn't publishing," she said, tossing it back at him. "They ought to go into breakfast cereal. It's more suited to their mentality."

"Yes, Amy, but they own us. So unless you want to look for a job right before Christmas, don't go signing any more literary lights. We can't afford them."

* * *

"I dreamed I went to the airport to catch my flight to Paris, but they wouldn't let me in first class. They said I was dirty, and badly dressed, and I had to fly coach. But all the coach seats were

taken so I had to go by Greyhound, and the bus got lost and ended up in this dreary farmhouse in the middle of Kansas."

The eminent psychiatrist, his kindly gray eyes moved to tears by the beautiful girl on the couch in front of him, sighed and stirred in his chair. How could he ever persuade her that she was clean enough, good enough, for first class?

* * *

Amy choked. "Roxanne. Dear. Where's the story?"

"It's here. In front of you. Have you forgotten how to read?"

"But your readers expect passion, romance. Nothing happens. The doctor doesn't even fall in love with Clarissa."

"Well, he does of course, but he keeps it to himself." Roxanne picked up the manuscript and thumbed through it. She began reading aloud, clicking her rings against the chair arm for emphasis.

Clarissa put her hand trustingly in the older man's. "You don't know how much this means to me, Doctor. To finally find someone who understands what I've been through."

Dr. Friedrich felt his flesh stir. His professional calm had never been pierced by any of his patients before, but this gaminelike waif, abused by father, abandoned by mother, so in need of trust and guidance, was different.

He longed to be able to say "My dear, I wish you would not think of me as your doctor, but your dearest friend as well. I long for nothing more than to protect you from the blasts of the stormy world beyond these walls." But if he spoke he would lose her precious trust forever.

Roxanne dropped the pages with a thump, as though that settled the point.

"Well, why can't he marry her?" Amy asked.

"Amy, you didn't read it, did you? He's already got a wife,

only she's in an institution for the criminally insane. But his compassion is so great he can't bring himself to divorce her. Then the Nazi-hunters confuse him with a man who was a prison-camp guard who looked like him, and he gets arrested. It turns out that the wife has turned him in—that her criminal insanity has given her a persecution complex and she blames him for all her troubles. So Clarissa has to find him, behind the Iron Curtain—this takes place in 1983—where he's been put into a gulag—and rescue him. And the wife has a brainstorm when she finds out he's been rescued. That kills her. But Clarissa has already become a nun. They sometimes dream about each other but they die without seeing one another again."

Amy blinked. "It seems a little downbeat for your readers, Roxanne. I wonder if—"

"Don't wonder at me, Amy," Roxanne snapped, her luminous eyes flashing magnificently. "Dr. Reindorf says happy endings are difficult to find. My readers need to learn that just as much as I do. If they keep expecting every book to be a panacea they'll be just as badly off as me, expecting every man I fall in love with to solve all my problems."

* * *

"I warned you," Clay snarled. "Send her off to the fucking shrinks and what happens? We get cheap psychology about her readers and a book no one will buy. The woman can't write, for Christ sake. If she loses her adolescent fantasy about true love she loses her audience."

"Maybe Dr. Reindorf will betray her as badly as Gerardo and Kenny, and that surgeon, her first husband, who gave us *A Clean Wound.*"

"We can't take that chance," Clay said. "You've got to do something."

"I'm sixty," Amy said. "I can take early retirement. You're the one who's worried about it. You do something. Get the publicity department to plant a story in the *National Enquirer* that Roxanne is getting therapy from a child molester."

She meant it as a joke but Clay thought it was worth an effort. His publicity staff turned him down.

"We can't plant stories about our own writers. Publishing is a community of gossips. Someone will know, they'll leak it to someone else who hates you, and the next thing you know Roxanne will be at Putnam and you'll be eating wiener-water soup."

Clay began to lose sleep. *Final Analysis,* done in silver with a suggestive couch on the cover, came well out of the gate, but word of mouth began killing it before the second printing was ready. It jumped onto the *Times* list in third place but stayed there only a week before plummeting to ninth. After five short weeks *Final Analysis* dropped off the list into the black hole of overstock and remainders.

The faxes from Brussels were hot enough to scorch the veneer from Clay Rossiter's desktop, while Roxanne's agent, Lila Trumbull, called daily to blame Clay for not marketing the book properly.

"But you can't market long, dull dreams and their interpretation," Clay howled to his secretary. "As I told Amy."

Clay fired Amy, to relieve his feelings, then had to rehire her the next morning: Roxanne had an editor clause in her contract. She could leave Gaudy if Amy did.

"Only, if she's going to keep turning out cheap psychology it won't matter. Pretty soon even Harlequin won't touch her. And, by the way, we won't be able to afford you. How long has she been seeing this damned shrink?"

"About nine months. And the last time she was in New York she only stayed overnight so as not to miss a session. So it doesn't seem to be following the course of her usual infatuations."

"He's not in New York? Where is he?"

"Santa Fe. This isn't the only town with psychiatrists in it, Clay."

"Yeah, they're like rats: wherever you find a human population, there they'll be, eating the garbage," Clay grumbled. "Maybe he can fall off a mesa."

When Amy left he stared at the clock. It was eleven in New York. Nine A.M. in New Mexico. He got up abruptly and took his coat from behind the door.

"I have the flu," he told his secretary. "If some moron calls from Brussels tell him I'm running a high fever and can't talk."

"You look healthy to me," she said.

"It's the hectic flush of fever."

He was out of the office before she could chide him further. He flagged a cab, then changed his mind. The cops were forever questioning cabdrivers. He took the long, slow subway ride to Queens.

On the flight to Albuquerque he wondered what he should do about renting a car. He'd paid cash for his ticket so that he could use an assumed name, but he'd need a driver's license and credit card to rent a car. When the man next to him got up to use the bathroom Clay went through his breastpocket. They didn't look anything alike, but no one ever inspected those photos. And fortunately the man's home was in New Mexico. He wouldn't miss his license until after Clay mailed it back to him, with cash for the price of the rental, of course.

It turned out to be easy. Pathetically easy. He called Dr. Reindorf and told him the truth, that he was Roxanne's publisher, that they were all worried about her, and could he have a word in confidence. Someplace quiet, remote, where they wouldn't run the risk of Roxanne seeing Clay and feeling spied upon. Reindorf suggested a mesa with a view of Santa Fe below it when he'd finished seeing patients for the day.

Clay made the red-eye back to New York with an hour to spare. The next morning Amy stuck her head around his door.

She started to ask him something, but decided he really did have the flu, his eyes were so puffy. It wasn't until later in the day that Roxanne called her, distraught at Reindorf's death.

"She somehow ended up going to the morgue to look at the body, don't ask me why," Amy told Clay's secretary, since Clay had gone home sick again. "It had been run over by a car several times before being thrown from the mesa. The cops hauled her ex-gardener in for questioning but they don't seem to have any suspects."

"The news should revive Clay," his secretary said.

* * *

Ancilla's hands fluttered at her sides like captive birds. "You don't understand, Karl. Papa is dead. His work—I never valued it properly, but I must try to carry it on."

"But, darling girl, it's too heavy a burden for you. It's just not a suitable job for a woman."

"Ah, if you knew what I felt, when I saw him—had to identify his body after the jackals had been at it—no burden could be too big for me now."

Karl felt pride stir within him. He had loved Ancilla when she had been a beautiful, willful girl, the toast of Vienna. But now, prepared to assume a woman's role in life—to shoulder a load most men would turn from—the spoiled child lines dropped from her cherry lips, giving her the mouth of a woman, firm, ripe, desirable.

* * *

"I love it," Clay said. "I'm ecstatic. And you're calling it *Life's Work*? You got her to change it from *An Unsuitable Job for a Woman*? Good going. It's been only seventeen weeks since that shrink died and she's already cured. We ought to be able to print a million, a million two, easy. I'll fax Brussels. We'll go out to celebrate."

"I'd rather celebrate right here." Amy shut his office door.

"We have a chance to sign a really brilliant new writer. Her name is Lisa Ferguson and she's written an extraordinary novel about life in western Kansas during the sixties. She's going to be the next Eudora Welty."

"No, Amy. Hispanic experience is good. African is possible. But rural Kansas is of no interest to anyone these days except you. I'm certainly not going to pitch it to Brussels."

Amy leaned over the desk. "Clay, Lila Trumbull called me seventeen weeks ago. The day after you went home sick with the flu."

"She's always calling. How can you know what day it was?"

"Because that was when Roxanne's shrink's body was found." Amy smiled and spoke softly, as if to Roxanne herself. "Lila thought she saw you in the Albuquerque airport the day before. She was stopping to see Roxanne on her way back to New York from L.A. and was sure you were renting a car when she was picking up her bags. She'd called to you, but you were in such a hurry you didn't hear her."

Clay shifted in his chair. When he spoke his voice came out in a croak.

"I—she—she should have asked at the rental counter. They could've told her no one rented a car in my name that day. Anyway, I couldn't have been there. I was home with the flu."

"That's what I told her, Clay. You were home sick—she must have been mistaken. And that's what I'll tell anyone else who asks. . . . I'll call Lisa Ferguson's agent and tell her thirty, okay?"

Clay stared at her glassily, like a stuffed owl. "Sure, Amy. You do that."

Amy stood up. "Oh—and, Clay, in case you're thinking how good I'd look at the bottom of a mesa—or under the IRT —I hope you remember Roxanne has an editor clause in her contract. And she's made it clear a dozen different ways that she won't work with you."

Clay's secretary came down to Amy's office a few minutes later. "Can you talk to old Mr. Jambon in Brussels? Clay's gone home sick again. I hope there isn't anything serious wrong with him."

Amy smiled. "He's fine. He just got a little overexcited this morning about Roxanne's new book."

ANNE PERRY

It is the last decade of the twentieth century, and the sensations associated with love have changed little over the ages. However, the conventions of love—its manners and mores—have shifted and mutated dramatically from one era to the next. Which is why, when the queen of the Victorian mystery novel, Anne Perry, delivers a delicious little puzzle with its origins in the nuances of respectable nineteenth-century courtship, careful attention must be paid to love's past and not its present. What may seem merely quaint today, when a man's word or a woman's honor apparently has no more than casual value, was once a matter of deadly importance.

In a world of discreet butlers, polished silver trays, and cravats "tied to perfection," Anne Perry is a peerless companion, as consummate an eavesdropper on this vanished, fascinating society as the blackmailer of her title.

Already one of the most popular mystery writers of the past couple of decades, the author has received enormous—if unwanted—attention for her recently discovered and revealed past. As a teenager in New Zealand, she and her best friend murdered the friend's mother while under the influence of a subsequently banned prescription drug. Her exemplary life since then has produced nothing more notorious than fictional violence that has brought her a vast readership.

—O.P.

The Blackmailer

BY ANNE PERRY

The butler closed the withdrawing room door behind him. "Excuse me, sir. There is a young gentleman called to see you." He held out the silver tray, offering Henry Rathbone the card on it.

Henry picked it up and read. The name James Darcy was only slightly familiar. It was half past nine on a January evening, and bitterly cold. The gas lamps in the street were haloed in fog, and the hansom cabs' wheels hissed in the damp, their horses' hooves muffled by the clinging darkness.

"He seems very agitated, sir," the butler said, watching Henry's face. "He begged me to ask if you would see him, as he is in some kind of difficulty, although of course he did not impart its nature to me."

"Then I suppose you had better show him in," Henry conceded. "I cannot imagine how he believes I may help." Nor could he. He was a mathematician and occasional inventor, a lover of fine watercolors which he collected when he could afford to, and an inveterate dabbler in shops which dealt in anything old. He liked the evidences of ordinary life, rather than the antiques of wealth.

The man who followed the butler into the room was of average height, fair coloring, and regular features. He was very well dressed. His cravat was tied to perfection, his boots gleamed, and in spite of his obvious anxiety, he bore himself with confidence.

"It is very good of you to receive me, sir," he said, extending his hand. "Most particularly since I have called at such an uncivil hour. To tell you the truth, I have been arguing with myself all afternoon as to what I should do, and whether or not I should approach you." He met Henry's eyes with disarming candor, and Henry saw the fear sharp and bright in them.

"Please sit down, Mr. Darcy," he invited. "A glass of brandy? You must be cold."

"Indeed I am. That is most kind of you." Darcy moved closer to the fire and stood for a moment. Then, as if his legs had collapsed, he sank into the chair, letting out his breath in a shaking sigh. "I am in a most terrible situation, Mr. Rathbone, and I cannot get myself out of it without the help of someone like yourself, a man of unquestioned honor. I am being blackmailed." He sat quite still, his blue eyes fixed on Henry's face, as if dreading his response, yet unable to move his gaze until he had seen it.

Henry poured the brandy and passed it across.

"I see. Do you know by whom?"

"Oh, yes," Darcy said quickly. "A man called James Albury. To my sorrow, I have a passing acquaintance with him."

Henry hesitated. He had never encountered blackmail before, but he was willing to do what he could to help this young man so obviously in distress. Whatever his weakness or failing, another man's attempt to profit from it in this manner was inexcusable. It was indelicate to ask, and yet in order to foresee the consequence of failure, he had to know the original offense.

As if reading his dilemma, Darcy spoke, leaning forward a little, the firelight warming the pallor of his face.

"I did not commit any crime, Mr. Rathbone, or I would not place you in the embarrassment of being party to it. If I tell you my story, you will understand."

Henry sat back and, without thinking, rested his feet on the fender. His slippers were already well scorched from the practice. "Please do," he said encouragingly.

Darcy sipped his brandy, cradling the glass in his hands.

"I was staying the weekend at the country house of Lord Wilbraham. There were several other guests, among them Miss Elizabeth Carlton, to whom I am betrothed." He took a deep breath and looked down. The flush in his cheeks was more than the reflection of the flames.

Henry did not interrupt.

"You will need to understand the geography of the house," Darcy continued. "The conservatory lies beyond a most agreeable morning room in which are hung some rather valuable pictures, most particularly some Persian miniatures painted upon bone. They are quite small, not more than a few inches across, most delicately wrought—with a single hair, so I have heard. There is no other door to the morning room except that into the hall."

Henry wondered where Darcy was leading. Presumably it had something to do with the miniatures.

Again Darcy seemed uncomfortable. His eyes left Henry's and he looked down at the carpet between them.

"Please believe me, Mr. Rathbone, I am devoted to Miss Carlton. She is everything a man could desire: honest, gentle, modest, of the sweetest nature . . ."

It occurred to Henry that these were euphemisms for saying that the girl was lacking in spirit or humor, and more than a little boring, but he smiled and said nothing.

Darcy bit his lip. "But I was rash enough to spend a great deal more of the evening than I should have in the company of another young lady, alone in the conservatory. I had gone in there, rather more by chance than design, and when I heard Lizzie . . . Miss Carlton, through the open doors into the morning room, I did not wish to be seen coming out with Miss Bartlett. She was . . . er . . . in high good humor, and . . . a trifle disheveled in her dress. She had caught her gown on a frond of one of the palm trees . . . and . . ." He opened his eyes wide and stared at Henry with wretchedness.

"I see," Henry said with considerable compassion. The truth of the matter might be as Darcy said, or it might not. It was not for him to judge. "Where do the miniatures come in to the matter?"

"Two of them were stolen," Darcy said huskily. "The alarm was raised as soon as it was noticed, and from the circumstances it was obvious that they were taken before Lizzie went into the morning room, although she said that she had not noticed their absence."

"And the blackmail?" Henry asked. "Is the suggestion that you took them as you passed through to the conservatory?"

"Yes. They were seen shortly before that!" Darcy's voice rose in anguish. "You perceive my dilemma? I was at all times with Miss Bartlett. She would swear for me that I did not, and could not, have taken them! But if she were to do so, then Lizzie would know that I was in the conservatory with Miss Bartlett . . . and I confess, Mr. Rathbone, that would be most painful for her, and some considerable embarrassment for me. Miss Bartlett's reputation is . . . less . . ."

"You do not need to spell it out for me." Henry leaned forward and poked the fire, putting on another two or three coals.

"Added to which," Darcy went on, "if I were to prove myself innocent, then it would leave poor Lizzie with the matter of proving herself innocent also. Of course she is! She is as honest as it is possible to be, and is an heiress to a considerable sum. It would not be more than unpleasant for her. No one could imagine . . . Nevertheless, I cannot . . ."

"I see your predicament," Henry said with feeling. Indeed, it was very apparent, as was his conflict of emotions over the wealthy Miss Carlton, who would not take a pleasing view of his dalliance, real or imagined, with Miss Bartlett.

"But I do not know how I can help. What does Mr. Albury require of you? You have not said."

"Oh, money!" Darcy answered with contempt. "And of course if I should pay him once, then there is nothing on earth to stop him returning again and again, as often as he pleases." His voice rose close to panic and there was desperation in his eyes. "If I once give in to him, he could bleed me till I have nothing left!" His hands were clenched before him. "But if I don't, he leaves me no alternative but to permit him either to ruin me or drive me to defend myself at Lizzie's cost, and the end of my betrothal and my future happiness." He bent forward and covered his face with his hands. "God, I was a fool to stay there in that damned conservatory, but there was no harm in it, I swear to that!"

Henry felt an intense pity for him. It was a piece of very mild foolishness, such as any young man might commit. Possibly most young men had, feeling the constraints of marriage and domestic ties closing around them, and taking a last opportunity for a gentle flirtation. Darcy had been caught by an extraordinary mischance. But Henry had no idea how he could help. He sought anything to say that would at least be of comfort, and found nothing.

Darcy looked up. "Mr. Rathbone, I can think of only one way in which this blackguard might be confounded. . . ."

"Indeed?" Henry was greatly relieved. "Pray tell me how, and I will do all I can to aid you, and with the greatest pleasure." He meant it profoundly.

Darcy straightened himself and set his shoulders square. He took another healthy sip of his brandy and then put the glass down.

"Mr. Rathbone, if you, and some highly reputable and esteemed gentleman of your acquaintance—I know there are many—were to come to my rooms and secrete yourselves in the adjoining chamber, with the door on the jar, I could face Albury and entice him to commit himself verbally to precisely what he is doing. Then he will have damned himself out of his own mouth. With witnesses against him such as yourself, a disinterested party whose reputation no man would question, then I think he will not dare to press his case further. He could have as much to lose as I, or perhaps even more. No man of honor can tolerate a blackmailer."

"Quite!" Henry said almost eagerly. "I do believe you have the answer, Mr. Darcy. And I have half a dozen acquaintances at the very least, who would be happy to dispatch such a fellow and count it a service to humanity to do so. Lord Jesmond leaps to mind most readily. If he is agreeable to you, I shall approach him tomorrow."

"Most agreeable, sir," Darcy said quickly. "An admirable gentleman, and his condemnation could ruin Albury, or any man fool enough to earn it. I cannot begin to express to you how grateful I am. I shall be forever in your debt, as will my dear Lizzie, although she will never know it." He rose to his feet and held out his hand impulsively. "Thank you, Mr. Rathbone, with all my heart!"

It was two days later on a sharp, frosty afternoon, with ice cracking in the puddles and a bleached winter sky that promised a bitter night, when Henry Rathbone and Lord Jesmond alighted from their hansom cab and presented themselves at Darcy's lodgings in Mayfair. They had not used Lord Jesmond's carriage in case its presence in the mews might cause the blackmailer to suspect a witness to his dealings.

They were welcomed at the door by Darcy, who was quite understandably in a state of considerable anxiety. His eyes were bright and his color feverish. He moved jerkily, all but drawing them inside, with a hand on Henry's arm which he released with a stammered apology as soon as he realized his unwarranted familiarity. Henry introduced him to Lord Jesmond.

"I am most heartily grateful, my lord," Darcy said earnestly. "It is an inestimable kindness for you to have taken up my cause in this way. I can never repay you."

"No need, my dear fellow," Jesmond assured him, taking the offered hand and shaking it warmly. "Dastardly thing, blackmail. Fellow deserves to be horsewhipped, but I daresay a damned good fright will serve the purpose, and without jeopardizing your good name or your future happiness. Now, where may we wait so as to observe this wretch without ourselves being seen?"

"This way, my lord." Darcy turned on his heel and led them into a most agreeable room furnished with armchairs and a small carved table of Oriental style. The fireplace was after the fashion of Adam, and above the mantel was a highly individual collection of paintings of the scenery of the Cape of Good Hope. There were brass candlesticks of some elegance at either end, and a brisk fire which made the room most comfortable.

Darcy led them to a door at the farther side, and the chilly, apparently unused, bedroom beyond, in which there was no furniture except a large Chinese silk screen.

"I'm sorry," he apologized. "I know it is miserably cold in here, but were I to set a fire, Albury might wonder why, and I am desperate to get this matter over with. I fear if I do not succeed this time, I shall not have another opportunity. He is a blackguard, but he is not a fool."

"Quite, my dear fellow," Lord Jesmond said immediately. "Might choose to meet you somewhere in the open next time, what? Damn the cold and the rain! This will do very well, I assure you. Handy having the screen there, in case he should look in. Daresay you thought of that, what?" He smiled, perhaps attempting to put Darcy in good heart.

Darcy smiled back. It was a pained expression, the specter of fear too sharp in it for Henry at least to miss.

"Don't worry," he said gently. "He won't raise the issue again, once we've caught him fairly at his game. But anxiety in your manner will be all to the good. Now pull the door to, and we will wait here, behind the screen."

"Thank you again, gentlemen," Darcy said with feeling, then did as he was bid. The next moment the door was all but closed, and Henry and Jesmond were alone, seeing nothing but the delicately embroidered silk of the screen. The silence was so complete it all but crackled. There were no footsteps or voices of domestic service. Possibly whoever cared for Darcy's needs had been sent out of the house on errands of one sort or another. There was not even the hiss of flames or the settling of coals beyond the door. The whole house seemed to have held its breath.

Then at last it came, a voice which was not Darcy's, a soft, insinuating, well-bred voice of a man used to charm and ease of good manners. But Henry heard in it the higher pitch of nervousness, the added sharpness, the little space for an indrawn breath of a man who knows he is about dangerous business, and has something to win or lose.

"Right, Darcy, let us not waste time with pleasantries neither of us means. I hope you are well. You wish I would meet with lethal mischance which would free you from all risk from me. Let us assume it has been said. But I am alive and in excellent health, and look set to remain so—unless you are rash enough to try to murder me! But I have taken some precautions against that." He laughed abruptly. "And it would seem an excessive reaction to what is, after all, a fairly modest request to a man of the means you will have when you have married Miss Elizabeth Carlton." There was a moment's silence.

"Damn you!" Darcy said chokingly.

"And I know of nothing which will prevent that," Albury went on, "except your failure to oblige me."

Darcy's voice came sharply. "In what manner 'oblige you'?"

"Oh, come!" Albury said in disgust. "Don't be coy with me. You understand me very well. We have already made our positions quite plain." There was no impatience in his voice. To Henry, standing in the chill behind the Chinese screen, there was a note of pleasure in it, as if he savored his power and was in no haste to have the moment over.

The same thought must have come to Darcy, because the next instant his voice came quite clearly, raised a little.

"You are enjoying this, you wretch! I used to consider you, if not a friend, at least a person worthy of respect. My God, how wrong I was! You are not fit to cross the threshold of any decent house!"

"You are in no position to criticize, my dear Darcy, let alone to fling insults," Albury replied with amusement. "How many thresholds do you suppose you would be permitted to cross were it generally known that you pocketed two of your host's most delicate and valuable Persian miniature paintings?"

"I did not!" Darcy said desperately. "I—"

"Indeed," Albury said with disbelief. "Then no doubt you will prove it and have me for false accusation when I tell everyone what I know."

"I . . ." Darcy was all but sobbing. Henry glanced at Jesmond. Darcy was playing his part extremely well. Perhaps he had less confidence in his plan than he had seemed to have earlier. Albury had apparently robbed him of his faith. Henry's anger against him almost boiled over. Blackmail was among the most despicable of crimes, a slow and quite deliberate torture.

"You could always pay me, as agreed," Albury said distinctly. "Twenty pounds a month, I think, will keep me in the luxuries to which I would like to accustom myself, quite without beggaring you. You will have to forgo a few of the pleasantries of life you now enjoy. Your good claret may have to go, your visits to the opera, your rather regular new shirts. You will have to wear your boots a trifle longer than you do now. And I daresay, at least until your marriage, you will not be able to be quite so generous to Miss Carlton."

"Damn you!" Darcy said fiercely. "That is blackmail!"

"Of course it is!" Albury replied, his tone filled with amusement. "Do you mean to say you have only just appreciated that?"

"No." Now the confidence was back, Darcy sounded like a different man. "No, I have always known it was; I simply wanted to hear you say so. Because blackmail is a crime, quite a severe one, and I have witnesses to our conversation. And that, I think, gives me an equal advantage with you."

"What?" Albury was aghast. "Where?"

Henry moved from behind the screen just as the door was flung wide and a dark, lean young man faced them, his mouth open, his eyes filled with horror.

"Mr. Darcy is quite correct," Henry said, moving forward to allow Lord Jesmond also to be seen. "We have overheard your entire exchange, Mr. Albury, and you would be well advised to leave here and never mention the matter to anyone as long as you live. Count yourself fortunate to have escaped ruin and prosecution. You will not get a penny from Darcy. In return, neither Lord Jesmond nor myself will speak of your contemptible behavior. It will remain as secret as it is now."

Albury backed away, turning to stare at Darcy with loathing.

"Nothing," Darcy reaffirmed, pointing to the farther door and the way out. "Leave my house and do not set foot here again. Should I chance to meet you socially, I shall treat you with civility, as if nothing had happened between us, for the sake of our bargain."

Henry and Jesmond came into the sitting room, glad of the warmth. The fire crackled in the grate. Darcy had set more coals in it. There was an ease in the air, a sense of victory.

"Bargain?" Albury looked from one to the other of them in rage and frustration. "I get nothing, and you get away with theft! What are those miniatures worth? A hundred, two hundred? More? You'll sell them and do very nicely."

"I didn't take them," Darcy said earnestly. "I have never stolen a thing in my life."

"No?" Albury's eyes widened in exaggerated disbelief.

"No," Darcy said firmly.

"Then why did you not say so at the time, and tell me to go to hell?" There was a smirk on Albury's face and his eyes were bright and hard.

"Because to do so I should have to admit that I was alone in the company of a young lady other than my betrothed, and for a longer time than she might understand. Also, it would provoke speculation that—" Darcy stopped suddenly, perhaps realizing he had said far more than he needed to, and raised the very questions he wanted to avoid.

Albury smiled, showing very fine teeth, transforming his face.

"You mean that it might suggest that Miss Carlton took them herself? Of course it might! In fact it would! And there would be a certain justice in that."

"It would be monstrous!" Darcy said furiously. He took a

step forward, his fists clenched by his sides. "Don't you dare say such a thing ever again. Do you hear me? Or I shall take great pleasure in thrashing you till you are obliged to eat your meals from the mantelpiece, sir."

"It would also be true," Albury returned without moving a step.

"You go too far, sir," Jesmond stepped forward at last. "To blacken a lady's name when she is not here to defend herself is inexcusable. You will retract your calumny immediately, and then leave while you still have a whole skin and can walk away with nothing but your honor injured."

Henry was staring at the two younger men and the emotions written so deeply in them. A strange thought was stirring in his mind.

"It makes no sense," Darcy protested. "Lizzie would never do such a thing. Anyone who knows her knows that! She has all the means she could wish, and she is as honest as the day."

"But a woman," Albury said, ignoring Lord Jesmond and looking only at Darcy. "And as capable of feeling jealousy as the next."

Darcy swallowed. "Jealousy?" he said hoarsely.

"Of course! Did you imagine she did not know you were in the conservatory with Belle Bartlett, or picture in her mind only too clearly what you may have been doing in between the orchids and the potted palms? Then you are a fool!"

Darcy gulped. He seemed to be shaking very slightly, as if in spite of the heat in the room he were cold within.

"She took them," Albury went on. "In order to compromise you. She knows of a surety, better than anyone else, that you did not take them. But either she will see you, or Miss Bartlett, accused of the theft, in thought if not in word, or failing that, she will hold it over your head for the rest of your life together."

"Never say that again!" Darcy said between dry lips, his voice strangled in his throat. "Never, do you hear me?"

Albury held out his hand. "Fifty pounds, once only."

Darcy turned and went to a small bureau at the far side of the room. He opened the top, and from a pigeonhole took out several Bank of England notes. Without a word, he held them out to Albury.

"Just a moment!" Henry reached across and closed his hand over Darcy's, preventing Albury from taking the money. "You do not need to pay him."

"Yes, I do!" Darcy said desperately. "God knows, I cannot marry Lizzie now. It would be a torment every day, every night. I should see this jealousy in her eyes each time I looked at her. Our life would be intolerable. Every time I spoke civilly to another woman I should fear what she might do. But one cannot kill the habit of love so easily, not in one blow, however hard. I shall protect her honor in the eyes of others. No one need know but herself and her father." He bit his lip. "I shall have to speak to him. Our understanding cannot remain. But I shall do this for her at least. Free my hand, sir."

Henry kept hold of it.

"What you wish to give Mr. Albury, or why, is your own affair, Mr. Darcy, but you do not need to pay him in order to protect Miss Carlton. She is guilty of nothing more than perhaps a misjudgment of character."

"I don't know what you mean," Darcy protested. "She has behaved despicably. She has attempted out of jealousy to brand Miss Bartlett a thief!"

"Because she knew that you and she were in the conservatory together?" Henry asked.

"Apparently."

"Then she knew that just as Miss Bartlett could swear to your innocence of theft, so you could, and would, swear to hers!

That would leave her own guilt suspect, in just the manner Mr. Albury has said."

Darcy paled, glanced at Albury, then back at Henry Rathbone. He made as if to speak, but no words came.

"But my dear chap, it makes no sense," Jesmond said in utter confusion. "You must be mistaken."

"It makes perfect sense," Henry explained. "If you consider the story from the beginning, not as Mr. Darcy would have us believe. Take all the facts as he described them. A young man, betrothed to one young lady, finds himself most attracted to another, perhaps more vivacious. He cannot break his word to the first. That is legally breach of promise, and socially suicidal to one who has considerable aspirations. Also it would be unlikely to gain him the hand of the lady he desires. Her father, also wealthy and of eminent position, would not countenance it."

Darcy was ashen now.

"He must find another way out," Henry continued. "The young lady will not leave him. He must create an honorable cause to leave her, one in which he remains untarnished, free to pursue his ambitions. At a country house party the opportunity presents itself and the idea is born. He needs only the help of a clever actor." He glanced at Albury, who was now in an extremity of embarrassment. "And two witnesses of reputations above question, and by nature honorable, eager to right a wrong, and perhaps a trifle innocent in the ways of young men with too few scruples and too much appetite for success."

"Good heavens!" Jesmond was appalled.

Henry looked again at Darcy.

"Don't feel you have failed entirely, Mr. Darcy. As soon as I acquaint Miss Carlton with the facts, she will free you to pursue Miss Bartlett, or whomsoever else you wish. Although I doubt Sir George Bartlett will accept you into his family, any more than I should. I have not been the service to you that you intended, but I have indeed served a purpose. Come, Jesmond." He led the way to the door, then, with Jesmond at his heels, turned back. "Don't forget you owe Mr. Albury for an excellent piece of acting! Good day, gentlemen!"

SHEL SILVERSTEIN

For anyone who ever dreamed of creating stories, or poems, of drawing, or writing songs and plays, but couldn't quite find the originality of expression that set them apart from the pedestrian, Shel Silverstein is their worst nightmare.

When he is asked to write the lyrics for a song, he needs no more than fifteen minutes. A play might need an entire weekend. When I asked him to write a story for this book, he said, "Well, I've never written a crime story in my life. Wait, I have an idea." He never paused for a breath between those two sentences. The fable that follows, not a story in the traditional form, is that idea. In his various homes, he has drawers full of songs and stories and fables and drawings and plays and poems that he's never gotten around to sending to his agent or his publishers. When he focused long enough to put together a book of his short pieces, it immediately made The New York Times *bestseller list. Not for two weeks. Not for two months.* The Light in the Attic *stayed on the list for more than two years!*

Shel Silverstein offered to write another piece if I compiled another anthology someday. I said, "What if you can't come up with an idea?" He looked absolutely baffled by the notion.

—O.P.

For What She Had Done

BY SHEL SILVERSTEIN

She had to die.
This Omoo knew.
He also knew he could not kill her.
Not even try to kill her.
Those eyes. Would look at him. Not even try. So, what to do?
There was one Ung. Who lived in a cave.
Beyond the hard mountain. A foul cave.
Far from the village.
Ung, who hunted with stones.
Who killed with his hands.
Who had killed two saber-tooths.
And one great bear, whose skin he now wore hanging from his hairy shoulders.
And Ung had killed men. Many men.
And, it was said, a woman.

Ung, who took the fresh meat left upon the flat rock for the
Spirit of the Sky.
And the Spirit of the Sky would go hungry.
And bring pain and darkness to the village.
But none dare say words to Ung.
Who had killed two saber-tooths.
And one great bear. And men, many men.
And, it was said, a woman.
He went to Ung.
Yes, said Ung, I will kill her.
For what she has done, said Omoo.
For equal weight, said Ung, in bear meat or lizard skins.
She is a large woman, said Omoo.
Equal weight, said Ung. Now you must come and show her
to me, that I may kill her.
That I cannot, said Omoo.
Then how will I know her?
Her hair is long, said Omoo.
Her eyes burn like the pools of night.
Many have the long hair, said Ung.
Many have eyes like the pools of night.
She will be bathing, said Omoo.
Tomorrow, as the sun dies.
She will be bathing. Washing her long hair at the falling water.
Many women will be bathing, said Ung.
Many long-haired, night-eyed women.
How will I know it is she?
Omoo thought.
Ah, he said, she shall be carrying flowers.
Bright hill flowers, that I shall gather and place in her hands,
before she goes to bathe at the falling water.
Then you will know her.
And you will kill her.

For equal weight, said Ung.
Yes, said Omoo, for equal weight.

And so was begun the custom
of giving bouquets and corsages.

DONNA TARTT

A problem common to many lauded novels by the new generation of writers is lack of story. While we may not always like the principal characters, they are well drawn and fully realized. The dialogue may be brittle and frequently predictable, but it is crisp and true. Places and ambience come into plain view, even if they are not necessarily where we would choose to be. But nothing happens. *The tales move along on a long stretch of road and then stop. The whole experience is as satisfying as one of those food bars consumed by astronauts. One tasted like steak and supplied the same nutrients, but it wasn't the real thing. Neither was the bar that tasted like chocolate ice cream.*

Donna Tartt's first novel, The Secret History, *on the other hand,* is *the real thing. All the terrific writing of other talented English majors, sure, but a real story too: a plot—that great rarity among "serious" writers of contemporary fiction. And, no less important, a* good *plot.*

The author is not a fast writer, so there has been no book to follow that huge initial success. Even her short stories take ages to produce.

As an admirer of her work, I wanted Donna Tartt to be in this book. The inflexible rule was that all stories had to be original, written especially for this book. We winked at the rule, as this is a poem. It had previously been read by about eleven subscribers to the Oxford Review.

—O.P.

True Crime

BY DONNA TARTT

Things were getting hot in Idaho. Smiling,
strangled, in his distinctive red-and-silver pickup,
he seethed with the name of actress Elke Sommer.
Full moons seemed to bring out the worst in him.
So did eighteen year old neighbor Debra Earl. Lake Charles,
Louisiana.
Prognosis: poor. Following a late dance at the VFW hall,
Authorities recovered a diary, a favorite rifle, a sales receipt
For antifreeze. "I have a problem. I'm
A cannibal." He spoke of plans
For a G.E.D. degree, a part-time candy business.
Stick figures of his first-grade sweetheart
Were scratched along the barrel of his gun.